IN GOD WE TRUST
All Others Pay Cash

IN GOD WE TRUST
All Others Pay Cash

JEAN SHEPHERD

MAIN STREET BOOKS

DOUBLEDAY
NEW YORK LONDON TORONTO SYDNEY AUCKLAND

A Main Street Book
PUBLISHED BY DOUBLEDAY
a division of Bantam Doubleday Dell Publishing Group, Inc.
1540 Broadway, New York, New York 10036

Main Street Books, Doubleday, and the portrayal of a
building with a tree are trademarks of Doubleday, a
division of Bantam Doubleday Dell Publishing Group, Inc.

Chapters 2, 8, 14, 16, 24, 26, 30 originally
appeared in *Playboy*, Copyright © 1964, 1965, 1966
by HMH Publishing Co., Inc.

To my Mother, and my Kid Brother
And the Rest of the Bunch . . .

CONTENTS

THERE ARE AT LEAST TWO KINDS OF EDUCATION.

. . . *George Ade*

IN GOD WE TRUST
All Others Pay Cash

I 🦢 WE MEET FLICK, THE FRIENDLY BARTENDER

I felt like a spy. It was the first time I had ever ridden a cab in my own hometown. When I had left it I was definitely not a cab rider. Now taking cabs was as natural as breathing or putting on shoes. I could see the cab driver giving me the eye in his rear-view mirror. He was wearing the standard Midwestern work uniform of lumberjacket, corduroy cap, and a red face.

"You from out of town?"

He caught me off guard. I had forgotten that out of New York people quite often spoke to other people.

"Uh. . . . what?"

"You from out of town?"

"Ah . . . yeah, I guess so." Making one of my famous instantaneous decisions, I opted for being from out of town.

"Yeah, well, I could tell. Where ya from?"

"New York. Now, that is."

He mopped his windshield with a greasy rag. The cab's heater was making the windows cloud up. Outside I could dimly see the grimy streets lined with dirty, hard ice and crusted drifts covered with that old familiar layer of blast-furnace dust; ahead of us a long line of dirt-encrusted cars carrying loads of steelworkers, refinery slaves, and railroad men to wherever they spent most of their lives. He went on:

"Yep. New York. Me and my wife went there once. For two weeks. We saw the Fair. I sure don't see how anyone can stand to live there."

We continued to rattle through the smoky gray Winter air. I watched a giant gas works drift by our port side. On the starboard a vast, undulating sea of junkyards rolled to the horizon.

"It's okay to visit."

I guess he threw that in so as not to hurt my feelings.

"Oh, you get used to it."

He blew his nose loudly into a red bandanna and laughed juicily.

"Yeah, I guess a guy can get used to anything. If he's gotta."

A crossing gate banged down in front of us, its flashers angrily blinking off and on. A warning bell clanged deafeningly as a giant Diesel locomotive swept across our bow, towing a short string of smelly tankers. Four brakemen clung to their sides, yelling to one another as they roared past.

"What was that?" I shouted.

"I SAID A GUY CAN GET USED TO ANYTHING." He bellowed back.

The gate went up. We were off again. I fished into my briefcase, at last finding the onionskin on which I had written, for my own use, a thumbnail description of the town I was now riding through, my own despised hometown. As we roared and squeaked on, I read over what I had written:

Hohman, Indiana, is located in the extreme Northwestern corner of the state, where the state line ends abruptly in the icy, detergent-filled waters of that queen of the Great Lakes, Lake Michigan. It clings precariously to the underbody of Chicago like a barnacle clings to the rotting hulk of a tramp steamer.

From time to time echoes of the Outside World arrive in Hohman, but they are muted and bear little relevance to the daily life of its inhabitants. Theirs is a world of belching furnaces, roaring Bessemer Converters, fragrant Petroleum distillation plants, and freight yards. Mostly, their

Social life is found in Bowling halls or Union halls or beer halls, not to mention dance halls and pool parlors.

Theirs is a sandy, rolling country, cooled, nay, frozen to rigidity in the Winter by howling gales that got their start near the Arctic Circle, picked up force over the frozen wastes of Lake Michigan, and petered out in downtown Hohman, after freezing ears, cracking blocks, and stunting the Summer hopes in many a breast.

In Summer the process is reversed, and the land lies still and sear under the blazing Midwestern sun. This is where the first faint beginnings of the Great Plains can be found. A gnarled cactus plant, rolling tumbleweeds; an occasional Snowy Owl. The residents of Hohman are hardly aware of this, although their truculent pride in being Hoosiers is seen everywhere.

Under the soil of most backyards, covered with a thin, drifting coat of blast-furnace dust and refinery waste, made fragrant by the soaked-in aroma of numerous soap factories, lie in buried darkness the arrowheads, stone axes, and broken pots of the departed Indian. Where the tribes danced in Indian summer now grow Used Car lots and vast, swampy junkyards.

Not far from downtown Hohman lie the onion sets and cantaloupe vines of the Dutch immigrant farmers, and then the endless, mile-after-mile monotony of the Indiana cornfields. To the West the sand dunes ring Lake Michigan almost to the border of Michigan itself. To the North—the Lake. And to the West and North—Chicago.

It is a place people never really come to, but mostly want to leave. And leave they do, to go to the fabled East or to the unbelievable California coast. They rarely talk about where they have come from. There isn't much to say. At night in Hohman the rabbits still hop through the backyard gardens. The trains thunder through the dark on their way to somewhere else. The sky is always lit by the eternal flames of the Open Hearths and blast furnaces.

Nothing much has changed, probably least of all those who were born and formed by the Northern Indiana mill-town existence.

Oh yeah? I answered myself. I have never been a fan of my particular style of Official Writer-ese, but, after all, it's a living. It's a hell of a lot better than working in the Tin Mill, which we were now passing.

We were getting into painfully familiar country: ragged vacant lots, clumps of signboards advertising paint, American Legion halls, bowling alleys, all woven together with a compact web of high tension wires, telephone poles, and gas stations.

Home is where the heart is. In fact, not more than two blocks from where we now waited for a light I had spent the festering years of my childhood.

I got out of the cab at the intersection and headed directly for Flick's Tavern, the tavern whose floors I had helped to clean as a tot, and where I had learned a few of Life's seamier lessons. Flick himself had been an old boyhood sidekick who had taken over the tavern from his father, long since passed away. I hadn't seen him since my Army days.

It was a cold, early December day and a few plastic wreaths were in evidence. The sign hanging out over the sidewalk read:

BOOZE

Flick's sense of humor obviously was still operating.

Inside I instantly saw the place had changed little. The bar was longer, the jukebox bigger; there was a color TV hanging from the wall, but the air was as gamy and rich as ever, if not more so, a thick oleo of dried beer suds, fermenting bar rags, sweaty overalls, and urinal deodorants. I breathed in a deep gulp to clear my brain, kicked some snow off my Italian shoes, and sat down at one of the stools near the window.

Down at the far end of the bar I saw a white-shirted back banging away at what appeared to be some sort of ice cabinet. He glanced up in the gloom and called out:

"What'll you have?"

"A beer."

"I'll be right with you."

He went on working. Through the window I could see a Used-Car lot where once, I recalled in the dim past, a stand of willows had grown. It was midafternoon, between shifts, so the tavern was empty. I looked back down the bar just in time to see the white-shirted figure draw a stein of draught, topping it off neatly with a good head. He sat it down in front of me.

"How the hell are you, Flick?" I went right at him in a frontal attack.

"Uh . . . okay. How're you?"

"Don't you remember me?"

He looked at me in that long, wary Bartender stare, suspecting, at first, a touch.

"Fer Chrissake!"

"Yep, it's me. Your old buddy."

"Fer cryin' out loud! What the hell're you doing back here in Hohman, Ralph?"

I will now lightly pass over the ensuing sickening scene of boyhood companions meeting after years of elapsed time. Back-slappings, hollerings, and other classical maneuvers were performed. I told him why I had come back, about the piece I was supposed to do for an Official magazine on The Return Of The Native To The Indiana Mill Town. He snorted. They don't think of Hohman as a mill town. It's just Hohman.

He had drawn a beer for himself and another for me, broken out a bag of pretzels, and we began to do some really good, solid Whatever-happened-to . . . ?, Did-she-ever-marry . . . ?, When-did-they-put-in-the-bowling-alley-down-at . . . ?, and all the rest of it. I could see that Flick was wearing a bowling shirt, white, with his team name stitched over the pocket. Bowling is the staff of life, the honey of existence, the *raison d'être* for most men in Hohman. Flick was no exception.

"Did you ever learn to control that hook, Flick?" I remembered him as a wild fastball bowler who lofted a lot and who had a wicked, uncontrollable hook.

"I'm getting my wood."

We sat for a long moment, sipping our beer and looking out

into the gray, gloomy day. A big red Christmas wreath hung over the cash register.

"Are you gonna be around for Christmas, Ralph?" he asked.

"I hope so."

He had reminded me of something that had crossed my mind a few days before. The Christmas season does things like that to you.

"Flick, do you remember that BB gun you used to have? That 200-shot Daisy pump gun?"

"That what?"

"Your BB gun."

"Hell, I still got it. It comes in handy sometimes."

"You won't believe it, Flick, but the other day, in New York, I'm sitting in the H & H . . ."

"The H & H?"

"The Horn & Hardart. The Automat."

"Oh yeah. I heard about those. You get pie right out of the wall."

"That's right, that's the H & H. Anyway. . . ."

"You know, I've never been to New York. I'd like to go there some day. I hear it's a rough place to live, but. . . ."

"Anyway, Flick, I'm in the H & H and this lady comes in and sits down, and she's got a button that says 'Disarm the Toy Industry' on it."

"Disarm the *Toy* Industry?"

"I guess she meant BB guns."

"Fer Chrissake, it's getting nuttier and nuttier." Flick's native Indiana humor struck to the core.

"Anyway, Flick, I'm sitting there talking to her, and I suddenly remember that BB gun I got for Christmas. Do you remember?"

"No kidding, Disarm the Toy Industry? Oh boy. . . ."

II ᒚᕽ DUEL IN THE SNOW, *or* RED RYDER NAILS THE CLEVELAND STREET KID

"DISARM THE TOY INDUSTRY"

Printed in angry block red letters the slogan gleamed out from the large white button like a neon sign. I carefully reread it to make sure that I had not made a mistake.

"DISARM THE TOY INDUSTRY"

That's what it said. There was no question about it.

The button was worn by a tiny Indignant-type little old lady wearing what looked like an upturned flowerpot on her head and, I suspect (viewing it from this later date) a pair of Ked tennis shoes on her feet, which were primly hidden by the Automat table at which we both sat.

I, toying moodily with my chicken pot pie, which of course is a specialty of the house, surreptitiously examined my fellow citizen and patron of the Automat. Wiry, lightly powdered, tough as spring steel, the old doll dug with Old Lady gusto into her meal. Succotash, baked beans, creamed corn, side order of Harvard beets. Bad news—a Vegetarian type. No doubt also a dedicated Cat Fancier.

Silently we shared our tiny Automat table as the great throng of pre-Christmas quick-lunchers eddied and surged in restless excitement all around us. Of course there were the usual H & H club members spotted here and there in the mob; out-of-work seal trainers, borderline bookies, ex-Opera divas, and panhandlers trying hard to look like Madison Avenue account men just getting out of the cold for a few minutes. It is an Art, the ability to nurse a single cup of coffee through an entire ten-hour day of sitting out of the biting cold of mid-December Manhattan.

And so we sat, wordlessly as is the New York custom, for long moments until I could not contain myself any longer.

"Disarm the Toy Industry?" I tried for openers.

She sat unmoved, her bright pink and ivory dental plates working over a mouthful of Harvard beets, attacking them with a venom usually associated with the larger carnivores. The red juice ran down over her powdered chin and stained her white lace bodice. I tried again:

"Pardon me, Madam, you're dripping."

"Eh?"

Her ice-blue eyes flickered angrily for a moment and then glowed as a mother hen's looking upon a stunted, dwarfed offspring. Love shone forth.

"Thank you, sonny."

She dabbed at her chin with a paper napkin and I knew that contact had been made. Her uppers clattered momentarily and in an unmistakably friendly manner.

"Disarm the Toy Industry?" I asked.

"It's an outrage!" she barked, causing two elderly gentlemen at the next table to spill soup on their vests. Loud voices are not often heard in the cloistered confines of the H & H.

"It's an outrage the way the toymakers are forcing the implements of blasphemous War on the innocent children, the Pure in Spirit, the tiny babes who are helpless and know no better!"

Her voice at this point rising to an Evangelical quaver, ringing from change booth to coffee urn and back again. Four gnarled atheists three tables over automatically, by reflex action alone, hurled four "Amen's" into the unanswering air. She continued:

"It's all a Government plot to prepare the Innocent for evil, Godless War! I know what they're up to! Our Committee is

on to them, and we intend to expose this decadent Capitalistic
evil!"

She spoke in the ringing, anvil-like tones of a True Believer,
her whole life obviously an unending fight against *They*, the
plotters. She clawed through her enormous burlap handbag,
worn paperback volumes of Dogma spilling out upon the floor
as she rummaged frantically until she found what she was searching for.

"Here, sonny. Read this. You'll see what I mean." She
handed me a smudgy pamphlet from some embattled group of
Right Thinkers, based—of course—in California, denouncing the
U.S. as a citadel of Warmongers, profit-greedy despoilers of the
young and promoters of world-wide Capitalistic decadence, all
through plastic popguns and Sears Roebuck fatigue suits for tots.

She stood hurriedly, scooping her dog-eared library back into
her enormous rucksack and hurled her parting shot:

"Those who eat meat, the flesh of our fellow creatures, the
innocent slaughtered lamb of the field, are doing the work of
the Devil!"

Her gimlet eyes spitted the remains of my chicken pot pie
with naked malevolence. She spun on her left Ked and strode
militantly out into the crisp, brilliant Christmas air and back
into the fray.

I sat rocking slightly in her wake for a few moments, stirring
my lukewarm coffee meditatively, thinking over her angry, mili-
tant slogan.

"DISARM THE TOY INDUSTRY"

A single word floated into my mind's arena for just an
instant—"Canal water!"—and then disappeared. I thought on:
As if the Toy industry has any control over the insatiable desire
of the human spawn to own Weaponry, armaments, and the
implements of Warfare. It's the same kind of mind that thought
if *making* whiskey were prohibited people would stop *drinking*.

I began to mull over my own youth, and, of course, its un-
ceasing quest for roscoes, six-shooters, and any sort of blue
hardware—simulated or otherwise—that I could lay my hands
on. It is no coincidence that the Zip Green was invented by

kids. The adolescent human carnivore is infinitely ingenious when confronted with a Peace movement.

Outside in the spanking December breeze a Salvation Army Santa Claus listlessly tolled his bell, huddled in a doorway to avoid the direct blast of the wind. I sipped my coffee and remembered another Christmas, in another time, in another place, and . . . a gun.

I remember clearly, itchingly, nervously, maddeningly the first time I laid eyes on it, pictured in a three-color, smeared illustration in a full-page back cover ad in *Open Road For Boys*, a publication which at the time had an iron grip on my aesthetic sensibilities, and the dime that I had to scratch up every month to stay with it. It was actually an early *Playboy*. It sold dreams, fantasies, incredible adventures, and a way of life. Its center foldouts consisted of gigantic Kodiak bears charging out of the page at the reader, to be gunned down in single hand-to-hand combat by the eleven-year-old Killers armed only with hunting knife and fantastic bravery.

Its Christmas issue weighed over seven pounds, its pages crammed with the effluvia of the Good Life of male Juvenalia, until the senses reeled and Avariciousness, the growing desire to own Everything, was almost unbearable. Today there must be millions of ex-subscribers who still can't pass Abercrombie & Fitch without a faint, keening note of desire and the unrequited urge to glom on to all of it. Just to have it, to feel it.

Early in the Fall the ad first appeared. It was a magnificent thing of balanced copy and pictures, superb artwork, and subtly contrived catch phrases. I was among the very first hooked, I freely admit it.

BOYS! AT LAST *YOU* CAN OWN AN *OFFICIAL RED RYDER* CARBINE ACTION TWO-HUNDRED SHOT *RANGE MODEL AIR RIFLE!*

This in block red and black letters surrounded by a large balloon coming out of Red Ryder's own mouth, wearing his enormous ten-gallon Stetson, his jaw squared, staring out at me manfully and speaking directly *to* me, eye to eye. In his hand was the knurled stock of as beautiful, as coolly deadly-looking a piece of weaponry as I'd ever laid eyes on.

YES, FELLOWS. . . .

Red Ryder continued under the gun:

YES, FELLOWS, THIS TWO-HUNDRED-SHOT CARBINE ACTION AIR RIFLE, JUST LIKE THE ONE I USE IN ALL MY RANCE WARS CHASIN' THEM RUSTLERS AND BAD GUYS CAN BE YOUR VERY OWN! IT HAS A SPECIAL BUILT-IN SECRET COMPASS IN THE STOCK FOR TELLING THE DIRECTION IF YOU'RE LOST ON THE TRAIL, AND ALSO AN OFFICIAL RED RYDER SUNDIAL FOR TELLING TIME OUT IN THE WILDS. YOU JUST LAY YOUR CHEEK 'GAINST THIS STOCK, SIGHT OVER MY OWN SPECIAL DESIGN CLOVERLEAF SIGHT, AND YOU JUST CAN'T MISS. TELL DAD IT'S GREAT FOR TARGET SHOOTING AND VARMINTS, AND IT WILL MAKE A SWELL CHRISTMAS GIFT!!

The next issue arrived and Red Ryder was even more insistent, now implying that the supply of Red Ryder BB guns was limited and to order now or See Your Dealer Before It's Too Late!

It was the second ad that actually did the trick on me. It was late November and the Christmas fever was well upon me. I thought about a Red Ryder air rifle in all my waking hours, seven days a week, in school and out. I drew pictures of it in my Reader, in my Arithmetic book, on my hand in indelible ink, on Helen Weathers' dress in front of me, in crayon. For the first time in my life the initial symptoms of genuine lunacy, of Mania, set in.

I imagined innumerable situations calling for the instant and irrevocable need for a BB gun, great fantasies where I fended off creeping marauders burrowing through the snow toward the kitchen, where only I and I alone stood between our tiny huddled family and insensate Evil. Masked bandits attacking my father, to be mowed down by my trusted cloverleaf-sighted deadly weapon. I seriously mulled over the possibility of an invasion of raccoons, of which there were several in the county. Acts of selfless Chivalry defending Esther Jane Alberry from escaped circus tigers. Time and time again I saw myself a miraculous crack shot, picking off sparrows on the wing to the gasps of admiring girls and envious rivals on Cleveland Street. There was one dream that involved my entire class getting lost on a field trip in the swamps, wherein I led the tired, hungry band back to civilization, using only my Red Ryder compass and sundial. There was no question about it. Not only should I have such a gun, it was an absolute *necessity!*

Early December saw the first of the great blizzards of that year. The wind howling down out of the Canadian wilds a few hundred miles to the north had screamed over frozen Lake Michigan and hit Hohman, laying on the town great drifts of snow and long, story-high icicles, and sub-zero temperatures where the air cracked and sang. Streetcar wires creaked under caked ice and kids plodded to school through forty-five-mile-an-hour gales, tilting forward like tiny furred radiator ornaments, moving stiffly over the barren, clattering ground.

Preparing to go to school was about like getting ready for extended Deep-Sea Diving. Longjohns, corduroy knickers, checkered flannel Lumberjack shirt, four sweaters, fleece-lined leatherette sheepskin, helmet, goggles, mittens with leatherette gauntlets and a large red star with an Indian Chief's face in the middle, three pair of sox, high-tops, overshoes, and a sixteen-foot scarf wound spirally from left to right until only the faint glint of two eyes peering out of a mound of moving clothing told you that a kid was in the neighborhood.

There was no question of staying home. It never entered anyone's mind. It was a hardier time, and Miss Bodkin was a hardier teacher than the present breed. Cold was something that was accepted, like air, clouds, and parents; a fact of Nature, and as such could not be used in any fraudulent scheme to stay out of school.

My mother would simply throw her shoulder against the front door, pushing back the advancing drifts and stone ice, the wind raking the living-room rug with angry fury for an instant, and we would be launched, one after the other, my brother and I, like astronauts into unfriendly Arctic space. The door clanged shut behind us and that was it. It was make school or die!

Scattered out over the icy waste around us could be seen other tiny befurred jots of wind-driven humanity. All painfully toiling toward the Warren G. Harding School, miles away over the tundra, waddling under the weight of frost-covered clothing like tiny frozen bowling balls with feet. An occasional piteous whimper would be heard faintly, but lost instantly in the sigh of the eternal wind. All of us were bound for geography lessons involving the exports of Peru, reading lessons dealing with fat cats and dogs named Jack. But over it all like a faint, thin, off-stage chorus was the building excitement. Christmas was on its way. Each day was more exciting than the last, because Christmas was one day closer. Lovely, beautiful, glorious Christmas, around which the entire year revolved.

Off on the far horizon, beyond the railroad yards and the great refinery tanks, lay our own private mountain range. Dark and mysterious, cold and uninhabited, outlined against the steel-gray skies of Indiana winter, the Mills. It was the Depression, and the natives had been idle so long that they no longer even considered themselves out of work. Work had ceased to exist, so how could you be out of it? A few here and there picked up a day or so a month at the Roundhouse or the Freight yards or the slag heaps at the Mill, but mostly they just spent their time clipping out coupons from the back pages of *True Romances* magazine, coupons that promised virgin territories for distributing ready-made suits door to door or offering untold riches repairing radios through correspondence courses.

Downtown Hohman was prepared for its yearly bacchanalia of peace on earth and good will to men. Across Hohman Avenue and State Street, the gloomy main thoroughfares—drifted with snow that had lain for months and would remain until well into Spring, ice encrusted, frozen drifts along the curbs—were

strung strands of green and red Christmas bulbs, and banners
that snapped and cracked in the gale. From the streetlights hung
plastic ivy wreaths surrounding three-dimensional Santa Claus
faces.

For several days the windows of Goldblatt's department store
had been curtained and dark. Their corner window was traditionally a major high-water mark of the pre-Christmas season.
It set the tone, the motif of their giant Yuletide Jubilee. Kids
were brought in from miles around just to see the window. Old
codgers would recall vintage years when the window had flowered
more fulsomely than in ordinary times. This was one of those
years. The magnificent display was officially unveiled on a
crowded Saturday night. It was an instant smash hit. First
Nighters packed earmuff to earmuff, their steamy breath clouding up the sparkling plate glass, jostled in rapt admiration before a golden, tinkling panoply of mechanized, electronic Joy.

This was the heyday of the Seven Dwarfs and their virginal
den mother, Snow White. Walt Disney's seven cutie-pies ham-
mered and sawed, chiseled and painted while Santa, bouncing
Snow White on his mechanical knee, ho-ho-ho'd through eight
strategically placed loudspeakers—interspersed by choruses of
"Heigh ho, heigh ho, it's off to work we go." Grumpy sat at
the controls of a miniature eight-wheel Rock Island Road steam
engine and Sleepy played a marimba, while in the background,
inexplicably, Mrs. Claus ceaselessly ironed a red shirt. Sparkling
artificial snow drifted down on Shirley Temple dolls, Flexible
Flyers, and Tinker Toy sets glowing in the golden spotlight. In
the foreground a frontier stockade built of Lincoln Logs was
manned by a company of kilted lead Highlanders who were
doughtily fending off an attack by six U. S. Army medium tanks.
(History has always been vague in Indiana.) A few feet away
stood an Arthurian cardboard castle with Raggedy Andy sitting
on the drawbridge, his feet in the moat, through which a Lionel
freight train burping real smoke went round and round. Dopey
sat in Amos and Andy's pedal-operated Fresh Air Taxicab beside a stuffed panda holding a lollipop in his paw, bearing the
heart-tugging legend, "Hug me." From fluffy cotton clouds

above, Dionne quintuplet dolls wearing plaid golf knickers hung from billowing parachutes, having just bailed out of a high-flying balsawood Fokker triplane. All in all, Santa's workshop made Salvador Dali look like Norman Rockwell. It was a good year. Maybe even a great one. Like a swelling Christmas balloon, the excitement mounted until the whole town tossed restlessly in bed—and made plans for the big day. Already my own scheme was well under way, my personal dream. Casually, carefully, calculatingly, I had booby-trapped the house with copies of *Open Road For Boys*, all opened to Red Ryder's slit-eyed face. My father, a great john reader, found himself for the first time in his life in alien literary waters. My mother, grabbing for her copy of *Screen Romances*, found herself cleverly euchred into reading a Red Ryder sales pitch; I had stuck a copy of *ORFB* inside the cover showing Clark Gable clasping Loretta Young to his heaving breast.

At breakfast I hinted that there was a rumor of loose bears in the neighborhood, and that I was ready to deal with them if I had the proper equipment. At first my mother and the Old Man did not rise to the bait, and I began to push, grow anxious, and, of course, inevitably overplayed my hand. Christmas was only weeks away, and I could not waste time with subtlety or droll innuendo.

My brother, occasionally emerging from under the daybed during this critical period, was already well involved in some private Little Brother persiflage of his own involving an Erector Set with motor, capable of constructing drawbridges, Eiffel towers, Ferris wheels, and operating guillotines. I knew that if he got wind of *my* scheme, all was lost. He would then begin wheedling and whining for what I wanted, which would result in nobody scoring, since he was obviously too young for deadly weapons. So I cleverly pretended that I wanted nothing more than a simple, utilitarian, unpretentious Sandy Andy, a highly symbolic educational toy popular at the time, consisting of a kind of funnel under which was mounted a tiny conveyor belt of little scooplike gondolas. It came equipped with a bag of white sand that was poured into the funnel. The sand trickling out of the bottom into the gondolas set the belt in motion. As each gondola was filled, it moved down the track to be replaced by another, which, when filled, moved down another notch. And endlessly they went, dumping sand out at the bottom of the track and starting up the back loop to be refilled again—on and on until all the sand was deposited in the red cup at the bottom of the track. The kid then emptied the cup into the funnel and it started all over again—ceaselessly, senselessly, round and round. How like Life itself; it was the perfect toy for the Depression. Other kids in the neighborhood were embarked on grandiose, pie-in-the-sky dreams of Lionel electric trains, gigantic Gilbert chemistry sets, and other totally unimaginable impossibilities.

Through my brain nightly danced visions of six-guns snapped from the hip and shattering bottles—and a gnawing nameless frenzy of impending ecstasy. Then came my first disastrous mistake. In a moment of unguarded rashness I brought the whole plot out into the open. I was caught by surprise while pulling on my high-tops in the kitchen, huddled next to the stove, the only source of heat in the house at that hour of the morning. My mother, leaning over a pot of simmering oatmeal, suddenly asked out of the blue:

"What would you like for Christmas?"

Horrified, I heard myself blurt: "A Red Ryder BB gun!"

Without pausing or even missing a stroke with her tablespoon, she shot back: "Oh no. You'll shoot out one of your eyes."

It was the classic Mother BB Gun Block! I was sunk! That deadly phrase, used many times before by hundreds of mothers, was not surmountable by any means known to Kid-dom. I had really booted it, but such was my mania, my desire for a Red Ryder carbine, that I immediately began to rebuild the dike.

"I was just kidding. Even though Flick is getting one. (A lie.) I guess . . . I guess . . . I sure would like a Sandy Andy, I guess."

I watched the back of her Chinese red chenille bathrobe anxiously, looking for any sign that my shaft had struck home.

"They're dangerous. I don't want anybody shooting their eyes out."

The boom had been lowered and I was under it. With leaden heart and frozen feet I waddled to school, bereft but undaunted.

At Recess time little knots of kids huddled together for warmth amid the gray craggy snowbanks and the howling gale. The telephone wires overhead whistled like banshees while the trapeze rings on the swings clanked hollowly as Schwartz and Flick and Bruner and I discussed the most important thing next to What I'm Going To Get For Christmas, which was What I'm Getting My Mother and Father For Christmas. We talked in hushed, hoarse whispers to guard against Security leaks. The selection of a present was always done with greater secrecy than that which usually surrounds a State Department White Paper on Underground Subversive Operations in a Foreign Country. Schwartz, his eyes darting over his shoulder as he spoke, leaned into the wind and hissed:

"I'm getting my father. . . ."

He paused dramatically, hunching forward to exclude unfriendly ears, his voice dropping even lower. We listened intently for his punchline.

". . . a new Flit gun!"

The sheer creative brilliance of it staggered us for a moment. Schwartz smiled smugly, his earmuffs bobbing jauntily as he leaned back into the wind, knowing he had scored. Flick, looking suspiciously at a passing female first grader who could be a spy for his mother, waited until the coast was clear and then launched his entry into the icy air.

"For my father I'm getting. . . ."

Again we waited, Schwartz with a superior smirk playing faintly on his chapped lips.

". . . a rose that *squirts!*"

We had all seen these magnificent appliances at George's Candy Store, and instantly we saw that this was a gift *anyone* would want. They were bright-red celluloid, with a white rubber bulb for pocket use. At this point, luckily, the bell rang, calling us back to our labors before I had to divulge my own gifts, which I knew did not come up to these magnificent strokes of genius.

I had not yet made an irrevocable choice for my mother, but I had narrowed the field down to two spectacular items I had been stealthily eying at Woolworth's for several weeks. The first was a tasteful string of beads about the size of small walnuts, brilliant ruby in color with tiny yellow flowers embedded in the glass. The other and more expensive gift—$1.98—was a pearl-colored perfume atomizer, urn-shaped, with golden lion's feet and matching gold top and squeeze bulb. It was not an easy choice. It was the age-old conflict between the Classic and the Sybaritic, and that is never easily resolved.

For my father, I had already made the down payment on a family-size can of Simoniz. One of my father's favorite proverbs, one he never tired of quoting, was:

"Motorists wise, Simoniz."

He was as dedicated a hood-shiner as ever bought a fourth-hand Graham-Paige, with soaring hopes and bad valves. I could hardly wait to see him unwrap the Simoniz on Christmas Eve, with the light of the red, yellow, green, and blue bulbs on the tree making that magnificent can glow like the deep flush of myrrh and frankincense. It was all I could do, a constant tortured battle, to keep myself from spilling the beans and thus destroying the magnificent moment of stunned surprise, the disbelieving delight which I knew would fell him like a thunderclap when he saw that I had gone all out.

In fact, several times over the supper table I had meaningfully asked:

"I'll bet you can't guess what I got you for Christmas, Dad."

Once, instead of saying: "Hmmmmmm," he answered by saying: "Hmmm. Let's see. Is it a new furnace?"

My kid brother fell over sideways in nutty little-kid laughter and knocked over his milk, because my father was one of the most feared Furnace Fighters in Northern Indiana.

"That clanky old son of a bitch," he called it, and many's the night with the snow drifting in through the Venetian blinds and the windows rattling like frozen tom-toms he would roar down the basement steps, knocking over Ball jars and kicking roller skates out of the way, bellowing:

"THAT SON OF A BITCH HAS GONE OUT AGAIN! THAT GOD-DAMN CLANKY SON OF A BITCH!!"

The hot-air registers breathed into the clammy air the whistling breath of the Antarctic. A moment of silence. The stillness of the tundra gripped the living room; the hoarfrost sparkled like jewels in the moonlight on my mother's Brillo pad in the kitchen sink.

CLANK! K-BOOM! CLANK! K-BOOM! *CLANK!*

"SONOFABITCH!"

CLANK! K-BOOM! K-BOOM! CLANKCLANK!

He would be operating something called The Shaker, a long iron handle that stuck out of the bottom of that zinc and tin monster called The Furnace.

"For Chrissake, open up the goddamn damper, willya! How the hell did it get turned all the way down again!? GODDAMMIT!"

My mother would leap out of bed and rush into the kitchen in the dark to pull a chain behind the broom closet door marked "Draft."

"FOR CHRISSAKE, STUPID, I SAID THE GODDAMN *DAMPER!*"

My kid brother and I would huddle under our baseball quilt in our Dr. Denton Sleepers, waiting for the uproar to strike us. That's why my brother knocked over the milk when my Old Man said the thing about a new furnace. Indiana wit is always pungent and to the point.

My father was also an expert Clinker Fisher. The furnace was always producing something called "clinkers" which got stuck in the grates, causing faint puffs of blue smoke to come out from under the daybed.

"Sonofabitch clinker!"

The Old Man would jump up at the first whiff and rush down into the basement for a happy night at the old iron fishing hole with his trusty poker. People in Northern Indiana fought Winter tooth and claw; bodily, and there was never a letup.

I had not yet decided on what to get my kid brother for Christmas. It was going to be either a rubber dagger or a Dick Tracy Junior Crimefighter Disguise Kit, containing three false noses and a book of instructions on how to trap crooks. Picking something for your kid brother is never easy, particularly if what you get him is something you yourself have always wanted. This can lead to nothing but bad blood, smoldering rivalries, and scuffling in the bathroom. I myself was lukewarm on rubber daggers at this point in the game, so I was inclined to figure that a good big one with a painted silver blade might do the trick. I was a little doubtful about the Dick Tracy Kit, since I sensed vaguely that there might be trouble over one of the noses, a large orange job with plastic horn-rimmed glasses attached. A dark-horse possibility was a tin zeppelin with red propellers and blue fins. I figured this was something you could really get your teeth into, and it was what I eventually decided on, not realizing that one of the hardest things to wrap in green tissue paper with Santa Claus stickers and red string is a silver zeppelin. Zeppelins are not easy to disguise.

It was now the second week of December and all the stores in town stayed open nights, which meant that things were really getting serious. Every evening immediately after supper we would pile into the car and drive downtown for that great annual folk rite, that most ecstatic, golden, tinseled, quivering time of all kidhood: Christmas shopping. Milling crowds of blue-jowled, agate-eyed foundry workers, gray-faced refinery men, and motley hordes of open-hearth, slag-heap, Bessemer-converter, tin-mill, coke-plant, and welding-shop fugitives trudged through the wildly pulsing department stores, through floor after floor of shiny, beautiful, unattainable treasures, trailed by millions of leatherette-jacketed, high-topped, mufflered kids, each with a gnawing hunger to Get It All. Worried-looking, flush-faced mothers wearing frayed cloth coats with ratty fox-fur collars, their hands chapped and raw from years of dishwater therapy, rode herd on the surging mob, ranging far and wide into the aisles and under the counters, cuffing, slapping, dragging whiners of all sizes from department to department.

At the far end of Toyland in Goldblatt's, on a snowy throne framed with red-and-white candy canes under a suspended squadron of plastic angels blowing silver trumpets in a glowing golden grotto, sat the Man, the Connection: Santa Claus himself. In Northern Indiana Santa Claus is a *big* man, both spiritually and physically, and the Santa Claus at Goldblatt's was officially recognized among the kids as being unquestionably THE Santa Claus. In person. Eight feet tall, shiny high black patent-leather boots, a nimbus cloud of snow-white beard, and a real, thrumming, belt-creaking stomach. No pillows or stuffing. I mean a real *stomach!*

A long line of nervous, fidgeting, greedy urchins wound in and out of the aisles, shoving, sniffling, and above all waiting, waiting to tell HIM what they wanted. In those days it was not easy to disbelieve fully in Santa Claus, because there wasn't much else to believe *in*, and there were many theological arguments over the nature of, the existence of, the affirmation and denial of his existence. However, ten days before zero hour, the air pulsing to the strains of "We Three Kings of Orient Are," the store windows garlanded with green-and-red wreaths, and the toy department bristling with shiny Flexible Flyers, there were few who *dared* to disbelieve. As each day crept on to the next like some arthritic glacier, the atheists among us grew moodier and less and less sure of ourselves, until finally in each scoffing heart was the floating, drifting, nagging suspicion:

"Well, you never can tell."

It did not pay to take chances, and so we waited in line for our turn. Behind me a skinny seven-year-old girl wearing a brown stocking cap and gold-rimmed glasses hit her little brother steadily to keep him in line. She had green teeth. He was wearing an aviator's helmet with the goggles pulled down over his eyes. His galoshes were open and his maroon corduroy knickers were damp. Behind them a fat boy in a huge sheepskin coat stood numbly, his eyes watering in vague fear, his nose red and running. Ahead of my brother and me, a long, uneven procession of stocking caps, mufflers, mittens, and earmuffs inched painfully forward, while in the hazy distance, in his magic glowing cave, Mister Claus sat each in turn on his broad red knee and listened to exultant dream after exultant dream whispered, squeaked, shouted, or sobbed into his shell-like, whisker-encased ear.

Closer and closer we crept. My mother and father had stashed us in line and disappeared. We were alone. Nothing stood between us and our confessor, our benefactor, our patron saint, our dispenser of BB guns, but 297 other beseechers at the throne. I have always felt that later generations of tots, products of less romantic upbringing, cynical nonbelievers in Santa Claus from birth, can never know the nature of the true dream. I was well into my twenties before I finally gave up on the Easter bunny, and I am not convinced that I am the richer for it. Even now there are times when I'm not so sure about the stork.

Over the serpentine line roared a great sea of sound: tinkling bells, recorded carols, the hum and clatter of electric trains, whistles tooting, mechanical cows mooing, cash registers dinging, and from far off in the faint distance the "Ho-ho-ho-ing" of jolly old Saint Nick.

One moment my brother and I were safely back in the Tricycle and Irish Mail department and the next instant we stood at the foot of Mount Olympus itself. Santa's enormous gleaming white snowdrift of a throne soared ten or fifteen feet above our heads on a mountain of red and green tinsel carpeted with flashing Christmas-tree bulbs and gleaming ornaments. Each kid in turn was prodded up a tiny staircase at the side of the mountain on Santa's left, as he passed his last customer on to his right and down a red chute—back into oblivion for another year.

Pretty ladies dressed in Snow White costumes, gauzy gowns glittering with sequins, and tiaras clipped to their golden, artificial hair, presided at the head of the line, directing traffic and keeping order. As we drew nearer, Santa seemed to loom larger and larger. The tension mounted. My brother was now whimpering steadily. I herded him ahead of me while, behind, the girl in the glasses did the same with *her* kid brother. Suddenly there was no one left ahead of us in the line. Snow White grabbed my brother's shoulder with an iron grip and he was on his way up the slope.

"Quit dragging your feet. Get moving," she barked at the toiling little figure climbing the stairs.

The music from above was deafening:

JINGLE BELLS, JINGLE BELLS, JINGLE ALL THE WAY. . . . sung by 10,000 echo-chambered, reverberating chipmunks. . . .

High above me in the sparkling gloom I could see my brother's yellow-and-brown stocking cap as he squatted briefly on Santa's gigantic knee. I heard a booming "Ho-ho-ho," then a high, thin, familiar, trailing wail, one that I had heard billions of times before, as my brother broke into his Primal cry. A claw dug into my elbow and I was launched upward toward the mountaintop.

I had long before decided to level with Santa, to really lay it on the line. No Sandy Andy, no kid stuff. If I was going to ride the range with Red Ryder, Santa Claus was going to have to get the straight poop.

"AND WHAT'S YOUR NAME, LITTLE BOY?"

His booming baritone crashed out over the chipmunks. He reached down and neatly hooked my sheepskin collar, swooping me upward, and there I sat on the biggest knee in creation, looking down and out over the endless expanse of Toyland and down to the tiny figures that wound off into the distance.

"Uhh . . . uhhh . . . uhhh. . . ."

"THAT'S A FINE NAME, LITTLE BOY! HO-HO-HO!"

Santa's warm, moist breath poured down over me as though from some cosmic steam radiator. Santa smoked Camels, like my Uncle Charles.

My mind had gone blank! Frantically I tried to remember what it was I wanted. I was blowing it! There was no one else in the world except me and Santa now. And the chipmunks.

"Uhhh . . . ahhhh. . . ."

"WOULDN'T YOU LIKE A NICE FOOTBALL?"

My mind groped. Football, football. Without conscious will, my voice squeaked out:

"Yeah."

My God, a football! My mind slammed into gear. Already Santa was sliding me off his knee and toward the red chute, and I could see behind me another white-faced kid bobbing upward.

"*I want a Red Ryder BB gun with a special Red Ryder sight and a compass in the stock with a sundial!*" I shouted.

"HO-HO-HO! *YOU'LL SHOOT YOUR EYE OUT, KID.* HO-HO-HO! MERRY CHRISTMAS!"

Down the chute I went.

I have never been struck by a bolt of lightning, but I know how it must feel. The back of my head was numb. My feet clanked leadenly beneath me as I returned to earth at the bottom of the chute. Another Snow White shoved the famous free gift into my mitten—a barely recognizable plastic Kris Kringle stamped with bold red letters: MERRY XMAS. SHOP AT GOLD-BLATT'S FREE PARKING—and spun me back out into Toyland. My brother stood sniveling under a counter piled high with Raggedy Ann dolls, from nowhere my mother and father appeared.

"Did you tell Santa what you wanted?" the Old Man asked.

"Yeah. . . ."

"Did he ask you if you had been a good boy?"

"No."

"Ha! Don't worry. He knows anyway. I'll bet he knows about the basement window. Don't worry. He knows."

Maybe *that* was it! My mind reeled with the realization that maybe Santa *did* know how rotten I had been and that the football was not only a threat but a punishment. There had been for generations on Cleveland Street a theory that if you were not "a good boy" you would reap your just desserts under the Christmas tree. This idea had been largely discounted by the more confirmed evildoers in the neighborhood, but now I could not escape the distinct possibility that there was something to it. Usually for a full month or so before the big day most kids walked the straight and narrow, but I had made a drastic slip from the paths of righteousness by knocking out a basement window with a sled runner and then compounding the idiocy by denying it when all the evidence was incontrovertible. This caused an uproar which had finally resulted in my getting my mouth washed out with Lux and a drastic curtailment of allowance to pay for the glass. I could see that either my father or Santa, or perhaps both, were not content to let bygones be bygones. Were they in league with each other? Or was Santa actually a mother in disguise?

The next few days groaned by. Now only three more school days remained before Christmas vacation, that greatest time of all the year. As it drew closer, Miss Iona Pearl Bodkin, my homeroom teacher, became more and more manic, whipping the class into a veritable frenzy of Yuletide joy. We belted out carol after carol. We built our own paper Christmas tree with cut-out ornaments. We strung long strings of popcorn chains. Crayon Santas and silver-paper wreaths poured out of our assembly line.

In the corner of the room, atop a desk decorated with crepe-paper rosettes, sat our Christmas grab bag. Every kid in the class had bought a gift for the grab bag, with someone's name—drawn from a hat—attached. I had bought for Helen Weathers a large, amazingly life-like, jet-black rubber tarantula. I cackled fiendishly as I wrapped it, and even now its beady green eyes glared from somewhere in the depths of the Christmas grab bag. I knew she'd like it.

Miss Bodkin, after recess, addressed us:

"I want all of you to write a theme. . . ."

A theme! A rotten theme before Christmas! There *must* be kids somewhere who love writing themes, but to a normal air-breathing human kid, writing themes is a torture that ranks only with the dreaded medieval chin-breaker of Inquisitional fame. A theme!

". . . entitled 'What I want for Christmas,'" she concluded.

The clouds lifted. I saw a faint gleam of light at the other end of the black cave of gloom which had enveloped me since my visit to Santa. Rarely had the words poured from my penny pencil with such feverish fluidity. Here was a theme on a subject that needed talking about if ever one did! I remember to this day its glorious winged phrases and concise imagery:

What I want for Christmas is a Red Ryder BB gun with a compass in the stock and this thing that tells time. I think everybody should have a Red Ryder BB gun. They are very good for Christmas. I don't think a football is a very good Christmas present.

I wrote it on blue-lined paper from my Indian Chief tablet, being very careful about the margins. Miss Bodkin was very snippy about uneven margins. The themes were handed in and I felt somehow that when Miss Bodkin read mine she would sympathize with my plight and make an appeal on my behalf to the powers that be, and that everything would work out, somehow. She was my last hope.

The final day before vacation dawned dank and misty, with swirling eddies of icy wind that rattled the porch swing. Warren G. Harding School glowed like a jeweled oasis amid the sooty snowbanks of the playground. Lights blazed from all the windows, and in every room the Christmas party spirit had kids writhing in their seats. The morning winged by, and after lunch Miss Bodkin announced that the rest of the afternoon would be party time. She handed out our graded themes, folded, with our names scrawled on the outside. A big red B in Miss Bodkin's direct hand glowed on my literary effort. I opened it, expecting Miss Bodkin's usual penciled corrections, which ran along the lines of "Watch margins" or "Check Sp." But this time a personal note leaped up, flew around the room, and fastened itself leech-like on the back of my neck:

"You'll shoot your eye out. Merry Christmas."

I sat in my seat, shipping water from every seam. Was there no end to this conspiracy of irrational prejudice against Red Ryder and his peacemaker? Nervously I pulled out of my desk the dog-eared back page of *Open Road For Boys*, which I had carried with me everywhere, waking and sleeping, for the past few weeks. Red Ryder's handsome orange face with the big balloon coming out of his mouth did not look discouraged or defeated. Red must have been a kid once himself, and they must have told him the same thing when he asked for his first Colt .44 for Christmas.

I stuffed my tattered dreams back into my geography book and gloomily watched other, happier, carefree, singing kids who were going to *get* what they wanted for Christmas as Miss Bodkin distributed little green baskets filled with hard candy. Somewhere off down the hall the sixth-grade glee club was singing "Oh little town of Bethlehem, how still we see thee lie. . . ."

Mechanically my jaws crunched on the concrete-hard rock candy and I stared hopelessly out of the window, past cut-out Santas and garlands of red and green chains. It was already getting dark. Night falls fast in Northern Indiana at that time of year. Snow was beginning to fall, drifting softly through the feeble yellow glow of the distant street lamps while around me unbridled merriment raged higher and higher.

By suppertime that night I had begun to resign myself to my fate. After all, I told myself, you can always use another football, and, anyway, there will be other Christmases.

The day before, I had gone with my father and mother to the frozen parking lot next to the Esso station where, after long and soul-searching discussion, we had picked out our tree.

"There's a bare spot on the back."

"It'll fluff out, lady, when it gets hot."

"Is this the kind the needles fall out?"

"Nah, that's them balsams."

"Oh."

Now it stood in the living room, fragrantly, toweringly, teeteringly. Already my mother had begun the trimming operations. The lights were lit, and the living room was transformed into a small, warm paradise.

From the kitchen intoxicating smells were beginning to fill the house. Every year my mother baked two pumpkin pies, spicy and immobilizingly rich. Up through the hot-air registers echoed the boom and bellow of my father fighting The Furnace. I was locked in my bedroom in a fever of excitement. Before me on the bed were sheets of green and yellow paper, balls of colored string, and cellophane envelopes of stickers showing sleighing scenes, wreaths, and angels blowing trumpets. The zeppelin was already lumpily done—it had taken me forty-five minutes—and now I struggled with the big one, the magnificent gleaming gold and pearl perfume atomizer, knowing full well that I was wrapping what would undoubtedly become a treasured family heirloom. I checked the lock on the door, and for double safety hollered:

"DON'T ANYONE OPEN THIS DOOR!"

I turned back to my labors until finally there they were—my masterworks of creative giving piled in a neat pyramid on the quilt. My brother was locked in the bathroom, wrapping the fly swatter he had bought for the Old Man.

Our family always had its Christmas on Christmas Eve. Other less fortunate people, I had heard, opened their presents in the chill clammy light of dawn. Far more civilized, *our* Santa Claus recognized that barbaric practice for what it was. Around midnight great heaps of tissuey, crinkly, sparkly, enigmatic packages appeared among the lower branches of the tree and half hidden among the folds of the white bedsheet that looked in the soft light like some magic snowbank.

Earlier, just after the tree had been finished, my father had taken me and my brother out in the Graham-Paige to "pick up a bottle of wine." When we returned, Santa had been there and gone! On the end table and the bookcase were bowls of English walnuts, cashews, and almonds and petrified hard candy. My brother circled around the tree, moaning softly, while I, cooler and more controlled, quickly eyed the mountain of revealingly wrapped largess—and knew the worst.

Out of the kitchen came my mother, flushed and sparkly-eyed, bearing two wineglasses filled with the special Walgreen drugstore vintage that my Old Man especially favored. Christmas had officially begun. As they sipped their wine we plunged into the cornucopia, quivering with desire and the ecstasy of unbridled avarice. In the background, on the radio, Lionel Barrymore's wheezy, friendly old voice spoke kindly of Bob Cratchit and Tiny Tim and the ghost of old Marley.

The first package I grabbed was tagged "To Randy from Santa." I feverishly passed it over to my brother, who always was a slow reader, and returned to work. Aha!

"To Ralphie from Aunt Clara"—on a largish, lumpy, red-wrapped gift that I suspected to be the crummy football. Frantically I tore off the wrappings. Oh no! OH NO! A pair of fuzzy, pink, idiotic, cross-eyed, lop-eared bunny slippers! Aunt Clara had for years labored under the delusion that I was not only perpetually four years old but also a girl. My mother instantly added oil to the flames by saying:

"Oh, aren't they sweet! Aunt Clara always gives you the nicest presents. Put 'em on; see if they fit."

They did. Immediately my feet began to sweat as those two fluffy little bunnies with blue button eyes stared sappily up at me, and I knew that for at least two years I would have to wear them every time Aunt Clara visited us. I just hoped that Flick would never spot them, as the word of this humiliation could easily make life at Warren G. Harding School a veritable hell.

Next to me in harness my kid brother silently, doggedly stripped package after package until he hit the zeppelin. It was the jackpot!

"WOW! A ZEPPELIN! WHOOPEE! WOW!"

Falling over sideways with an ear-splitting yell, he launched it upward into the middle branches of the tree. Two glass angels and a golden bugle crashed to the floor, and a string of lights winked out.

"It's not supposed to fly, you nut," I said.

"AHH, WHAT GOOD IS A ZEPPELIN THAT DON'T FLY!?"

"It rolls. And beeps."

Instantly he was on his knees pushing the Graf Zeppelin, beeping fiendishly, propellers clacking, across the living-room rug. It was a sound that was to become sickeningly familiar in the months ahead. I suspect even at that moment my mother knew that one day the zeppelin would mysteriously disappear, never to beep again.

My father was on his feet with the first blink of the dying tree lights. He loved nothing better than to track down the continual short circuits and burned-out bulbs of Christmas tree light strings. Oblivious, I continued to ravage my gifts, feigning unalloyed joy at each lousy Sandy Andy, dump truck, and Monopoly game. My brother's gift to me was the only bright spot in an otherwise remarkably mediocre haul: a rubber Frankenstein face which I knew would come in handy. I immediately put it on and, peering through the slit eyes, continued to open my booty.

"Oh, how terrible!" my mother said. "Take it off and put it away."

"I think it looks good on him," my father said. I stood up and did my already famous Frankenstein walk, clumping stiff-legged around the living room and back to the tree.

Finally it was all over. There were no more mysterious packages under the tree, only a great pile of crumpled tissue paper, string, and empty boxes. In the excitement I had forgotten Red Ryder and the BB gun, but now it all came back. Skunked! Well, at least I had a Frankenstein face. And there was no denying that I had scored heavily with the Simoniz and the atomizer, as well as the zeppelin. The joy of giving can uplift the saddened heart.

My brother lay dozing amid the rubble, the zeppelin clasped in one hand and his new fire truck in the other. My father bent over from his easy chair, his eighth glass of wine in his hand.

"Say, don't I see something over there stuck behind the drapes? Why, I think there *is* something over there behind the drapes."

He was right! There *was* a tiny flash of red under the ecru curtains. Like a shot I was off, and milliseconds later I knew that old Santa had come through! A long, heavy, red-wrapped package, marked "To Ralphie from Santa" had been left somehow behind the curtains. In an instant the wrappings were off, and there it was! A Red Ryder carbine-action range-model BB gun lay in its crinkly white packing, blue-steel barrel graceful and taut, its dark, polished stock gleaming like all the treasures of the Western world. And there, burned into the walnut, his level gaze unmistakable, his jaw clean and hard, was Red Ryder himself coolly watching my every move. His face was even more beautiful and malevolent than the pictures in the advertisements showed.

Over the radio thundered a thousand-voiced heavenly choir: "JOY TO THE WORLD, THE LORD HAS COME. . . ."

My mother sat and smiled a weak, doubtful smile while my Old Man grinned broadly from behind his wineglass.

The magnificent weapon came equipped with two heavy tubes of beautiful Copproteck BBs, gleaming gold and as hard as sin itself. Covered with a thin film of oil they poured with a "ssshhhing" sound into the 200-shot magazine through a BB-size hole in the side of that long blue-steel tube. They added weight and a feeling of danger to the gun. There were also printed targets, twenty-five of them, with a large bull's-eye inside concentric rings marked "One-Two-Three-Four," and the bull's-eye was printed right in the middle of a portrait of Red Ryder himself.

I could hardly wait to try it out, but the instruction booklet said, in Red Ryder's own words:

Kids, never fire a BB gun in the house. They can really shoot. And don't ever shoot at other kids. I never shoot anybody but bad guys, and I don't want any of my friends hurt.

It was well past midnight anyway and, excitement or no, I was getting sleepy. Tomorrow was Christmas Day, and the relatives were coming over to visit. That would mean even more loot of one kind or another.

In my warm bed in the cold still air I could hear the falling snow brushing softly against the dark window. Next to me in the blackness lay my oiled blue-steel beauty, the greatest Christmas gift I had ever received. Gradually I drifted off to sleep—

pranging ducks on the wing and getting off spectacular hip-shots as I dissolved into nothingness.

Dawn came. As the gray light crept around the shades and over the quilt, I was suddenly and tinglingly awake. Stealthily I dressed in my icy maroon corduroy knickers, my sheepskin coat, and my plaid sweater. I pulled on my high-tops and found my mittens, crept through the dark living room, fragrant with Christmas tree, and out onto the porch. Inside the house the family slept the sleep of the just and the fulfilled.

During the night a great snow had fallen, covering the gritty remains of past snowfalls. The trees hung rich and heavy with fluffy down. The sun, soaring bright and brilliantly sharp over Pulaski's Candy Store, lit up the soft, rolling moonscape of snow with orange and gold splashes of color. Overnight the temperature had dropped thirty degrees or more, and the brittle, crackling air was still and clean, and it hurt the lungs to breathe it. The temperature stood at perhaps fifteen to twenty below zero, cold enough to make the telephone wires creak and groan in agony. From the eaves of the front porch gnarled crystal icicles stretched all the way to the drifts on the buried lawn.

I trudged down the steps, barely discernible in the soft fluff, and now I stood in the clean air, ready to consummate my great, long, painful, ecstatic love affair. Brushing the snow off the third step, I propped up a gleaming Red Ryder target, the black rings and bull's-eye standing out starkly against the snowy whiteness. Above the bull's-eye Red Ryder watched me, his eyes following my every move. I backed off into the snow a good twenty feet, slammed the stock down onto my left kneecap, holding the barrel with my mittened left hand, flipped the mitten off my right and, hooking my fingers in the icy carbine lever, cocked my blue-steel buddy for the first time. I heard the BB click down into the chamber; the spring inside twanged sharply, and with a clunk she rested taut, hard, and loaded in my chapped, rapidly bluing hands.

For the first time I sighted down over that cold barrel, the heart-shaped rear sight almost brushing my nose and the blade of the front sight wavering back and forth, up and down, and finally coming to rest sharply, cutting the heart and laying dead on the innermost ring. Red Ryder didn't move a muscle, his Stetson flaring out above the target as he waited.

Slowly I squeezed the frosty trigger. Back . . . back . . . back. For one instant I thought wildly: It doesn't work! We'll have to send it back! And then:

CRRAAACK!

The gun jerked upward and for a brief instant everything stood still. The target twitched a tiny tick—and then a massive wallop, a gigantic, slashing impact crashed across the left side of my face. My horn-rimmed glasses spun from my head into a snowbank. For several seconds I stood, not knowing what had happened, warm blood trailing down over my cheek and onto the walnut stock of my Red Ryder 200-shot range-model BB gun.

I lowered the barrel convulsively. The target still stood; Red Ryder was unscratched. A ragged, uncontrolled tidal wave of pain, throbbing and singing, rocked my head. The ricocheting BB had missed my eye by perhaps a half inch, and a long, angry, bloody welt extended from my cheekbone almost to my ear. It was divine retribution! Red Ryder had struck again! Another bad guy had been gunned down!

Frantically I scrambled for my glasses. And then the most catastrophic blow of all—they were pulverized! Few things brought such swift and terrible retribution on a kid during the Depression as a pair of busted glasses. The left lens was out as clean as a whistle, and for a moment I thought: I'll fake it! They'll never know the lens is gone! But then, gingerly fingering my rapidly swelling black eye, I realized that here was a shiner on the way that would top even the one I got the time I fought Grover Dill.

As I put the cold horn-rims back on my nose, the front door creaked open just a crack and I could make out the blur of my mother's Chinese-red chenille bathrobe.

"Be careful. Don't shoot out your eye! Just be careful now."

She hadn't seen! Rapidly my mind evolved a spectacular fantasy involving a falling icicle and how it had hit the gun barrel which caused the stock to bounce up and cut my cheek and break my glasses and I tried to get out of the way but the icicle fell off the roof and hit the gun and it bounced up and hit me and. . . . I began to cry uproariously, faking it at first, but then the shock and fear took over and it was the real thing —heaving, sobbing, retching.

I was now in the bathroom, my mother bending over me, telling me:

"There now, see, it's just a little bump. You're lucky you didn't cut your eye. Those icicles sometimes even kill people. You're really lucky. Here, hold this rag on it, and don't wake your brother."

I HAD PULLED IT OFF!

I sipped the bitter dregs of coffee that remained in my cup, suddenly catapulted by a falling tray back into the cheerful, impersonal, brightly lit clatter of Horn & Hardart. I wondered whether Red Ryder was still dispensing retribution and frontier justice as of old. Considering the number of kids I see with broken glasses, I suspect he is.

. . . Flick topped off our glasses.

"How 'bout some more pretzels?"

He brought the beers back to where we were sitting. I took a deep swallow of cold beer. The old pipes were dry.

Flick went on:

"Do you remember Tom Mix and the TM Bar Ranch?"

"And the Old Wrangler? And that Lucky Horse-shoe Ring? As a matter of fact, you will notice that my index finger is still faintly green from that ring."

Above us the monster color TV set loomed menacing and silent.

"When it's Ralston time at breakfast. . . .
And the something something's something. . . .
Something, something, Jane and Jimmy, too. . . .
Something, something. . . ."

Flick was trying to ad-lib the theme song of the TM Bar Ralston radio show which had formed a bulwark of our childhood morality. I raised my hand imperiously.

"Stop, Flick. I will sing the greatest theme song of them all.

"Who's that little chatterbox . . . ?
The one with curly golden locks. . . ."

He blenched. "My God!"

"Who do I see . . . ?
It's Little Orphan Annie. . . ."

IV 🦢 THE COUNTERFEIT SECRET CIRCLE MEMBER GETS THE MESSAGE, *or* THE ASP STRIKES AGAIN

Every day when I was a kid I'd drop anything I was doing, no matter what it was—stealing wire, having a fistfight, siphoning gas—no matter what, and tear like a blue streak through the alleys, over fences, under porches, through secret short-cuts, to get home not a second too late for the magic time. My breath rattling in wheezy gasps, sweating profusely from my long cross-country run I'd sit glassy-eyed and expectant before our Crosley Notre Dame Cathedral model radio.

I was never disappointed. At exactly five-fifteen, just as dusk was gathering over the picturesque oil refineries and the faint glow of the muttering Open Hearths was beginning to show red against the gloom, the magic notes of an unforgettable theme song came rasping out of our Crosley:

> *"Who's that little chatterbox . . . ?*
> *The one with curly golden locks. . . .*
> *Who do I see . . . ?*
> *It's Little Orphan Annie."*

Ah, they don't write tunes like that any more. There was one particularly brilliant line that dealt with Sandy, Little Orphan Annie's airedale sidekick. Who can forget it?

Arf goes Sandy.

I think it was Sandy more than anyone else that drew me to the Little Orphan Annie radio program. Dogs in our neighborhood never went "Arf." And they certainly were a lot of things, but never faithful.

Little Orphan Annie lived in this great place called Tompkins Corners. There were people called Joe Corntassle and Uncle. They never mentioned the poolroom. There were no stockyards or fistfights. Or drunks sleeping in doorways in good old Tompkins Corners. Orphan Annie and Sandy and Joe Corntassle were always out chasing pirates or trapping smugglers, neither of which we ever had in Indiana as far as I knew. We had plenty of hubcap stealers and once even a guy who stole a lawn. But no pirates. At least they didn't call them that.

She also had this friend named The Asp, who whenever she was really in a tight spot would just show up and cut everybody's head off. I figured that if there was anything a kid of seven needed it was somebody named The Asp. Especially in our neighborhood. He wore a towel around his head.

Immediately after the nightly adventure, which usually took place near the headwaters of the dreaded Orinoco, on would come a guy named Pierre André, the *definitive* radio announcer.

"FELLAS AND GALS. GET SET FOR A MEETING OF THE LITTLE ORPHAN ANNIE SECRET CIRCLE!"

His voice boomed out of the Crosley like some monster, maniacal pipe organ played by the Devil himself. Vibrant, urgent, dynamic, commanding. Pierre André. I have long had a suspicion that an entire generation of Americans grew up feeling inferior to just the *names* of the guys on the radio. Pierre André. Harlow Wilcox. Vincent Pelletier. Truman Bradley. Westbrook Van Voorhees. André Baruch. Norman Brokenshire. There wasn't a Charlie Shmidlap in the lot. Poor little Charlie crouching next to his radio—a born Right Fielder. Playing right field all of his life, knee-deep in weeds, waiting for a flyball that never comes and more than half afraid that one day they *will* hit one in his direction.

"OKAY, KIDS. TIME TO GET OUT YOUR SECRET DECODER PIN. TIME FOR ANOTHER SECRET MESSAGE DIRECT FROM LITTLE

ORPHAN ANNIE TO MEMBERS OF THE LITTLE ORPHAN ANNIE
SECRET CIRCLE."

I got no pin. A member of an Out Group at the age of seven.
And the worst kind of an Out Group. I am living in a non-
Ovaltine-drinking neighborhood.

"ALL RIGHT. SET YOUR PINS TO B-7. SEVEN . . . TWENTY-TWO
. . . NINETEEN . . . EIGHT . . . *FORTY-NINE* . . . SIX . . .
THIRTEEN . . . *THREE!* . . . TWENTY-TWO . . . ONE . . . FOUR
. . . NINETEEN."

Pierre André could get more out of just numbers than Orson
Welles was able to squeeze out of *King Lear*.

"FOURTEEN . . . NINE . . . THIRTY-TWO. OKAY, FELLAS AND
GALS, OVER AND OUT."

Then—silence. The show was over and you had a sinister
feeling that out there in the darkness all over the country there
were millions of kids—decoding. And all I could do was to go
out into the kitchen where my mother was cooking supper and
knock together a salami sandwich. And plot. Somewhere kids
were getting the real truth from Orphan Annie. The message.
And I had no pin. I lived in an Oatmeal-eating family and
listened to an Ovaltine radio show. To get into the Little
Orphan Annie Secret Circle you had to send in the silver inner
seal from a can of what Pierre André called "that rich chocolate-
flavored drink that all the kids love." I had never even *seen* an
Ovaltine can in my life.

But as the old truism goes, every man has his chance, and
when yours comes you had better grab it. They do not make
appointments for the next day. One day while I am foraging my
way home from school, coming down one of my favorite alleys,
knee-deep in garbage and the thrown-out effluvia of kitchen life,
there occurred an incident which forever changed my outlook on
Existence itself, although of course at the time I was not aware
of it, believing instead that I had struck the Jackpot and was
at last on my way into the Big Time.

There was a standard game played solo by almost every male
kid I ever heard of, at least in our neighborhood. It was simple,
yet highly satisfying. There were no rules except those which

the player improvised as he went along. The game had no name and is probably as old as creation itself. It consisted of kicking a tin can or tin cans all the way home. This game is not to be confused with a more formal athletic contest called Kick The Can, which *did* have rules and even teams. This kicking game was a solitary, dogged contest of kid against can, and is quite possibly the very earliest manifestation of the Golf Syndrome.

Anyway, I am kicking condensed milk cans, baked bean cans, sardine cans along the alley, occasionally changing cans at full gallop, when I suddenly found myself kicking a can of a totally unknown nature. I kicked it twice; good, solid, running belts, before I discovered that what I was kicking was an Ovaltine can, the first I had ever seen. Instantly I picked it up, astounded by the mere presence of an Ovaltine drinker in our neighborhood, and then discovered that they had not only thrown out the Ovaltine can but had left the silver inner seal inside. Some rich family had thrown it *all* away! Five minutes later I've got this inner seal in the mail and I start to wait. Every day I would rush home from school and ask:

"Is there any mail for me?"

Day after day, eon after eon. Waiting for three weeks for something to come in the mail to a kid is like being asked to build the Pyramids singlehanded, using the ⚹3 Erector set, the one without the motor. We never did get much mail around our house anyway. Usually it was bad news when it *did* come. Once in a while a letter marked OCCUPANT arrived, offering my Old Man $300 on his signature only, no questions asked, "Even your employer will not be notified." They began with:

"Friend, are you in Money troubles?"

My Old Man could never figure out how they knew, especially since they only called him OCCUPANT. Day after day I watched our mailbox. On Saturdays when there was no school I would sit on the front porch waiting for the mailman and the sound of the yelping pack of dogs that chased him on his appointed rounds through our neighborhood, his muffled curses and thumping kicks mingling nicely with the steady uproar of snarling and yelping. One thing I knew. Trusty old Sandy never chased a mailman. And if he *had,* he would have caught him.

Everything comes to he who waits. I guess. At last, after at least 200 years of constant vigil, there was delivered to me a big, fat, lumpy letter. There are few things more thrilling in Life than lumpy letters. That rattle. Even to this day I feel a wild surge of exultation when I run my hands over an envelope that is thick, fat, and pregnant with mystery.

I ripped it open. And there it was! My simulated gold plastic Decoder pin. With knob. And my membership card.

It was an important moment. Here was a real milestone, and I knew it. I was taking my first step up that great ladder of becoming a real American. Nothing is as important to an American as a membership card with a seal. I know guys who have long strings of them, plastic-enclosed: credit cards, membership cards, identification cards, Blue Cross cards, driver's licenses, all strung together in a chain of Love. The longer the chain, the more they feel they belong. Here was my first card. I was on my way. And the best of all possible ways—I was making it as a Phony. A non-Ovaltine drinking Official Member.

BE IT KNOWN TO ALL AND SUNDRY THAT MR. RALPH WESLEY PARKER IS HEREBY APPOINTED A MEMBER OF THE LITTLE ORPHAN ANNIE SECRET CIRCLE AND IS ENTITLED TO ALL THE HONORS AND BENEFITS ACCRUING THERETO.

Signed: Little Orphan Annie. Countersigned: Pierre André. In ink.

Honors and benefits. Already, at the age of seven, I am *Mister* Parker. They hardly ever even called my Old Man that.

That night I can hardly wait until the adventure is over. I want to get to the real thing, the message. That's what counts. I had spent the entire day sharpening pencils, practicing twirling the knob on my plastic simulated gold Decoder pin. I had lined up plenty of paper and was already at the radio by three-thirty, sitting impatiently through the drone of the late afternoon Soap Operas and newscasts, waiting for my direct contact with Tompkins Corners, my first night as a full Member.

As five-fifteen neared, my excitement mounted. Running waves of goose pimples rippled up and down my spine as I hunched next to our hand-carved, seven-tube Cathedral in the living room. A pause, a station break. . . .

> "Who's that little chatterbox. . . .
> The one with curly golden locks. . . .
> Who do I see . . . ?
> It's Little Orphan Annie."

Let's get on with it! I don't need all this jazz about smugglers and pirates. I sat through Sandy's arfing and Little Orphan Annie's perils hardly hearing a word. On comes, at long last, old Pierre. He's one of *my* friends now. I am In. My first secret meeting.

"OKAY, FELLAS AND GALS. GET OUT YOUR DECODER PINS. TIME FOR THE SECRET MESSAGE FOR ALL THE REGULAR PALS OF LITTLE ORPHAN ANNIE, MEMBERS OF THE LITTLE ORPHAN ANNIE SECRET CIRCLE. ALL SET? HERE WE GO. SET YOUR PINS AT B-12."

My eyes narrowed to mere slits, my steely claws working with precision, I set my simulated gold plastic Decoder pin to B-12.

"ALL READY? PENCILS SET?"

Old Pierre was in great voice tonight. I could tell that tonight's message was really important.

"SEVEN . . . TWENTY-TWO . . . THIRTEEN . . . NINETEEN . . . EIGHT!"

I struggled furiously to keep up with his booming voice dripping with tension and excitement. Finally:

"OKAY, KIDS. THAT'S TONIGHT'S SECRET MESSAGE. LISTEN AGAIN TOMORROW NIGHT, WHEN YOU HEAR. . . ."

> "Who's that little chatterbox. . . .
> The one with curly golden locks. . . ."

Ninety seconds later I am in the only room in the house where a boy of seven could sit in privacy and decode. My pin is on one knee, my Indian Chief tablet on the other. I'm starting to decode.

7. . . .

I spun the dial, poring over the plastic scale of letters. Aha! B. I carefully wrote down my first decoded number. I went to the next.

22. . . .

Again I spun the dial. E . . .

The first word is B-E.

13 . . . S . . .

It was coming easier now.

19 . . . U.

From somewhere out in the house I could hear my kid brother whimpering, his wail gathering steam, then the faint shriek of my mother:

"Hurry up! Randy's gotta go!"

Now what!

"I'LL BE RIGHT OUT, MA! GEE WHIZ!"

I shouted hoarsely, sweat dripping off my nose.

S . . . U . . . 15 . . . R . . . E. BE SURE! A message was coming through!

Excitement gripped my gut. I was getting The Word. BE SURE . . .

14 . . . 8 . . . T . . . O . . . BE SURE TO what? What was Little Orphan Annie trying to say?

17 . . . 9 . . . DR . . . 16 . . 12 . . 1 . . . 9 . . . N . . K . . . 32 . . . OVA . . 19 . . LT . . .

I sat for a long moment in that steamy room, staring down at my Indian Chief notebook. A crummy commercial!

Again a high, rising note from my kid brother.

"I'LL BE RIGHT OUT, MA! FOR CRYING OUT LOUD."

I pulled up my corduroy knickers and went out to face the meat loaf and the red cabbage. The Asp had decapitated another victim.

V 🦢 I POKE AT AN OLD WOUND

. . . I sat staring sorrowfully into my flat beer. Flick, in his best Bartender's barside manner developed over years of sympathizing with despondent drunks, said philosophically:

"Well, chicks come and chicks go. They all want *something* from you."

I did not answer. He went on:

"Have you ever had an Ovaltine stinger? I'll whip one up for you if you'd like to try it."

"No, Flick, I'll stick with beer this afternoon." I was now rapidly approaching one of my Reflective moods.

"Flick, not only was I undone by Little Orphan Annie, but do you remember a girl named Junie Jo Prewitt?"

He stared for a moment out at the Used-Car lot, thinking hard.

"No, I don't believe I do."

"Well, Flick, I do. . . ."

VI ∾ THE ENDLESS STREETCAR RIDE INTO THE
NIGHT, AND THE TINFOIL NOOSE

Mewling, puking babes. That's the way we all start. Damply
clinging to someone's shoulder, burping weakly, clawing our way
into life. *All* of us. Then gradually, surely, we begin to divide
into two streams, all marching together up that long yellow
brick road of life, but on opposite sides of the street. One crowd
goes on to become the Official people, peering out at us from
television screens; magazine covers. They are forever appearing
in newsreels, carrying attaché cases, surrounded by banks of
microphones while the world waits for their decisions and state-
ments. And the rest of us go on to become . . . just us.

They are the Prime Ministers, the Presidents, Cabinet members, Stars, dynamic molders of the Universe, while we remain
forever the onlookers, the applauders of their real lives.

Forever down in the dark dungeons of our souls we ask ourselves:

"How did they get away from me? When did I make that first
misstep that took me forever to the wrong side of the street, to
become eternally part of the accursed, anonymous Audience?"

It seems like one minute we're all playing around back of the
garage, kicking tin cans and yelling at girls, and the next instant
you find yourself doomed to exist as an office boy in the Mail
Room of Life, while another ex-mewling, puking babe sends

down Dicta, says "No comment" to the Press, and lives a real, genuine *Life* on the screen of the world.

Countless sufferers at this hour are spending billions of dollars and endless man hours lying on analysts' couches, trying to pinpoint the exact moment that they stepped off the track and into the bushes forever.

It all hinges on one sinister reality that is rarely mentioned, no doubt due to its implacable, irreversible inevitability. These decisions cannot be changed, no matter how many brightly cheerful, buoyantly optimistic books on HOW TO ACHIEVE A RICHER, FULLER, MORE BOUNTIFUL LIFE or SEVEN MAGIC GOLDEN KEYS TO INSTANT DYNAMIC SUCCESS or THE SECRET OF HOW TO BECOME A BILLIONAIRE we read, or how many classes are attended for instruction in handshaking, back-slapping, grinning, and making After-Dinner speeches. Joseph Stalin was not a Dale Carnegie graduate. He went all the way. It is an unpleasant truth that is swallowed, if at all, like a rancid, bitter pill. A star is a star; a numberless cipher is a numberless cipher.

Even more eerie a fact is that the Great Divide is rarely a matter of talent or personality. Or even luck. Adolf Hitler had a notoriously weak handshake. His smile was, if anything, a vapid mockery. But inevitably his star zoomed higher and higher. Cinema luminaries of the first order are rarely blessed with even the modicum of Talent, and often their physical beauty leaves much to be desired. What is the difference between Us and Them, We and They, the Big Ones and the great, teeming rabble?

There are about four times in a man's life, or a woman's, too, for that matter, when unexpectedly, from out of the darkness, the blazing carbon lamp, the cosmic searchlight of Truth shines full upon them. It is how we react to those moments that forever seals our fate. One crowd simply puts on its sunglasses, lights another cigar, and heads for the nearest plush French restaurant in the jazziest section of town, sits down and orders a drink, and ignores the whole thing. While we, the Doomed, caught in the brilliant glare of illumination, see ourselves inescapably for what we are, and from that day on skulk in the weeds, hoping no one else will spot us.

Those moments happen when we are least able to fend them off. I caught the first one full in the face when I was fourteen. The fourteenth summer is a magic one for all kids. You have just slid out of the pupa stage, leaving your old baby skin behind, and have not yet become a grizzled, hardened, tax-paying beetle. At fourteen you are made of cellophane. You curl easily and everyone can see through you.

When I was fourteen, Life was flowing through me in a deep, rich torrent of Castoria. How did I know that the first rocks were just ahead, and I was about to have my keel ripped out on the reef? Sometimes you feel as though you are alone in a rented rowboat, bailing like mad in the darkness with a leaky bailing can. It is important to know that there are at least two billion other ciphers in the same boat, bailing with the same leaky can. They all think they are alone and are crossed with an evil star. They are right.

I'm fourteen years old, in my sophomore year at high school. One day Schwartz, my purported best friend, sidled up to me edgily outside of school while we were waiting on the steps to come in after lunch. He proceeded to outline his plan:

"Helen's old man won't let me take her out on a date on Saturday night unless I get a date for her girlfriend. A double date. The old coot figures, I guess, that if there are four of us there won't be no monkey business. Well, how about it? Do you want to go on a blind date with this chick? I never seen her."

Well. For years I had this principle—absolutely *no* blind dates. I was a man of perception and taste, and life was short. But there is a time in your life when you have to stop taking and begin to give just a little. For the first time the warmth of sweet Human Charity brought the roses to my cheeks. After all, Schwartz was my friend. It was little enough to do, have a blind date with some no doubt skinny, pimply girl for your best friend. I would do it for Schwartz. He would do as much for me.

"Okay. Okay, Schwartz."

Then followed the usual ribald remarks, feckless boasting, and dirty jokes about dates in general and girls in particular. It was decided that next Saturday we would go all the way. I had a morning paper route at the time, and my life savings stood at about $1.80. I was all set to blow it on one big night.

I will never forget that particular Saturday as long as I live. The air was as soft as the finest of spun silk. The scent of lilacs hung heavy. The catalpa trees rustled in the early evening breeze from off the Lake. The inner Me itched in that nameless way, that indescribable way that only the fourteen-year-old Male fully knows.

All that afternoon I had carefully gone over my wardrobe to select the proper symphony of sartorial brilliance. That night I set out wearing my magnificent electric blue sport coat, whose shoulders were so wide that they hung out over my frame like vast, drooping eaves, so wide I had difficulty going through an ordinary door head-on. The electric blue sport coat that draped voluminously almost to my knees, its wide lapels flapping soundlessly in the slightest breeze. My pleated gray flannel slacks began just below my breastbone and indeed chafed my armpits. High-belted, cascading down finally to grasp my ankles in a vise-like grip. My tie, indeed one of my most prized possessions, had been a gift from my Aunt Glenn upon the state occasion of graduation from eighth grade. It was of a beautiful silky fabric, silvery pearly colored, four inches wide at the fulcrum, and of such a length to endanger occasionally my zipper in moments of haste. Hand-painted upon it was a magnificent blood-red snail.

I had spent fully two hours carefully arranging and rearranging my great mop of wavy hair, into which I had rubbed fully a pound and a half of Greasy Kid Stuff.

Helen and Schwartz waited on the corner under the street-light at the streetcar stop near Junie Jo's home. Her name was Junie Jo Prewitt. I won't forget it quickly, although she has, no doubt, forgotten mine. I walked down the dark street alone, past houses set back off the street, through the darkness, past privet hedges, under elm trees, through air rich and ripe with promise. Her house stood back from the street even farther than the others. It sort of crouched in the darkness, looking out at me, kneeling. Pregnant with Girldom. A real Girlfriend house.

The first faint touch of nervousness filtered through the marrow of my skullbone as I knocked on the door of the screen-enclosed porch. No answer. I knocked again, louder. Through the murky screens I could see faint lights in the house itself. Still no answer. Then I found a small doorbell button buried in the sash. I pressed. From far off in the bowels of the house I heard two chimes "Bong" politely. It sure didn't sound like our doorbell. We had a real ripper that went off like a broken buzz saw, more of a BRRRAAAAKKK than a muffled Bong. This was a rich people's doorbell.

The door opened and there stood a real, genuine, gold-plated Father: potbelly, underwear shirt, suspenders, and all.

"Well?" he asked.

For one blinding moment of embarrassment I couldn't remember her name. After all, she was a blind date. I couldn't just say:

"I'm here to pick up some girl."

He turned back into the house and hollered:

"JUNIE JO! SOME KID'S HERE!"

"Heh, heh. . . ." I countered.

He led me into the living room. It was an itchy house, sticky stucco walls of a dull orange color, and all over the floor this Oriental rug with the design crawling around, making loops and sworls. I sat on an overstuffed chair covered in stiff green mohair that scratched even through my slacks. Little twisty bridge lamps stood everywhere. I instantly began to sweat down the back of my clean white shirt. Like I said, it was a very itchy house. It had little lamps sticking out of the walls that looked like phony candles, with phony glass orange flames. The rug started moaning to itself.

I sat on the edge of the chair and tried to talk to this Father. He was a Cub fan. We struggled under water for what seemed like an hour and a half, when suddenly I heard someone coming down the stairs. First the feet; then those legs, and there she was. She was magnificent! The greatest-looking girl I ever saw in my life! I have hit the double jackpot! And on a blind date! Great Scot!

My senses actually reeled as I clutched the arm of that bilge-green chair for support. Junie Jo Prewitt made Cleopatra look like a Girl Scout!

Five minutes later we are sitting in the streetcar, heading toward the bowling alley. I am sitting next to the most fantastic creation in the Feminine department known to Western man. There are the four of us in that long, yellow-lit streetcar. No one else was aboard; just us four. I, naturally, being a trained gentleman, sat on the aisle to protect her from candy wrappers and cigar butts and such. Directly ahead of me, also on the aisle, sat Schwartz, his arm already flung affectionately in a death grip around Helen's neck as we boomed and rattled through the night.

I casually flung my right foot up onto my left knee so that she could see my crepe-soled, perforated, wing-toed, Scotch bluchers with the two-toned laces. I started to work my famous charm on her. Casually, with my practiced offhand, cynical, cutting, sardonic humor I told her about how my Old Man had cracked the block in the Oldsmobile, how the White Sox were going to have a good year this year, how my kid brother wet his pants when he saw a snake, how I figured it was going to rain, what a great guy Schwartz was, what a good second baseman I was, how I figured I might go out for football. On and on I rolled, like Old Man River, pausing significantly for her to pick up the conversation. Nothing.

Ahead of us Schwartz and Helen were almost indistinguishable one from the other. They giggled, bit each other's ears, whispered, clasped hands, and in general made me itch even more.

From time to time Junie Jo would bend forward stiffly from the waist and say something I could never quite catch into Helen's right ear.

I told her my great story of the time that Uncle Carl lost his false teeth down the airshaft. Still nothing. Out of the corner of my eye I could see that she had her coat collar turned up, hiding most of her face as she sat silently, looking forward past Helen Weathers into nothingness.

I told her about this old lady on my paper route who chews tobacco, and roller skates in the backyard every morning. I still couldn't get through to her. Casually I inched my right arm up over the back of the seat behind her shoulders. The acid test. She leaned forward, avoiding my arm, and stayed that way.

"Heh, heh, heh. . . ."

As nonchalantly as I could, I retrieved it, battling a giant cramp in my right shoulder blade. I sat in silence for a few seconds, sweating heavily as ahead Schwartz and Helen are going at it hot and heavy.

It was then that I became aware of someone saying something to me. It was an empty car. There was no one else but us. I glanced around, and there it was. Above us a line of car cards looked down on the empty streetcar. One was speaking directly to me, to me alone.

DO YOU OFFEND?

Do I *offend?!*

With no warning, from up near the front of the car where the motorman is steering I see this thing coming down the aisle directly toward *me*. It's coming closer and closer. I can't escape it. It's this blinding, fantastic, brilliant, screaming blue light. I am spread-eagled in it. There's a pin sticking through my thorax. I see it all now.

I AM THE BLIND DATE!

ME!!

I'M the one they're being nice to!

I'm suddenly getting fatter, more itchy. My new shoes are like bowling balls with laces; thick, rubber-crepe bowling balls. My great tie that Aunt Glenn gave me is two feet wide, hanging down to the floor like some crinkly tinfoil noose. My beautiful hand-painted snail is seven feet high, sitting up on my shoulder, burping. Great Scot! It is all clear to me in the searing white

light of Truth. My friend Schwartz, I can see him saying to
Junie Jo:

"I got this crummy fat friend who never has a date. Let's
give him a break and. . . ."

I AM THE BLIND DATE!

They are being nice to *me!* She is the one who is out on a
Blind Date. A Blind Date that didn't make it.

In the seat ahead, the merriment rose to a crescendo. Helen
tittered; Schwartz cackled. The marble statue next to me stared
gloomily out into the darkness as our streetcar rattled on. The
ride went on and on.

I AM THE BLIND DATE!

I didn't say much the rest of the night. There wasn't much
to be said.

"You sure you don't want a shot? A little bourbon maybe?" Flick asked, oozing sympathy. He went on:

"Do you remember the time Jane Hutchinson left me standing in a snowdrift for four hours? While she had a date with Claude Eaton!"

"Whatever happened to her?"

"I hear she moved out somewhere near Cedar Lake." Flick mopped the bar pensively.

"Cedar Lake! I haven't heard of Cedar Lake for years! The Dance Hall! The Roller Rink! The Smell! Is it still out there, Flick? How *is* Cedar Lake?"

Flick paused meaningfully in his swabbing, savoring to the full his next statement.

"Cedar Lake. It's the first time I ever heard of 'em doing it to a lake. It's Condemned."

VIII 🦢 HAIRY GERTZ AND THE FORTY-SEVEN CRAPPIES

Life, when you're a Male kid, is what the Grownups are doing. The Adult world seems to be some kind of secret society that has its own passwords, handclasps, and countersigns. The thing is to get In. But there's this invisible, impenetrable wall between you and all the great, unimaginably swinging things that they seem to be involved in. Occasionally mutterings of exotic secrets and incredible pleasures filter through. And so you bang against it, throw rocks at it, try to climb over it, burrow under it; but there it is. Impenetrable. Enigmatic.

Girls somehow seem to be already involved, as though from birth they've got the Word. Lolita has no Male counterpart. It does no good to protest and pretend otherwise. The fact is inescapable. A male kid is really a *kid*. A female kid is a *girl*. Some guys give up early in life, surrender completely before the impassable transparent wall, and remain little kids forever. They are called "Fags," or "Homosexuals," if you are in polite society.

The rest of us have to claw our way into Life as best we can, never knowing when we'll be Admitted. It happens to each of us in different ways—and once it does, there's no turning back.

It happened to me at the age of twelve in Northern Indiana —a remarkably barren terrain resembling in some ways the surface of the moon, encrusted with steel mills, oil refineries, and honky-tonk bars. There was plenty of natural motivation for Total Escape. Some kids got hung up on kite flying, others on pool playing. I became the greatest vicarious angler in the history of the Western world.

I say vicarious because there just wasn't any actual fishing to be done around where I lived. So I would stand for hours in front of the goldfish tank at Woolworth's, landing fantails in my mind, after incredible struggles. I read *Field & Stream*, *Outdoor Life*, and *Sports Afield* the way other kids read *G-8 And His Battle Aces*. I would break out in a cold sweat reading about these guys portaging to Alaska and landing rare salmon; and about guys climbing the High Sierras to do battle with the wily golden trout; and mortal combat with the steelheads. I'd read about craggy, sinewy sportsmen who discover untouched bass lakes where they have to beat off the pickerel with an oar, and the saber-toothed, raging smallmouths chase them ashore and right up into the woods.

After reading one of these fantasies I would walk around in a daze for hours, feeling the cork pistol grip of my imaginary trusty six-foot, split-bamboo bait-casting rod in my right hand and hearing the high-pitched scream of my Pflueger Supreme reel straining to hold a seventeen-pound Great Northern in check.

I became known around town as "the-kid-who-is-the-nut-on-fishing," even went to the extent of learning how to tie flies, although I'd never been fly casting in my life. I read books on the subject. And in my bedroom, while the other kids are making balsa models of Curtiss Robins, I am busy tying Silver Doctors, Royal Coachmen, and Black Gnats. They were terrible. I would try out one in the bathtub to see whether it made a ripple that might frighten off the wily rainbow.

"Glonk!"

Down to the bottom like a rock, my floating dry fly would go. Fishing was part of the mysterious and unattainable Adult world. I wanted In.

My Old Man was In, though he was what you might call a once-in-a-while-fisherman-and-beer-party-goer; they are the same thing in the shadow of the blast furnaces. (I knew even then that there are people who Fish and there are people who Go Fishing; they're two entirely different creatures.) My Old Man did not drive 1500 miles to the Atlantic shore with 3000 pounds of Abercrombie & Fitch fishing tackle to angle for stripers. He was the kind who would Go Fishing maybe once a month during the summer when it was too hot to Go Bowling and all of the guys down at the office would get The Itch. To them, fishing was a way of drinking a lot of beer and yelling. And getting away from the women. To me, it was a sacred thing. To *fish*.

He and these guys from the office would get together and go down to one of the lakes a few miles from where we lived— but never to Lake Michigan, which wasn't far away. I don't know why; I guess it was too big and awesome. In any case, nobody ever really thought of fishing in it. At least nobody in my father's mob. They went mostly to a mudhole known as Cedar Lake.

I will have to describe to you what a lake in the summer in Northern Indiana is like. To begin with, heat, in Indiana, is something else again. It descends like a 300-pound fat lady onto a picnic bench in the middle of July. It can literally be sliced into chunks and stored away in the basement to use in winter; on cold days you just bring it out and turn it on. Indiana heat is not a meteorological phenomenon—it is a solid element, something you can grab by the handles. Almost every day in the summer the whole town is just shimmering in front of you. You'd look across the street and skinny people would be all fat and wiggly like in the fun-house mirrors at Coney Island. The asphalt in the streets would bubble and hiss like a pot of steaming Ralston.

That kind of heat and sun produces mirages. All it takes is good flat country, a nutty sun, and insane heat and, by George, you're looking at Cleveland 200 miles away. I remember many times standing out in center field on an incinerating day in mid-August, the prairie stretching out endlessly in all directions, and way out past the swamp would be this kind of tenuous, shadowy, cloud-like thing shimmering just above the horizon. It would be the Chicago skyline, upside down, just hanging there in the sky. And after a while it would gradually disappear.

So, naturally, fishing is different in Indiana. The muddy lakes, about May, when the sun starts beating down on them, would begin to simmer and bubble quietly around the edges. These lakes are not fed by springs or streams. I don't know what feeds them. Maybe seepage. Nothing but weeds and truck axles on the bottom; flat, low, muddy banks, surrounded by cotton-wood trees, cattails, smelly marshes, and old dumps. Archetypal dumps. Dumps gravitate to Indiana lakes like flies to a hog killing. Way down at the end where the water is shallow and soupy are the old cars and the ashes, busted refrigerators, oil drums, old corsets, and God knows what else.

At the other end of the lake is the Roller Rink. There's *always* a Roller Rink. You can hear that old electric organ going, playing "Heartaches," and you can hear the sound of the roller skates:

"Shhhhhh . . . sssshhhhhhhhh . . . sssssshhhhhhhhhhhhh-hhh. . . ."

And the fistfights breaking out. The Roller Rink Nut in heat. The Roller Rink Nut was an earlier incarnation of the Drive-In Movie Nut. He was the kind who was very big with stainless steel diners, motels, horror movies, and frozen egg rolls. A close cousin to the Motorcycle Clod, he went ape for chicks with purple eyelids. You know the crowd. Crewcuts, low fore-heads, rumbles, hollering, belching, drinking beer, roller skating on one foot, wearing black satin jackets with SOUTH SIDE A. C. lettered in white on the back around a white-winged roller-skated foot. The kind that hangs the stuff in the back windows of their '53 Mercuries; a huge pair of foam-rubber dice, a skull and crossbones, hula-hula dolls, and football players —Pro, of course, with heads that bob up and down. The guys with ball fringe around the windows of their cars, with phony

Venetian blinds in the back, and big white rubber mudguards hanging down, with red reflectors. Or they'll take some old heap and line it with plastic imitation mink fur, pad the steering wheel with leopard skin and ostrich feathers until it weighs seventeen pounds and is as fat as a salami. A TV set, a bar, and a folding Castro bed are in the trunk, automatically operated and all lined with tasteful Sears Roebuck ermine. You know the crew—a true American product. We turn them out like Campbell's Pork & Beans.

This is the system of aesthetics that brought the Roller Rink to Cedar Lake, Indiana, when I was a kid.

About 150 yards from the Roller Rink was the Cedar Lake Evening In Paris Dance Hall. Festering and steamy and thronged with yeasty refugees from the Roller Rink. These are the guys who can't skate. But they can do other things. They're down there jostling back and forth in 400-per-cent humidity to the incomparable sounds of an Indiana dancehall band. Twelve non-Union cretinous musicians—Mickey Iseley's Moonlight Serenaders—blowing "Red Sails In the Sunset" on Montgomery Ward altos. The lighting is a tasteful combination of naked light bulbs, red and blue crepe paper, and orange cellophane gels.

In between the Roller Rink and the Dance Hall are seventeen small shacks known as Beer Halls. And surrounding this tiny oasis of civilization, this bastion of bonhomie, is a gigantic sea of total darkness, absolute pitch-black Stygian darkness, around this tiny island of totally decadent, bucolic American merriment. The roller skates are hissing, the beer bottles are crashing, the chicks are squealing, Mickey's reed men are quavering, and Life is full.

And in the middle of the lake, several yards away, are over 17,000 fishermen, in wooden rowboats rented at a buck and a half an hour. It is 2 A.M. The temperature is 175, with humidity to match. And the smell of decayed toads, the dumps at the far end of the lake, and an occasional *soupçon* of Standard Oil, whose refinery is a couple of miles away, is enough to put hair on the back of a mud turtle. Seventeen thousand guys clumped together in the middle, fishing for the known sixty-four crappies in that lake.

Crappies are a special breed of Midwestern fish, created by God for the express purpose of surviving in waters that would kill a bubonic-plague bacillus. They have never been known to fight, or even faintly struggle. I guess when you're a crappie, you figure it's no use anyway. One thing is as bad as another. They're just down there in the soup. No one quite knows what they eat, if anything, but everybody's fishing for them. At two o'clock in the morning.

Each boat contains a minimum of nine guys and fourteen cases of beer. And once in a while, in the darkness, is heard the sound of a guy falling over backward into the slime:

SSSSGLUNK!

"Oh! Ah! Help, help!" A piteous cry in the darkness. Another voice:

"Hey, for God's sake, Charlie's fallen in again! Grab the oar!"

And then it slowly dies down. Charlie is hauled out of the goo and is lying on the bottom of the boat, urping up dead lizards and Atlas Prager. Peace reigns again.

The water in these lakes is not the water you know about. It is composed of roughly ten per cent waste glop spewed out by Shell, Sinclair, Phillips, and the Grasselli Chemical Corporation; twelve per cent used detergent; thirty-five per cent thick gruel composed of decayed garter snakes, deceased toads, fermenting crappies, and a strange, unidentifiable liquid that holds it all together. No one is quite sure *what* that is, because everybody is afraid to admit what it really is. They don't want to look at it too closely.

So this mélange lays there under the sun, and about August it is slowly simmering like a rich mulligatawny stew. At two in the morning you can hear the water next to the boat in the darkness:

"Gluuummp . . . Bluuuummmp."

Big bubbles of some unclassified gas come up from the bottom and burst. The natives, in their superstitious way, believe that it is highly inflammable. They take no chances.

The saddest thing of all is that on these lakes there are usually about nineteen summer cottages to the square foot, each equipped with a large motorboat. The sound of a 40-horsepower Chris-Craft going through a sea of number-ten oil has to be heard to be believed.

RRRRRRRAAAAAAAAAHHHHHHHHHWWWWWWWWWWWWWRRRRRRRRRR-R!

The prow is sort of parting the stuff, slowly stirring it into a sluggish, viscous wake.

Natives actually *swim* in this water. Of course, it is impossible to swim near the shore, because the shore is one great big sea of mud that goes all the way down to the core of the earth. There are stories of whole towns being swallowed up and stored in the middle of the earth. So the native rows out to the middle of the lake and hurls himself off the back seat of his rowboat.

"GLURP!"

It is impossible to sink in this water. The specific gravity and surface tension make the Great Salt Lake seem dangerous for swimming. You don't sink. You just bounce a little and float there. You literally have to hit your head on the surface of these lakes to get under a few inches. Once you do, you come up streaming mosquito eggs and dead toads—an Indiana specialty—and all sorts of fantastic things which are the offshoot of various exotic merriments which occur outside the Roller Rink.

The bottom of the lake is composed of a thick incrustation of old beer cans. The beer cans are at least a thousand feet thick in certain places.

And so 17,000 fishermen gather in one knot, because it is rumored that here is where The Deep Hole is. All Indiana lakes have a Deep Hole, into which, as the myth goes, the fish retire to sulk in the hot weather. Which is always.

Every month or so an announcement would be made by my Old Man, usually on a Friday night, after work.

"I'm getting up early tomorrow morning. I'm going fishing."

Getting up early and going fishing with Hairy Gertz and the crowd meant getting out of the house about three o'clock in the afternoon, roughly. Gertz was a key member of the party. He owned the Coleman lamp. It was part of the folklore that if you had a bright lantern in your boat the fish could not resist it. The idea was to hold the lantern out over the water and the fish would have to come over to see what was going on. Of course, when the fish arrived, there would be your irresistible worm, and that would be it.

Well, these Coleman lamps may not have drawn fish, but they worked great on mosquitoes. One of the more yeasty experiences in Life is to occupy a tiny rented rowboat with eight other guys, knee-deep in beer cans, with a blinding Coleman lamp hanging out of the boat, at 2 A.M., with the lamp hissing like Fu Manchu about to strike and every mosquito in the Western Hemisphere descending on you in the middle of Cedar Lake.

ZZZZZZZZZZZZZZZZZZZZTTTTTTTTTTTT

They *love* Coleman lamps. In the light they shed the mosquitoes swarm like rain. And in the darkness all around there'd be other lights in other boats, and once in a while a face would float above one. Everyone is coated with an inch and a half of something called citronella, reputedly a mosquito repellent but actually a sort of mosquito salad dressing.

The water is absolutely flat. There has not been a breath of air since April. It is now August. The surface is one flat sheet of old used oil laying in the darkness, with the sounds of the Roller Rink floating out over it, mingling with the angry drone of the mosquitoes and muffled swearing from the other boats. A fistfight breaks out at the Evening In Paris. The sound of sirens can be heard faintly in the Indiana blackness. It gets louder and then fades away. Tiny orange lights bob over the dance floor.

"Raaahhhhhd sails in the sawwwwnnnnsehhhht. . . ."

It's the drummer who sings. He figures some day Ted Weems will be driving by, and hear him, and. . . .

". . . haaaahhhhwwww brightlyyyy they shinneee. . . ."

There is nothing like a band vocalist in a rotten, struggling Mickey band. When you've heard him over 2000 yards of soupy, oily water, filtered through fourteen billion feeding mosquitoes in the August heat, he is particularly juicy and ripe. He is overloading the ten-watt Allied Radio Knight amplifier by at least 400 per cent, the gain turned all the way up, his chrome-plated bullet-shaped crystal mike on the edge of feedback.

"Raaahhhhhd sails in the sawwwwnnnnsehhhht. . . ."

It is the sound of the American night. And to a twelve-year-old kid it is exciting beyond belief.

Then my Old Man, out of the blue, says to me:

"You know, if you're gonna come along, you got to clean the fish."

Gonna come along! My God! I wanted to go fishing more than anything else in the world, and my Old Man wanted to drink beer more than anything else in the world, and so did Gertz and the gang, and more than even *that*, they wanted to get away from all the women. They wanted to get out on the lake and tell dirty stories and drink beer and get eaten by mosquitoes; just sit out there and sweat and be Men. They wanted to get away from work, the car payments, the lawn, the mill, and everything else.

And so here I am, in the dark, in a rowboat with The Men. I am half-blind with sleepiness. I am used to going to bed at nine-thirty or ten o'clock, and here it is two, three o'clock in the morning. I'm squatting in the back end of the boat, with 87,000,000 mosquitoes swarming over me, but I am *fishing!* I am out of my skull with fantastic excitement, hanging onto my pole.

In those days, in Indiana, they fished with gigantic cane poles. They knew not from Spinning. A cane pole is a long bamboo pole that's maybe twelve or fifteen feet in length; it weighs a ton, and tied to the end of it is about thirty feet of thick green line, roughly half the weight of the average clothesline, three big lead sinkers, a couple of crappie hooks, and a bobber.

One of Sport's most exciting moments is when 7 Indiana

fishermen in the same boat simultaneously and without consulting one another decide to pull their lines out of the water and recast. In total darkness. First the pole, rising like a huge whip:

"Whoooooooooooooop!"

Then the lines, whirling overhead:

"Wheeeeeeeeeeeeooooooooooo!"

And then:

"OH! FOR CHRISSAKE! WHAT THE HELL?"

Clunk! CLONK!

Sound of cane poles banging together, and lead weights landing in the boat. And such brilliant swearing as you have never heard. Yelling, hollering, with somebody always getting a hook stuck in the back of his ear. And, of course, all in complete darkness, the Coleman lamp at the other end of the rowboat barely penetrating the darkness in a circle of three or four feet.

"Hey, for God's sake, Gertz, will ya tell me when you're gonna pull your pole up!? Oh, Jesus Christ, look at this mess!"

There is nothing worse than trying to untangle seven cane poles, 200 feet of soggy green line, just as they are starting to hit in the other boats. Sound carries over water:

"Shhhhh! I got a bite!"

The fishermen with the tangled lines become frenzied. Fingernails are torn, hooks dig deeper into thumbs, and kids huddle terrified out of range in the darkness.

You have been sitting for twenty hours, and nothing. A bobber just barely visible in the dark water is one of the most beautiful sights known to man. It's not doing anything, but there's always the feeling that at any instant it might. It just lays out there in the darkness. A luminous bobber, a beautiful thing, with a long, thin quill and a tiny red-and-white float, with just the suggestion of a line reaching into the black water. These are special bobbers for *very* tiny fish.

I have been watching my bobber so hard and so long in the darkness that I am almost hypnotized. I have not had a bite—ever—but the excitement of being there is enough for me, a kind of delirious joy that has nothing to do with sex or any of the

more obvious pleasures. To this day, when I hear some guy
singing in that special drummer's voice, it comes over me. It's
two o'clock in the morning again. I'm a kid. I'm tired. I'm
excited. I'm having the time of my life.

And at the other end of the lake:

"Raaahhhhhd sails in the sawwwwnnnnsehhhht. . . ."

The Roller Rink drones on, and the mosquitoes are humming.
The Coleman lamp sputters, and we're all sitting together in
our little boat.

Not really together, since I am a kid, and they are Men,
but at least I'm there. Gertz is stewed to the ears. He is down
at the other end. He has this fantastic collection of rotten
stories, and early in the evening my Old Man keeps saying:

"There's a kid with us, you know."

But by two in the morning all of them have had enough so
that it doesn't matter. They're telling stories, and I don't care.
I'm just sitting there, clinging to my cane pole when, by God,
I get a nibble!

I don't believe it. The bobber straightens up, jiggles, dips,
and comes to rest in the gloom. I whisper:

"I got a bite!"

The storytellers look up from their beer cans in the darkness.

"What . . . ? Hey, whazzat?"

"Shhhhh! Be quiet!"

We sit in silence, everybody watching his bobber through the
haze of insects. The drummer is singing in the distance. We
hang suspended for long minutes. Then suddenly all the bobbers
dipped and went under. The crappies are hitting!

You never saw anything like it! We are pulling up fish as
fast as we can get them off the hooks. Crappies are flying
into the boat, one after the other, and hopping around on the
bottom in the darkness, amid the empty beer cans. Within
twenty minutes we have landed forty-seven fish. We are knee-
deep in crappies. The jackpot!

Well, the Old Man just goes wild. They are all yelling and
screaming and pulling the fish in—while the other boats around
us are being skunked. The fish have come out of their hole or

whatever it is that they are in at the bottom of the lake, the beer cans and the old tires, and have decided to eat.

You can hear the rest of the boats pulling up anchors and rowing over, frantically. They are thumping against us. There's a big, solid phalanx of wooden boats around us. You could walk from one boat to the other for miles around. And still they are skunked. *We* are catching the fish!

By 3 A.M. they've finally stopped biting, and an hour later we are back on land. I'm falling asleep in the rear seat between Gertz and Zudock. We're driving home in the dawn, and the men are hollering, drinking, throwing beer cans out on the road, and having a great time.

We are back at the house, and my father says to me as we are coming out of the garage with Gertz and the rest of them:

"And now Ralph's gonna clean the fish. Let's go in the house and have something to eat. Clean 'em on the back porch, will ya, kid?"

In the house they go. The lights go on in the kitchen; they sit down and start eating sandwiches and making coffee. And I am out on the back porch with forty-seven live, flopping crappies.

They are well named. Fish that are taken out of muddy, rotten, lousy, stinking lakes are muddy, rotten, lousy, stinking fish. It is as simple as that. And they are made out of some kind of hard rubber.

I get my Scout knife and go to work. Fifteen minutes and twenty-one crappies later I am sick over the side of the porch. But I do not stop. It is part of Fishing.

By now, nine neighborhood cats and a raccoon have joined me on the porch, and we are all working together. The August heat, now that we are away from the lake, is even hotter. The uproar in the kitchen is getting louder and louder. There is nothing like a motley collection of Indiana office workers who have just successfully defeated Nature and have brought home the kill. Like cave men of old, they celebrate around the camp-fire with song and drink. And belching.

I have now finished the last crappie and am wrapping the

clean fish in the editorial page of the *Chicago Tribune.* It
has a very tough paper that doesn't leak. Especially the editorial
page.

The Old Man hollers out:

"How you doing? Come in and have a Nehi."

I enter the kitchen, blinded by that big yellow light bulb,
weighted down with a load of five-and-a-half-inch crappies,
covered with fish scales and blood, and smelling like the far end
of Cedar Lake. There are worms under my fingernails from
baiting hooks all night, and I am feeling at least nine feet
tall. I spread the fish out on the sink—and old Hairy Gertz says:

"My God! Look at those *speckled beauties!*" An expression
he had picked up from *Outdoor Life.*

The Old Man hands me a two-pound liverwurst sandwich
and a bottle of Nehi orange. Gertz is now rolling strongly, as
are the other eight file clerks, all smelly, and mosquito-bitten,
eyes red-rimmed from the Coleman lamp, covered with worms
and with the drippings of at least fifteen beers apiece. Gertz
hollers:

"Ya know, lookin' at them fish reminds me of a story." He
is about to uncork his cruddiest joke of the night. They all
lean forward over the white enamel kitchen table with the
chipped edges, over the salami and the beer bottles, the rye
bread and the mustard. Gertz digs deep into his vast file
of obscenity.

"One time there was this Hungarian bartender, and ya know,
he had a cross-eyed daughter and a bowlegged dachshund. And
this. . . ."

At first I am holding back, since I am a kid. The Old
Man says:

"Hold it down, Gertz. You'll wake up the wife and she'll
raise hell."

He is referring to My Mother.

Gertz lowers his voice and they all scrunch their chairs forward amid a great cloud of cigar smoke. There is only one
thing to do. I scrunch forward, too, and stick my head into
the huddle, right next to the Old Man, into the circle of leering,

snickering, fishy-smelling faces. Of course, I do not even remotely comprehend the gist of the story. But I know that it is rotten to the core.

Gertz belts out the punch line; the crowd bellows and beats on the table. They begin uncapping more Blatz.

Secretly, suddenly, and for the first time, I realize that I am In. The Eskimo pies and Nehi oranges are all behind me, and a whole new world is stretching out endlessly and wildly in all directions before me. I have gotten The Signal!

Suddenly my mother is in the doorway in her Chinese-red chenille bathrobe. Ten minutes later I am in the sack, and out in the kitchen Gertz is telling another one. The bottles are rattling, and the file clerks are hunched around the fire celebrating their primal victory over The Elements.

Somewhere off in the dark the Monon Louisville Limited wails as it snakes through the Gibson Hump on its way to the outside world. The giant Indiana moths, at least five pounds apiece, are banging against the window screens next to my bed. The cats are fighting in the backyard over crappie heads, and fish scales are itching in my hair as I joyfully, ecstatically slide off into the great world beyond.

"It hasn't changed a bit," Flick said.

Two truckdrivers had taken places at the far end of the bar. Flick ambled down; served them up a pair of boilermakers. One of them got up immediately, crossed to the jukebox, dropped in a coin, pressed the buttons, and returned to his stool. Immediately a wavering reddish-purple light filled the room as the enormous plastic jukebox glowed into vivid neon life. Waterfalls cascaded through its plastic sides. I watched it for a moment, and, forgetting where I was, said:

"Pure Pop Art."

Flick paused in his glass-polishing.

"Pure what?"

It was too late to back out.

"Pop Art, Flick. Pure Pop Art. That jukebox."

"What's Pop Art?"

"That's hard to explain, Flick. You've got to be With It."

"What do you mean? I'm With It."

I sipped my beer to stall for time.

"Flick, have you ever heard of the Museum of Modern Art in New York?"

"Yeah. What about it?"

"Well, Flick. . . ."

X 🦢 MY OLD MAN AND THE LASCIVIOUS SPECIAL AWARD THAT HERALDED THE BIRTH OF POP ART

I "hmmmmed" meaningfully yet noncommittally as I feigned interest in the magnificent structure before us. "Hmmmm," I repeated, this time in a slightly lower key, watching carefully out of the corner of my eye to see whether she was taking the lure.

A 1938 Hupmobile radiator core painted gaudily in gilt and fuchsia revolved on a Victrola turntable before us. From its cap extended the severed arm of a female plastic mannequin. It reached toward the vaulted ceiling high above us. Its elegantly contorted hand clutched a can of Bon Ami, the kitchen cleanser. The Victrola repeated endlessly a recording of a harmonica band playing "My Country 'Tis Of Thee." The bronze plaque at its base read: IT HASN'T SCRATCHED YET.

The girl nodded slowly and deliberately in deep appreciation of the famous contemporary masterwork, the central exhibit in the Museum's definitive Pop Art Retrospective Panorama, as the Sunday supplements called it. I closed in:

"He's got it down."

I paused adeptly, waited a beat or two and then, using my clipped, put-down voice:

". . . *all* of it."

She rose to the fly like a hungry she-salmon:

"It's The Bronx, all right. Fordham Road, squared. Let 'em laugh *this* off on the Grand Concourse!"

I moved in quickly.

"You can say that again!"

Hissing in the venomous sibilant accents of a lifelong Coffee Shop habitué that I always used in the Museum of Modern Art on my favorite late afternoon time-killer—Girl Tracking—which is the art most fully explored and pursued at the Museum of Modern Art. Nowhere in all of New York is it easier, nor more pleasant, to snare and net the complaisant, rebellious, burlap-skirted, sandal-wearing CCNY undergraduate. Amid the throngs of restless Connecticut matrons and elderly Mittel European art nuts there is always, at the Museum, a roving eddying gulf stream of Hunters and the Hunted.

It was the work of an instant to bundle her off to the outdoor tables in the garden where we sat tensely; date and cream cheese sandwiches between sips of watery Museum of Modern Art orange drink.

"Marcia, how many of these clods *really* dig?" I shrugged toward all the other tables around us. "It's really sickening!!"

"Bastards!"

She whistled through her teeth. I sensed the stirrings, faint but unmistakable, of an Afternoon Love. Up to her pad off the NYU campus, down to the Village by subway for a hamburger, and then. . . .

"Only the other day," she continued, "at the Fig, I said to Claes: 'Pop Shmop. Art is Art, the way I see it'. . . ."

She trailed off moodily and then bit viciously into the raisin nut bread, her Mexican serape sweeping the ashes from her cigarette into my salad.

"Good old Claes." I followed her lead, "He lays it on the Phonies!"

I wondered frantically for a brief instant who the hell Claes was!

"And they lap it up," she added.

Our love duet was meshing nicely now. Point and counterpoint we wove our fabric of Protest, Tristan and Isolde of the Hip.

A light fog-like rain descended on us from what passes for sky in New York. We ignored the dampness as we clutched and groped toward one another in the psychic gloom.

"What do these Baby Machines know of Pop Art?"

I nodded toward a covey of Connecticut ladies eating celery near us. Our eyes met intensely for a long, searing moment. Hers smoldered; mine watered, but I hung in there grimly. And then, her voice low, quivering with emotion, deliberately she spoke:

"Pop Art, as these fools call it, is the essential dissection of Now-ness, the split atom of the Here moment."

We looked deep into each other's souls for another looping instant. I took three deliberate beats and countered:

"Now-ness is us, baby. The *Now* of Here!"

Her hand clutched convulsively at the smudged and dog-eared paperback copy of *Sexus*. A Henry Miller. I knew my harpoon had struck pay dirt!

Suddenly, without warning, she stood up and called out in a loud voice:

"Steve! Oh Stevie, over here!"

I turned and saw striding toward us over the marble palazzo, past a Henry Moore fertility symbol, a tall broad-shouldered figure wearing black cowboy boots and tight leather pants. Marcia hurriedly darted forward.

"I've been waiting, Stevie. You're late."

Stevie, her high cheekbones topped by two angry embers for eyes, snapped:

"Let's go, baby. I'm double-parked. And the fuzz tag a Harley-Davidson around here quicker than a kick in the ass. Let's go."

Her rich bass voice echoed from statue to statue. Marcia, weakly indicating me, said:

"Uh . . . this is . . . uh . . . uh. . . ."

"Pleased ta meetcha, Bud," Stevie barked manfully, her thin moustache bristling in cheery greeting. They were off arm in arm. Once again I was alone amid the world's art treasures.

"You can't win 'em all."

I muttered under my breath as I wolfed down what remained of Marcia's sandwich, salvaging what little I could from the fiasco. The competition for girls in New York is getting rougher and more complex by the moment. I ironically raised my paper cup of tepid orange drink to the gray heavens, sighting over its waxen brim the glowering bronze head of Rodin's *Balzac* outlined craggily against the jazzily lit museum interior, the pink plaster arm of IT HASN'T SCRATCHED YET seeming to reach out of Balzac's neck.

"To good old Claes. And Pop Shmop."

I drained the miserable orange drink with a single strangled gulp. Then it happened. Somewhere way off deep down in that dark, buried coal bin of my subconscious a faint but unmistakable signal squeaked and then was silent. A signal about what? Why? What was Balzac trying to say? Or was it Rodin? Once again I sighted over the statue's head and aligned the mannequin arm at exactly the same position that had set off that faint ringing. The rain drifted down silently while I waited. Nothing.

I tried again; still nothing. My eye fell on Marcia's half-empty cup. Could there be a connection? Carefully realigning the arm and statue, I sipped the sickening liquid. Far off, unmistakably, once again the bell tolled for me. There was no question about it. Unmistakably there was a connection between the orange drink and that arm, not to mention glowering old Balzac, the original woman hater.

By now the rest of the tables had been deserted by my fellow Pop Art lovers. Alone, I sat in the museum garden, contemplating the inexplicable. The pieces began to assemble themselves with no help from me. I slowly began to realize that I had been fortunate enough to be present at the very birth of Pop Art itself. And had, in fact, known intimately the very first Pop Art fanatic who had endured, like all true avant-garde have always, the scorn and jibes of those nearest to them. His dedication to his aesthetic principles almost wrecked our happy home. My father was a full generation ahead of his time, and he never knew it.

The Depression days were the golden age of the newspaper Puzzle Contest. Most newspapers had years before given up the futile struggle to print News, since nothing much ever happened and had turned their pages over to comic strips and endless Fifty Thousand Dollar Giant Jackpot Puzzle Contests. Dick Tracy became a national hero. Andy Gump was more widely quoted than the President. Orphan Annie's editorializing swayed voters by the million. Popeye raised the price of spinach to astronomical heights, and Wimpy spawned a chain of hamburger joints.

As for puzzles, when one ended, another began immediately and occasionally as many as three or four colossal contests ran simultaneously. NAME THE PRESIDENTS, MYSTERY MOVIE STARS, FAMOUS FIGURES IN HISTORY, MATCH THE BABY PICTURES. On and on the contests marched, all variations on the same theme, page after page of distorted and chopped-up pictures of movie stars, kings, novelists, and ballplayers, while in the great outer darkness, for the price of a two-cent newspaper, countless millions struggled nightly to Hit The Jackpot. They were all being judged for Originality, Neatness, and Aptness of Thought. All decisions, of course, were final.

Occasionally the tempo varied with a contest that featured daily a newspaper camera shot taken of a crowd at random—walking across a street, waiting for a light, standing at a bus stop. IS YOUR FACE CIRCLED? IF IT IS, CALL THE HERALD EXAMINER AND CLAIM FIVE HUNDRED DOLLARS!! The streets were full of roving bands of out-of-work contestants, hoping to have their faces circled. My father was no exception. One of his most treasured possessions was a tattered newspaper photo that he carried for years in his wallet, a photo of a crowd snapped on Huron Street that showed, not more than three inches away from the circled face, a smudged figure wearing a straw skimmer, looking the wrong way. He swore it was him. He had invented an involved story to corroborate this, which he told at every company picnic for years.

He was particularly hooked on FIND THE HIDDEN OBJECTS and HOW MANY MISTAKES ARE IN THIS PICTURE?, which consisted of three-legged dogs, ladies with eight fingers, and smoke-stacks with smoke blowing in three directions. He was much better at this game than the Historical Figures. No one in Hohman had ever even heard of Disraeli, but they sure knew a lot about smokestacks and how many horns a cow had, and whether birds flew upside down or not.

Contest after contest spun off into history. Doggedly my father labored on. Every night the *Chicago American* spread out on the dining-room table, paste pot handy, scissors and ruler, pen and ink, he clipped and glued; struggled and guessed. He was not the only one in that benighted country who pasted a white wig on Theodore Roosevelt and called him John Quincy Adams, or confused Charlemagne with Sitting Bull. But to the faithful and the persevering and to he who waits awards will come. The historic day that my father "won a prize" is still a common topic of conversation in Northern Indiana.

The contest dealt with GREAT FIGURES FROM THE WORLD OF SPORTS. It was sponsored by a soft-drink company that manufactured an artificial orange drink so spectacularly gassy that violent cases of The Bends were common among those who bolted it down too fast. The color of this volatile liquid was a blinding iridescent shimmering, luminous orange that made *real* oranges pale to the color of elderly lemons by comparison. Taste is a difficult thing to describe, but suffice it to say that this beverage, once quaffed, remained forever in the gastronomical memory as unique and galvanic.

All popular non-alcoholic drinks were known in those days by a single generic term—"Pop." What this company made was called simply "Orange pop." The company trademark, seen everywhere, was a silk-stockinged lady's leg, realistically flesh-colored, wearing a black spike-heeled slipper. The knee was crooked slightly and the leg was shown to the middle of the thigh. That was all. No face; no torso; no dress—just a stark, disembodied, provocative leg. The name of this pop was a play on words, involving the lady's knee. Even today in the windows of dusty, fly specked Midwestern grocery stores and poolrooms this lady's leg may yet be seen.

The first week of the contest was ridiculously easy: Babe Ruth, Bill Tilden, Man O' War, and the Fighting Irish. My Old Man was in his element. He had never been known to read anything *but* the Sport page. His lifetime subscription to the *St. Louis Sporting News* dated back to his teen-age days. His memory and knowledge of the minutia and trivia of the Sporting arenas was deadening. So naturally he whipped through the first seven weeks without once even breathing hard.

Week by week the puzzlers grew more obscure and esoteric. Third-string utility infielders of Second-Division ball clubs, substitute Purdue halfbacks, cauliflower-eared canvas-backed Welterweights, selling platers whose only distinction was a nineteen-length defeat by Man O' War. The Old Man took them all in his stride. Night after night, snorting derisively, cackling victoriously, consulting his voluminous records, he struggled on toward the Semi-Finals.

A week of nervous suspense and a letter bearing the imprint of a lady's leg informed him that he was now among the Elect. He had survived all preliminary eliminations and was now entitled to try for the Grand Award of $50,000, plus "hundreds of additional valuable prizes."

Wild jubilation gripped the household, since no one within a thirty-mile radius had ever gotten this far in a major contest, least of all the Old Man. He usually petered out somewhere along the fourth set of FAMOUS FACES and went back to his Chinese nail puzzle and the ball scores. That night we had ice cream for supper.

The following week the first set of puzzles in the final round arrived in a sealed envelope. They were killers! Even the Old Man was visibly shaken. His face ashen, a pot of steaming black coffee at his side, the kids locked away in the bedroom so as not to disturb his massive struggle, he labored until dawn. The pop company had pulled several questionable underhanded ploys. Water Polo is not a common game in Hohman and its heroes are not on everyone's tongue. Hop Skip & Jump champions had never been lionized in Northern Indiana. No one had even *heard* of Marathon Walking! It was a tough night.

His solutions were mailed off, and again we waited. Another set of even more difficult puzzles arrived. Again the sleepless ordeal, the bitter consultations with poolroom scholars, the sense of imminent defeat, the final hopeless guesses, the sealed envelope. Then silence. Days went by with no word of any kind. Gaunt, hollow-eyed, my father watched the mailman as he went by, occasionally pausing only to drop off the gas bill or flyers offering neckties by mail. It was a nervous, restless time. Sudden flareups of temper, outbursts of unmotivated passion. At night the wind soughed emptily and prophetically through the damp clotheslines of the haunted backyards.

Three weeks to a day after the last mailing, a thin, neat, crisp envelope emblazoned with the sinister voluptuous insignia lay enigmatically on the dining-room table, awaiting my father's return from work. The minute he roared into the kitchen that night he knew.

"It's come! By God! Where is it?"

What had come? Fifty thousand dollars? Fame? A trip to the moon? The end of the rainbow? News of yet another failure?

With palsied hand and bulging eye he carefully slit the crackling envelope. A single typewritten sheet:

CONGRATULATIONS. YOU HAVE WON A MAJOR AWARD IN OUR FIFTY THOUSAND DOLLAR "GREAT HEROES FROM THE WORLD OF SPORTS" CONTEST. IT WILL ARRIVE BY SPECIAL MESSENGER DELIVERED TO YOUR ADDRESS. YOU ARE A WINNER. CONGRATULATIONS.

That night was one of the very few times my father ever actually got publicly drunk. His cronies whooped and hollered, guzzled and yelled into the early morning hours, knocking over chairs and telling dirty stories. My mother supplied endless sandwiches and constantly mopped up. Hairy Gertz, in honor of the occasion, told his famous dirty story about the three bartenders, the Franciscan monk, and the cross-eyed turtle. Three times. It was a true Victory Gala of the purest sort.

Early the next morning the first trickle of a flood of envy-tinged congratulations began to come in. Distant uncles, hazy second cousins, real estate agents, and Used-Car salesmen called to offer heartfelt felicitations and incidental suggestions for highly rewarding investments they had at their disposal. The Old Man immediately, once his head had partially cleared, began to lay plans. Perhaps a Spanish adobe-type house in Coral Gables, or maybe he'd open up his own Bowling Alley. Victory is heady stuff, and has often proved fatal to the victors.

The next afternoon a large unmarked delivery truck stopped in front of the house. Two workmen unloaded a square, sealed, waist-high cardboard carton, which was lugged into the kitchen. They left and drove off. Somehow an air of foreboding surrounded their stealthy, unexplained operation.

The Old Man, his face flushed with excitement, fumbling in supercharged haste to lay bare his hard-won symbol of Victory, struggled to open the carton. A billowing mushroom of ground excelsior surged up and out. In he plunged. And there it was.

The yellow kitchen light bulb illumined the scene starkly and yet with a touch of glowing promise. Tenderly he lifted from its nest of fragrant straw the only thing he had ever won in his life. We stood silent and in awe at the sheer shimmering, unexpected beauty of the "Major Award."

Before us in the heavy, fragrant air of our cabbage-scented kitchen stood a *life-size* lady's leg, in true blushing-pink flesh tones and wearing a modish black patent leather pump with spike heel. When I say life-size I am referring to a rather large lady who obviously had dined well and had matured nicely. It was a well filled-out leg!

It was so realistic that for a brief instant we thought that we had received in the mail the work of an artist of the type that was very active at that period—the Trunk Murderer. For some reason this spectacular form of self-expression has declined, but in those days something in the air caused many a parson's daughter to hack up her boyfriend into small segments which were then shipped separately to people chosen at random from the phone book. Upon being apprehended and tried, she was almost always aquitted, whereupon she accepted numerous offers to appear in Vaudeville as a featured headliner, recalling her days as a Trunk Murderer complete with props and a dramatized stage version of the deed.

For a split instant it seemed as though our humble family had made the headlines.

My mother was the first to recover.

"What is it?"

"A . . . leg," my father incisively shot back.

It was indeed a leg, more of a leg in fact than any leg any of us had ever seen!

"But . . . what is it?"

"Well, it's a leg. Like a statue, I guess."

"A *statue?*"

Our family had never owned a statue. A statue was always considered to be a lady wearing a wreath and concrete robes, holding aloft a torch in one hand and a book in the other. This was the only kind of statue outside of generals sitting on horses that we had ever heard about. They all had names like VICTORY or PEACE. And if this was a statue, it could only have one name:

WHOOPEE!

My mother was trying to get herself between the "statue" and the kids.

"Isn't it time for bed?"

"Holy Smokes, would you look at that!"

My father was warming up.

"Holy Smokes, would you *look* at that? Do you know what this is?"

My mother did not answer, just silently edged herself between my kid brother and the magnificent limb.

"Would you believe it, it's a LAMP!"

It was indeed a lamp, a lamp in its own way a *Definitive* lamp. A master stroke of the lightoliers' art. It was without question the most magnificent lamp that we had ever seen.

This was the age of spindly, artificially antiqued, teetery brass contrivances called "bridge lamps." These were usually of the school of design known as WPA Nco-Romanticism, a school noted for its heavy use of brass flower petals and mottled parchment shades depicting fauns and dryads inscribed in dark browns and greens. The light bulbs themselves were often formed to emulate a twisted, spiraled candle flame of a peculiar yellow-orange tint. These bulbs were unique in that they contrived somehow to make a room even dimmer when they were turned on. My mother was especially proud of her matched set, which in addition to brass tulip buds teetered shakily on bases cleverly designed to look like leopards' paws.

On the kitchen table stood the lamp that was destined to play a subtle and important role in our future. My Old Man dove back into the box, burrowing through the crackling packing.

"AHA! Here's the shade!"

A monstrous, barrel-shaped bulging tube of a shade, a striking Lingerie pink in color, topped by a glittering cut-crystal orb, was lifted reverently up and put onto the table. Never had shade so beautifully matched base. Within an instant the Old Man had screwed it atop the fulsome thigh, and there it stood, a full four feet from coquettishly pointed toe to sparkling crystal. His eyes boggled behind his Harold Lloyd glasses.

"My God! Ain't that great? Wow!!"

He was almost overcome by Art.

"What a great lamp!"

"Oh . . . I don't know."

My mother was strictly the crocheted-doily type.

"What a great lamp! Wow! This is exactly what we need for the front window. Wow!"

He swept up the plastic trophy, his symbol of Superiority, and rushed out through the dining room and into the living room. Placing the lamp squarely in the middle of the library table, he aligned it exactly at the center of the front window. We trailed behind him, applauding and yipping. He was unrolling the cord, down on all fours.

"Where's the damn plug?"

"Behind the sofa."

My mother answered quietly, in a vaguely detached tone.

"Quick! Go out in the kitchen and get me an extension!"

Our entire world was strung together with "extensions." Outlets in our house were rare and coveted, each one buried under a bakelite mound of three-way, seven-way, and ten-way plugs and screw sockets, the entire mess caught in a twisted, snarling Gordian knot of frayed and cracked lamp cords, radio cords, and God knows what. Occasionally in some houses a critical point was reached and one of these electrical bombs went off, sometimes burning down whole blocks of homes, or more often blowing out the main fuse, plunging half the town into darkness.

"Get the extension from the toaster!"

He shouted from under the sofa where he was burrowing through the electrical rat's nest.

I rushed out into the kitchen, grabbed the extension, and scurried back to the scene of action.

"Give it to me! Quick!"

His hand reached out from the darkness. For a few moments —full silence, except for clickings and scratchings. And deep breathing from behind the sofa. The snap of a few sparks, a quick whiff of ozone, and the lamp blazed forth in unparalleled glory. From ankle to thigh the translucent flesh radiated a vibrant, sensual, luminous orange-yellow-pinkish nimbus of Pagan fire. All it needed was tom-toms and maybe a gong or two. And a tenor singing in a high, quavery, earnest voice:

"A pretty girl/Is like a melody. . . ."

It was alive!

"Hey, look."

The Old Man was reading from the instruction pamphlet which had been attached to the cord.

"It's got a two-way switch. It says here: 'In one position it's a tasteful Night Light and in the other an effective, scientifically designed Reading Lamp.' Oh boy, is this great!"

He reached up under the shade to throw the switch.

"Why can't you wait until the kids are in bed?"

My mother shoved my kid brother behind her. The shade had a narrow scallop of delicate lace circling its lower regions.

"Watch this!"

The switch clicked. Instantly the room was flooded with a wave of pink light that was pure perfume of illumination.

"Now that is a real lamp!"

The Old Man backed away in admiration.

"Hey wait. I want to see how it looks from the outside."

He rushed into the outer darkness, across the front porch and out onto the street. From a half block away he shouted:

"Move it a little to the left. Okay. That's got it. You oughta see it from out here!"

The entire neighborhood was turned on. It could be seen up and down Cleveland Street, the symbol of his victory.

The rest of that evening was spent in honest, simple Peasant admiration for a thing of transcendent beauty, very much like the awe and humility that we felt before such things as Christmas trees and used cars with fresh coats of Simonize. The family went to bed in a restless mood of festive gaiety. That is, everyone except my mother, who somehow failed to vibrate on the same frequency as my father's spectacular Additional Major Award.

That night, for the first time, our home had a Night Light. The living room was bathed through the long, still, silent hours with the soft glow of electric Sex. The stage was set; the principal players were in the wings. The cue was about to be given for the greatest single fight that ever happened in our family.

Real-life man and wife, mother and father battles rarely even remotely resemble the Theatrical or Fictional version of the Struggle between the Sexes. Homes have been wracked by strife and dissension because of a basic difference of opinion over where to go on a vacation, or what kind of car to buy, or a toaster that made funny noises, or a sister-in-law's false teeth, not to mention who is going to take out the garbage. And why.

In all my experience I have never known homes that had the kind of fights that appear in plays by Edward Albee and Tennessee Williams. It would never have occurred to my father to bellow dramatically in the living room, after twenty-seven Scotches:

"You bitch! You're not going to emasculate *me!*"

The Old Man would not have even known what the word "emasculate" *meant*, much less figure that that's what my mother was up to.

On the other hand, my mother thought "emasculation" had something to do with women getting the vote. But, in any event, Sex is rarely argued and fought over in any household I ever heard of, outside of heaving novels and nervous plays. That was not the kind of fights we had at home. There was no question of Emasculation or Role Reversal. My mother was a *Mother*. She knew it. My Old Man was . . . the Old Man. *He* knew it. There was no problem of Identity, just a gigantic clash of two opposing physical presences: the Immovable Body and the Force That Is Not To Be Denied.

The lamp stood in the middle of the window for months. Every night my mother would casually, without a word, draw the curtains shut, while Bing Crosby sang from the old Gothic Crosley:

"Hail KMH/Hail to the foe
Onward to victory/Onward we must go. . . ."

the theme song of the Kraft Music Hall. The Old Man would get up out of his chair. Casually. He would pull the curtain back, look out—pretending to be examining the weather—and leave it that way. Ten minutes later my mother would get up out of her chair, casually, saying:

"Gee, I feel a draft coming in from somewhere."

This slowly evolving ballet spun on through the Winter months, gathering momentum imperceptively night after night. Meanwhile, the lamp itself had attracted a considerable personal following among cruising prides of pimply-faced Adolescents who night after night could hardly wait for darkness to fall and the soft, sinuous radiation of Passion to light up the drab, dark corners of Cleveland Street.

The pop company enjoyed sales of mounting intensity, even during the normally slack Winter months. Their symbol now stood for far more than a sickeningly sweet orange drink that produced window-rattling burps and cavities in Adolescent teeth of such spectacular dimensions as to rival Mammoth Cave.

Night after night kids' eyes glowed in the darkness out on the street before our house, like predatory carnivores of the jungle in full cry. Night after night the lady's leg sent out its silent message.

The breaking point came, as all crucial moments in History do, stealthily and on cats' feet, on a day that was notable for its ordinariness. We never know when lightning is about to strike, or a cornice to fall. Perhaps it is just as well.

On the fateful day I came home from school and immediately opened the refrigerator door, looking for Something To Eat. Seconds later I am knocking together a salami sandwich. My Old Man—it was his day off—is in the john. Hollering, as he always did, accompanied by the roar of running water, snatches of song, complaints about No Pressure—the usual. My mother is somewhere off in the front of the house, puttering about. Dusting.

Life is one long song. The White Sox have won a ball game, and it's only spring training. The Old Man is singing. My brother is under the daybed, whimpering. The salami is as sweet as life itself.

The first fireflies were beginning to flicker in the cottonwoods. Northern Indiana slowly was at long last emerging from the iron grip of the Midwestern Winter. A softness in the air; a quickening of the pulse. Expectations long lying dormant in the blackened rock ice of Winter sent out tentative tender green shoots and yawned toward the smoky sun. Somewhere off in the distance, ball met bat; robin called to robin, and a screen door slammed.

In the living room my mother is talking to the aphids in her fern plant. She fought aphids all of her life. The water roared. I started on a second sandwich. And then:

CAAA-RAASHH!

". . . oh!" A phony, stifled gasp in the living room.

A split second of silence while the fuse sputtered and ignited, and it began.

The Old Man *knew*. He had been fearing it since the very

first day. The bathroom door slammed open. He rushed out, dripping, carrying a bar of Lifebuoy, eyes rolling wildly.

"What broke!? What happened?! WHAT BROKE!!?"

". . . the lamp." A soft, phony voice, feigning heartbreak.

For an instant the air vibrated with tension. A vast magnetic charge, a static blast of human electricity made the air sing. My kid brother stopped in mid-whimper. I took the last bite, the last bite of salami, knowing that this would be my last happy bite of salami forever.

The Old Man rushed through the dining room. He fell heavily over a footstool, sending a shower of spray and profanity toward the ceiling.

"Where is it? WHERE IS IT!?"

There it was, the shattered kneecap under the coffee table, the cracked, well-turned ankle under the radio; the calf—that voluptuous poem of feminine pulchritude—split open like a rotten watermelon, its entrails of insulated wire hanging out limply over the rug. That lovely lingerie shade, stove in, had rolled under the library table.

"Where's my glue? My glue! OH, MY LAMP!"

My mother stood silently for a moment and then said:

"I . . . don't know what happened. I was just dusting and . . . ah. . . ."

The Old Man leaped up from the floor, his towel gone, in stark nakedness. He bellowed:

"YOU ALWAYS WERE JEALOUS OF THAT LAMP!"

"Jealous? Of a *plastic leg?*"

Her scorn ripped out like a hot knife slicing through soft oleomargarine. He faced her.

"You were jealous 'cause I WON!"

"That's ridiculous. Jealous! Jealous of what? That was the ugliest lamp I ever saw!"

Now it was out, irretrievably. The Old Man turned and walked to the window. He looked out silently at the soft gathering gloom of Spring. Suddenly he turned and in a flat, iron voice:

"Get the glue."

"We're *out* of glue," my mother said.

My father always was a superb user of profanity, but now he
came out with just one word, a real Father word, bitter and
hard.

"DAMMIT!"

Without another word he stalked into the bedroom; slammed
the door, emerged wearing a sweatshirt, pants and shoes, and his
straw hat, and out he went. The door of the Oldsmobile
slammed shut out in the driveway.

"K-runch. Crash!"—a tinkle of glass. He had broken the
window of the one thing he loved, the car that every day he
polished and honed. He slammed it in Reverse.

RRRRAAAWWWWWRRRRR!

We heard the fender drag along the side of the garage. He
never paused.

RRRRAAAWWWWWRRROOOOMMMM!

And he's gone. We are alone. Quietly my mother started
picking up the pieces, something she did all her life. I am
hiding under the porch swing. My kid brother is now down
in the coal bin.

It seemed seconds later:

BBBRRRRRAAAAAWWWRRRRR . . . eeeeeeeeeh!

Up the driveway he charged in a shower of cinders and
burning rubber. You could always tell the mood of the Old
Man by the way he came up that driveway. Tonight there
was no question.

A heavy thunder of feet roared up the back steps, the kitchen
door slammed. He's carrying three cans of glue. Iron glue. The
kind that garage mechanics used for gaskets and for gluing back
together exploded locomotives. His voice is now quiet.

"Don't touch it. *Don't touch that lamp!*"

He spread a newspaper out over the kitchen floor and carefully, tenderly laid out the shattered fleshy remains. He is on all
fours now, and the work began. Painfully, hopelessly he tried
to glue together the silk-stockinged, life-size symbol of his great
victory.

Time and again it looked almost successful, but then he
would remove his hand carefully. . . . BOING! . . . the kneecap

kept springing up and sailing across the kitchen. The ankle didn't fit. The glue hardened into black lumps and the Old Man was purple with frustration. He tried to fix the leg for about two hours, stacking books on it. A Sears Roebuck catalog held the instep. The family Bible pressed down on the thigh. But it wasn't working.

To this day I can still see my father, wearing a straw hat, swearing under his breath, walking around a shattered plastic lady's leg, a Freudian image to make Edward Albee's best efforts pale into insignificance.

Finally he scooped it all up. Without a word he took it out the back door and into the ashbin. He sat down quietly at the kitchen table. My mother is now back at her lifelong station, hanging over the sink. The sink is making the Sink noise. Our sink forever made long, gurgling sighs, especially in the evening, a kind of sucking, gargling, choking retch.

Aaaagggghhhh—and then a short, hissing wheeze and silence until the next attack. Sometimes at three o'clock in the morning I'd lie in my bed and listen to the sink——Aaaaaggggghhhh.

Once in a while it would go: gaaaaaggggghhhh . . . PTUI!—— and up would come a wad of Mrs. Kissel's potato peelings from next door. She, no doubt, got our coffee grounds. Life was real.

My mother is hanging over her sink, swabbing eternally with her Brillo pad. If mothers had a coat of arms in the Midwest, it would consist of crossed Plumbers' Helpers rampant on a field of golden Brillo pads.

The Old Man is sitting at the kitchen table. It was white enamel with little chipped black marks all around the edge. They must have been made that way, delivered with those flaws. A table that smelled like dishrags and coffee grounds and kids urping. A kitchen-table smell, permanent and universal, that defied all cleaning and disinfectant—the smell of Life itself.

In dead silence my father sat and read his paper. The battle had moved into the Trench Warfare or Great Freeze stage. And continued for three full days. For three days my father spoke not. For three days my mother spoke likewise. There was only

the sink to keep us kids company. And, of course, each other,
clinging together in the chilly subterranean icy air of a great
battle. Occasionally I would try.

"Hey Ma, ah . . . you know what Flick is doing . . .
uh. . . ."

Her silent back hunched over the sink. Or:

"Hey Dad, Flick says that. . . ."

"WHADDAYA WANT?"

Three long days.

Sunday was sunny and almost like a day in Midsummer.
Breakfast, usually a holiday thing on Sundays, had gone by in
stony silence. So had dinner. My father was sitting in the living
room with the sun streaming in unobstructed through the front
window, making a long, flat, golden pattern on the dusty
Oriental rug. He was reading Andy Gump at the time. My
mother was struggling over a frayed elbow in one of my
sweaters. Suddenly he looked up and said:

"You know. . . ."

Here it comes! My mother straightened up and waited.

"You know, I like the room this way."

There was a long, rich moment. These were the first words
spoken in seventy-two hours.

She looked down again at her darning, and in a soft voice:

"Uh . . . you know, I'm sorry I broke it."

"Well . . ." he grew expansive, "It was . . . it was really
pretty jazzy."

"No," she answered, "I thought it was very *pretty!*"

"Nah. It was too pink for this room. We should get some kind
of brass lamp for that window."

She continued her darning. He looked around for a moment,
dropped the Funnies noisily to get attention, and then announced in his Now For The Big Surprise voice:

"How 'bout let's all of us going to a movie? How 'bout it?
Let's all take in a movie!"

Ten minutes later we're all in the Oldsmobile, on our way to
see Johnny Weismuller.

The drizzle had become a full rain by the time I realized I was the only one left in the windswept garden of the Museum of Modern Art. The lights were on inside, warm and glowing, and I could see a pink arm reaching skyward. I went back in to have another last, loving look at IT HASN'T SCRATCHED YET.

"How come they called it that?"

I laughed my notorious ironic cackle:

"It's some kind of soap or something."

"You mean they named a statue after *soap?*"

Flick squeezed his bar rag juicily onto the duckboards behind the mahogany. I had a vague feeling that the beer was beginning to get to me.

"Well . . . it's a slogan."

Behind us, all around us, everywhere, the jukebox boomed heavily and then stopped abruptly.

"Fer Chrissake, I can't see why they named a statue after soap."

"Well, I told you, you gotta be With It."

"Nuts."

Once again I was reminded forcibly that I was back in the Midwest, very far from the effete East.

An uproar broke out in one of the booths back in the gloom near the wall. Two structural ironworkers were loudly Indian-wrestling.

"I'll be right back."

Flick's jaw squared as he darted from behind the bar. I watched in the mirror as he quelled the battle, fed the combatants two more boilermakers, and returned.

"I'm not as tough as I used to be," said Flick matter-of-factly. "I argue more these days."

I remembered the day well when Flick in his salad period had thrown three Tin Mill Reckoners out on the street in quick succession, which is the Hohman equivalent of taking on King Kong, Gargantua, and Gorgeous George simultaneously.

"I noticed they stopped," I said.

"Well, they're on my bowling team. They'd better."

We sat silently for a moment as old friends will when in the midst of a reminiscing orgy. Flick slid another beer toward me.

"That reminds me, Flick. Is it still where it used to be?"

"Yep."

A minute later I was back at the bar, ready for more action and more beer. A faint snow was falling from the lead-colored skies. The wind rattled the plate glass windows of Flick's Tavern. Across the street the plastic streamers snapped and fluttered over the rows of like-new, mint-condition, creampuff, fully loaded, ready-to-go-specials. The Used-Car lot is a kind of shrine in Northern Indiana.

"You mean girls ride *motorcycles* in New York?"

"That is not *all* they do."

"Boy. New York sure sounds like a crazy place. I wanted to take my wife to see the Fair, but I couldn't get away."

"You didn't miss much."

Flick snapped a pretzel in two, moodily.

"Just the same, I'd a liked to have gone. I sure remember that one they had in Chicago."

"Oh come on, Flick. We were just little tiny kids."

"Yeah. But I remember it."

I sipped my beer and thought about that for a few seconds.

"You know, Flick, I read somewhere that John Dillinger, the old bank robber, used to go to that fair and ride the Sky Ride, between heists."

"I'll be damned. He was from Indiana, wasn't he?" Flick's Hoosier pride welled to the surface.

"You're damn right, Flick. You know, I remember only one thing about that fair."

XII ⮞ THE MAGIC MOUNTAIN

Right there on the Lake, next to the Outer Drive, they began to build a model of Fort Sheridan. This was a fort that was operating during Indian times on the site of Chicago. It was the scene of several very bloody Indian battles. And here they were once again putting this fort together log by log in a perfect reproduction of the original. It sat there looking out over the cold blue water, and you could see it from the car. It was brown and low, and looked like it was made out of Lincoln Logs. To a kid, forts are very big things. I asked my father, driving the Olds:

"What is that?"

"Fort Sheridan."

"Oh."

"Yup. They're building a World's Fair."

At that time the shore stretched empty and white, with little tufts of grass here and there, almost to the Fields Museum and down to the cold water, with only Fort Sheridan in the middle of the emptiness.

And, sure enough, a World's Fair began to grow. It spread outward like a mushroom patch from the tiny fort, and grew and grew and grew. Month by month, year by year, great blue and yellow and orange buildings right out of the land of Oz blotted out the Lake, until the tiny fort disappeared behind them all. Mile after mile was covered with this fantasy, this wonderland, this land of real, genuine, absolute Magic.

And I lived in a land that was eminently, very very unmagical. The least magic of all neighbhorhoods, a pure Oatmeal neighborhood—lumpy Oatmeal. And so the idea and the vision of the World's Fair began to be a true Fairyland. The Emerald City had come to the South Side.

It took hold of my imagination until there was room for nothing else, and I was not alone. All the newspapers ran stories, tremendous reams of copy, wondrous descriptions of what it was going to be like, this Shangri-La right there on the shores of Lake Michigan. And then the story began to spread about a special Kid thing that was going to be at the Fair. This Something grabbed me by the ankles and dragged me right into the vortex, and I will never forget it. It was a tremendous thing in my life. Treasure Island!

Treasure Island was a tiny World's Fair within the World's Fair. There was the Hall of Science, the Hall of Communications, the Hall of Man; all these great, wonderful halls that were dedicated to the proposition that Man was the most magnificent thing in the world, and that he was just beginning. A Century Of Progress! Over the horizon was even more magnificence and greatness, and in the middle of it all—Treasure Island!

The *Tribune* printed pictures of Treasure Island and told how it was going to be. I clipped them out and saved them, tons of them. One day I would be there myself.

This was a time in history before television, and kids didn't go to the movies very much because movies cost money and over the land lay the Depression. It was *not* just another show in a succession of shows. It *was* Treasure Island!

Spring came, and the day approached when the Fair was to open. Already the flags were flying. The Avenue of Flags. We would drive past in the Oldsmobile and try to see through the modernistic fence, and we could catch glimpses of Martian landscapes and golden pagodas. It was a magnificent sight outlined against the blue water of the Lake.

During the Depression it rained a lot, and things were gray and there were a lot of fistfights, but then, suddenly, *this!*

One bright Sunday the Fair actually opened. There were speeches and parades, and I sat next to the radio and listened to everything that happened. The word was out that we would go "when the weather got warmer." At least that was the explanation my brother and I got. No one talked to us much about money.

The Fair was all that anyone talked about for weeks, and a couple of my cousins had actually *been* there. It was impossible even to talk to them about it. They were speechless. They were like veterans of some indescribable war. They could understand each other, but we who hadn't been there were on the outside.

I would ask: "How about Treasure Island? The Magic Mountain? How about it? What was it like?"

They would just look at each other. What can you say?

Our time finally came. I am in the Fair! I am looking at the flags, and I see the great Halls of Science. I am a tiny, tiny squirt, but it made a colossal impression on me, the first truly immense impression of my life.

Green, yellow, gold, orange buildings! The Skyride! The unreal Fantasy World's Fair architecture. World's Fair buildings have no relationship to real buildings. It was truly beyond all my expectations, whatever they were. It *was* the Emerald City. Nothing was real, nothing, not even the people. Everything was just swirling around me—lights and colors and sounds and funny, sweet food, and more excitement than I could stand. And then, Treasure Island!

And right in the middle of Treasure Island, the vortex, the center, and as far as I was concerned the *reason* for the entire World's Fair—The Magic Mountain! I had never heard of Thomas Mann at that point. This mountain had certain parallels with Thomas Mann's *Magic Mountain* that did not become apparent until later.

Treasure Island was a true island. There was water all around it, with little boats and swans, and Indian canoes and rocky grottoes, and even a pirate ship riding at anchor. Everything great, all in one place. Everything that kids want to see was there.

I am just absolutely out of my skull. I am wild. The sun is shining down, the birds are singing, Kid music is playing; it is all there.

And right in the middle of it, the Magic Mountain, rising high up into the sky, six or seven, maybe even ten stories high. It's made out of that stuff that they build fantasies of. It's made of whatever they make things out of that they're going to knock down in a year. It had snow painted 'way up there near the summit. It was a real mountain. A mountain, in the Midwest, is really a *mountain* mountain. They don't have mountains in the Midwest, except in stories and cowboy movies, and here is a real mountain. My kid brother and I just couldn't believe it.

Only kids were allowed on the Magic Mountain. No grownups, even mothers, just kids. Kids under ten. We went in through the turnstiles and got in line, a long line of kids, jostling cheek by jowl, snaking into the Magic Mountain.

The line led onto a ramp that wound its way in a spiral round and round the sides of the mountain, and up and up. Slowly we climbed, higher and higher. I'm wondering what's happening to the kids at the top. I can hardly wait.

About every thirty or forty feet there's an attendant on the ramp, wearing a red cap and a blue jacket.

"Come on, you kids. Move along there. Straighten up. Come on, straighten up that line. Dress it up. Come on, you kids, quit shovin'. You, there. Hey, cut it out. Move along."

And so we inched along slowly, higher and higher. I am looking down over the railing from a tremendous height, maybe ten stories high above the Fair. I can see all the people down below, like ants. My mother is way down there. Flags flying. What a great thing!

I am hanging onto the railing and moving upward, my kid brother right behind, until finally, the last turn and I am at the summit—a flat wooden platform. There was only one kid ahead of me. And the Chief Attendant. He was taking each kid as they arrived on top of the platform, pushing him, shoving him into a dark doorway. A dark doorway, like a cave into the side of the mountain, right up at the very peak, where the snow was painted on. He grabs this skinny kid ahead of me by the shoulders and gives him a shove into the darkness.

"Aaaaiiiiiiiii!" And the kid is gone!

I am facing this black door. Alone! This is the moment I have been waiting for for maybe two or three years. I am at the core of my entire life. I have been building my existence on this, and now I am terrified. It's a black hole! Just a black hole! Nothing!

The guy with the cap grabs my shoulders.

"Come on, kid. Move."

"NO! NO!" Remember, I'm five or six.

"NO! NO!"

"Come on, kid, get in there. You're holding up the line."

He shoves me. I am in a hollow tube, a black, inky hollow tube, flat on my back. I start moving. Faster and faster in the darkness! A thousand miles a minute, round and round and round!

"AAAIIIiiii!" I'm spinning round and round in total blackness. I can't catch my breath. I'm getting green, purple, red. Faster and Faster!

zzzwwooooomp! I shoot out feet first in the sunlight, onto a pad.

"Aaaaiiiiiii!" Immediately another guy with a cap on grabs me and shoves a red plastic fire hat on my head, with a sign on it:

"ED WYNN, The Texaco Fire Chief!"

"Get moving, kid, here comes another one."

I could hear coming out of the black hole behind me: "AAiiiiiiiiiiiii!"

My brother flew out. Purple and green.

"Klonk." The fire hat on his head.

"Aiiiiiiiii!" Another kid shoots out into the sunlight.

"Klonk." Another fire hat.

We went out through the turnstile together. And there was my mother, eating a taffy apple.

"How was it?"

How was it! I have never been able to tell her. I have never been able to tell her about the Magic Mountain. It was then that I began to learn about dreams, that center hard core of dreams.

"Get in there, kid, you're holding up the line."

XIII 🦢 FLICK DREDGES UP A NOTORIOUS SON OF A BITCH

"Do you remember that robot they had at the Fair?" Flick asked.

"What robot?"

"Well, they had this robot. That smoked cigars. My Old Man took me to see it. That's the only thing I remember."

"That's the way it is with fairs. You never know what you'll remember." Beer brings out the philosopher in me.

The two ironworkers were now having a loud artistic argument in front of the jukebox. The boilermakers had done their work well. Flick's blue jaw tightened and once again he left the bar to go into combat. I watched from the corner of my eye as he loomed over the truculent music lovers. A few seconds later, all was peace as the two were eased out of the side door and into the cold air. Flick returned to his station and slapped his bar rag angrily into the brass trough.

"If it ain't one thing, it's another. You never get no peace around here." He continued:

"One day I'm gonna kick that son of a bitch in the ass so hard he'll never forget it!"

I looked out into the gray street and watched the belligerent, unsteady pair as they struggled against the wind in search of another, friendlier tavern. There was something vaguely familiar

about the short, wide one on the left, the one carrying the battered lunch bucket.

"Hey, Flick, who is that short guy on the left?"

"Grover Dill, that son of a bitch."

"No kidding! Really? Grover Dill! Flick, you shoulda sic'd
me on that bastard. It woulda scared him out of his wits."

Flick stared at me for a moment uncomprehendingly, and
then the dawn came up like thunder on his simple Midwestern
map. He leaned over the bar on his elbows.

"That's right! Boy, I will never forget *that* day!"

I put up two fingers in my best Biltmore Men's Bar manner.

"That calls for two fingers of the Real Stuff, Flick."

"You said it, Ralph!" He poured two neat ones.

"So that old son of a bitch Grover Dill hasn't changed a
bit, has he?"

Flick tossed his off.

"If anything, he's worse."

XIV 〰 GROVER DILL AND THE TASMANIAN DEVIL

The male human animal, skulking through the impenetrable fetid jungle of Kidhood, learns early in the game just what sort of animal he is. The jungle he stalks is a howling tangled wilderness, infested with crawling, flying, leaping, nameless dangers. There are occasional brilliant patches of rare, passionate orchids and other sweet flowers and succulent fruits, but they are rare. He daily does battle with horrors and emotions that he will spend the rest of his life trying to forget or suppress. Or recapture.

His jungle is a wilderness he will never fully escape, but those first early years when the bloom is on the peach and the milk teeth have just barely departed are the crucial days in the Great Education.

I am not at all sure that girls have even the slightest hint that there *is* such a jungle. But no man is really qualified to say. Most wildernesses are masculine, anyway.

And one thing that must be said about a wilderness, in contrast to the supple silkiness of Civilization, is that the basic, primal elements of existence are laid bare and raw. And can't be ducked. It is in that jungle that all men find out about themselves. Things we all know, but rarely admit. Say, for example, about that beady red-eyed, clawed creature, that ravening Car-

nivore, that incorrigibly wild, insane, scurrying little beast—
the Killer that is in each one of us. We pretend it is not there
most of the time, but it is a silly idle sham, as all male ex-kids
know. They have seen it and have run fleeing from it more
than once. Screaming into the night.

One quiet Summer afternoon, leafing through a library book,
with the sun slanting down on the oaken tables, I came across
a picture in a Nature book of a creature called the Tasmanian
Devil. He glared directly at me out of the page, with an un-
wavering red-eyed gaze, and I have never forgotten it. I was
looking at my soul!

The Tasmanian Devil is well named, being a nocturnal mar-
supial of extraordinary ferocity, being strictly carnivorous, and
when cornered fighting with a nuttiness beyond all bounds of
reason. In fact, it is said that he is one of the few creatures on
earth that *looks forward* to being cornered.

I looked him in the eye; he looked back, and even from
the flat, glossy surface of the paper I could feel his burning
rage, a Primal rage that glowed white hot like the core of a
nuclear explosion. A chord of understanding was struck between us. He knew and I knew. We were Killers. The only thing
that separated us was the sham. He admitted it, and I have been
attempting to cover it up all of my life.

I remember well the first time my own Tasmanian Devil
without warning screamed out of the darkness and revealed
himself for what he was—a fanged, maniacal meat eater. Every
male child sweats inside at a word that is rarely heard today:
the Bully. That is not to say that bullies no longer exist.
Sociologists have given them other and softer-sounding labels,
an "over-aggressive child," for example, but they all amount to
the same thing—Meatheads. Guys who grow up banging grilles
in parking lots and becoming captains of Industry or Mafia
hatchet men. Every school had at least five, and they usually
gathered followers and toadies like barnacles on the bottom of
a garbage scow. The lines were clearly drawn. You were either a
Bully, a Toady, or one of the nameless rabble of Victims who
hid behind hedges, continually ran up alleys, ducked under

porches, and tried to get a connection with City Hall, City Hall being the Bully himself.

I was an accomplished Alley Runner who did not wear sneakers to school from choice but to get off the mark quicker. I was well qualified to endorse Keds Champions with:

"I have outrun some of the biggest Bullies of my time wearing Keds, and I am still here to tell the tale."

It would make a great ad in *Boys' Life*:

"KIDS! When that cold sweat pours down your back and you are facing the Moment Of Truth on the way home from the store, don't you wish you had bought Keds? Yes, our new Bully-Beater model has been endorsed by skinny kids with glasses from coast to coast. That extra six feet may mean the difference between making the porch and you-know-what!"

Many of us have grown up wearing mental Keds and still ducking behind filing cabinets, water coolers, and into convenient men's rooms when that cold sweat trickles down between the shoulder blades. My Moment of Truth was a kid named Grover Dill.

What a rotten name! Dill was a Running Nose type of Bully. His nose was *always* running, even when it wasn't. He was a yelling, wiry, malevolent, sneevily snively Bully who had quelled all insurgents for miles around. I did not know one kid who was not afraid of Dill, mainly because Dill was truly aggressive. This kind of aggression later in life is often called "Talent" or "Drive," but to the great formless herd of kids it just meant a lot of running, getting belted, and continually feeling ashamed.

If Dill so much as said "Hi" to you, you felt great and warm inside. But mostly he just hit you in the mouth. Now a true Bully is not a flash in the pan, and Dill wasn't. This went on for years. I must have been in about second grade when Dill first belted me behind the ear.

Maybe the terrain had something to do with it. Life is

very basic in Northern Indiana. Life is more Primal there than in, say, New York City or New Jersey or California. First of all, Winters are really *Winters* there. Snow, ice, hard rocky frozen ground that doesn't thaw out until late June. Kids played baseball all Winter on this frozen lumpy tundra. Ground balls come galloping: "K-tunk K-tunk K-tunk K-tunk" over the Arctic concrete. And then summer would come. The ground would thaw and the wind would start, whistling in off the Lake, a hot Sahara gale. I lived the first ten years of my life in a continual sandstorm. A sandstorm in the Dunes region, with the temperature at 105 and no rain since the first of June, produces in a kid the soul of a Death Valley prospector. The Indiana Dunes—in those days no one thought they were special or spectacular—they were just the Dunes, all sand and swamps and even timber wolves. There were rattlesnakes in the Dunes, and rattlesnakes in fifth grade. Dill was a Puff-Adder among garden worms.

This terrain grew very basic kids who fought the elements all their lives. We'd go to school in a sandstorm and come home just before a tornado. Lake Michigan is like an enormous flue that stretches all the way up into the Straits of Mackinac, into the Great North Woods of Canada, and the wind howls down that lake like an enormous chimney. We lived at the bottom of this immense stovepipe. The wind hardly ever stops. Winter, Spring, Summer, Fall—whatever weather we had was made twenty times worse by the wind. If it was warm, it seared you like the open door of a blast furnace. If it was cold, the wind sliced you to little pieces and then put you back together again and sliced you up the other way, then diced and cubed you, ground you up, and put you back together and started all over again. People had red faces all year round from the wind.

When the sand is blowing off the Dunes in the Summer, it does something to the temper. The sand gets in your shoes and always hurts between the toes. The kids would cut the sides of their sneakers so that when the sand would get too much, just stick your foot up in the air and the sand would squirt out and you're ready for another ten minutes of action. It breeds a different kind of kid, a kid whose foot is continually

cut. One time Kissel spent two entire weeks with a catfish
hook in his left heel. He couldn't get it out, so he just kept going
to school and walked with one foot in the air. One day Miss
Siefert insisted that he go down and see the school nurse, who
cut the hook out. Kissel's screaming and yelling could be
heard all over the school. So you've got the picture of the
Jungle.

Grover Dill was just another of the hostile elements of
Nature, like the sand, the wind, and the stickers. Northern
Indiana has a strange little green burr that has festered fingers
and ankles for countless centuries. One of the great moments
in life for a kid was to catch a flyball covered with a thick furr
of stickers in a barehand grab, driving them in right to the
marrow of the knuckle bones.

One day, without warning of any kind, it happened. Monumental moments in our lives are rarely telegraphed. I am coming home from school on a hot, shimmering day, totally unaware that I was about to meet face to face that Tasmanian
Devil, that clawed, raging maniac that lurks inside each of us.
There were three or four of us eddying along, blown like leaves
through vacant lots, sticker patches, asphalt streets, steaming
cindered alleys and through great clouds of Indiana grass-
hoppers, wading through clouds of them, big ones that spit
tobacco juice on your kneecaps and hollered and yelled in the
weeds on all sides. The eternal locusts were shrieking in the
poplars and the Monarch butterflies were on the wing amid the
thistles. In short, it was a day like any other.

My kid brother is with me and we have one of those little
running ball games going, where you bat the ball with your
hand back and forth to each other, moving homeward at the
same time. The traveling game. The ball hops along; you field
it; you throw it back; somebody tosses it; it's grabbed on the
first bounce, you're out, but nobody stops moving homeward.
A moving ball game. Like a floating crap game.

We were about a block or so from my house, bouncing the
ball over the concrete, when it happened. We are moving along
over the sandy landscape, under the dark lowering clouds of

Open-Hearth haze that always hung between us and the sun. I
dart to my right to field a ground ball. A foot lashes out unexpectedly and down I go, flat on my face on the concrete road.
I hit hard and jarring, a bruising, scraping jolt that cut my lip
and drew blood. Stunned for a second, I look up. It is the
dreaded Dill!

To this day I have no idea how he materialized out of nowhere to trip me flat and finally to force the issue.

"Come on, kid, get out of the way, will ya?" He grabs the
ball and whistles it off to one of his Toadies. He had yellow
eyes. So help me God, yellow eyes!

I got up with my knees bleeding and my hands stunned and
tingling from the concrete, and without any conception at all
of what I was doing I screamed and rushed. My mind a total
red, raging, flaming blank. I know I screamed.

"YAAAAAAHHHH!"

The next thing I knew we are rolling over and over on the
concrete, screaming and clawing. I'm out of my skull! I am
pounding Dill against the concrete and we're rolling over and
over, battering at each other's faces. I was screaming continually.
I couldn't stop. I hit him over and over in the eyes. He rolled
over me, but I was kicking and clawing, gouging, biting, tearing.
I was vaguely conscious of people coming out of houses and
down over lawns. I was on top. I grabbed at his head. I caught
both of Grover Dill's ears in either hand and I began to pound
him on the concrete, over and over again.

I have since heard of people under extreme duress speaking
in strange tongues. I became conscious that a steady torrent
of obscenities and swearing was pouring out of me as I screamed.
I could hear my brother running home, hysterically yelling for
my mother, but only dimly. All I knew is that I was tearing and
ripping and smashing at Grover Dill, who fought back like a
fiend! But I guess it was the first time he had ever met face to
face with an unleashed Tasmanian Devil.

I continued to swear fantastically, as though I had no control
over it. I was conscious of it and yet it was as though it was
coming from something or someone outside of me. I swore as I

have never sworn since as we rolled screaming on the ground. And suddenly we just break apart. Dill, the back of his head all battered, his eyes puffed and streaming, slashed by my claws and fangs, was hysterical. There was hardly a scratch on me, except for my scraped knees and cut lip.

I learned then that Bravery does not exist. Just a kind of latent Nuttiness. If I had thought about attacking Dill for ten seconds before I had done it, I'd have been four blocks away in a minute flat. But something had happened. A wire broke. A fuse blew. And I had gone out of my skull.

But I had sworn! Terribly! Obscenely! In our house kids didn't swear. The things I called Dill I'm sure my mother had not even heard. And *I* had only heard once or twice, coming out of an alley. I had woven a tapestry of obscenity that as far as I know is still hanging in space over Lake Michigan. And my mother had heard!

Dill by this time is wailing hysterically. This had never happened to him before. They're dragging the two of us apart amid a great ring of surging grownups and exultant, scared kids who knew more about what was happening than the mothers and fathers ever would. My mother is looking at me. She said:

"What did you say?"

That's all. There was a funny look on her face. At that instant all thought of Grover Dill disappeared from what was left of my mind and all I could think of was the incredible shame of that unbelievable tornado of obscenity I had sprayed over the neighborhood.

I go into the house in a daze, and my mother's putting water on me in the bathroom, pouring it over my head and dabbing at my eyes which are puffed and red from hysteria. My kid brother is cowering under the dining-room table, scared. Kissel, next door, has been hiding in the basement, under the steps, scared. The whole neighborhood is scared, and so am I. The water trickles down over my hair and around my ears as I stare into the swirling drainage hole in the sink.

"You better go in and lie down on the daybed. Take it easy. Just go in and lie down."

She takes me by the shoulder and pushes me down on the daybed. I lie there scared, really scared of what I have done. I felt no sense of victory, no sense of beating Dill. All I felt was this terrible thing I had said and done.

The light was getting purple and soft outside, almost time for my father to come home from work. I'm just lying there. I can see that it's getting dark, and I know that he's on his way home. Once in a while a gigantic sob would come out, half hysterically. My kid brother by now is under the sink in the john, hiding among the mops, mewing occasionally.

I hear the car roar up the driveway and a wave of terror breaks over me, the terror that a kid feels when he knows that retribution is about to be meted out for something that he's been hiding forever—his rottenness. The basic rottenness has been uncovered, and now it's the Wrath of God, which you are not only going to get but which you deserve!

I hear him in the kitchen now. I'm in the front bedroom, cowering on the daybed. The normal sounds—he's hollering around with the newspaper. Finally my mother says:

"Come on, supper's ready. Come on, kids, wash up."

I painfully drag myself off the daybed and sneak along the woodwork, under the buffet, sneaking, skulking into the bathroom. My kid brother and I wash together over the sink. He says nothing.

Then I am sitting at the kitchen table, toying with the red cabbage. My Old Man looks up from the Sport page:

"Well, what happened today?"

Here it comes! There is a short pause, and then my mother says:

"Oh, not much. Ralph had a little fight."

"Fight? What kind of fight!"

"Oh, you know how kids are," she says.

The axe is poised over my naked neck! There is no way out! Mechanically I continue to shovel in the mashed potatoes and red cabbage, the meat loaf. But I am tasting nothing, just eating and eating.

"Oh, it wasn't much. I gave him a talking to. By the way, I see the White Sox won today. . . ."

About two thirds of the way through the meal I slowly began to realize that I was not about to be destroyed. And then a very peculiar thing happened. A sudden unbelievable twisting, heaving stomach cramp hit me so bad I could feel my shoes coming right up through my ears.

I rushed back into the bathroom, so sick to my stomach that my knees were buckling. It was all coming up, pouring out of me, the conglomeration of it all. The terror of Grover Dill, the fear of yelling the things that I had yelled, my father coming home, my obscenities . . . I heaved it all out. It poured out of me in great heaving rushes, splattering the walls, the floor, the sink. Old erasers that I had eaten years before, library paste that I had downed in second grade, an Indian Head penny that I had gulped when I was two! It all came up in thunderous, retching heaves.

My father hovered out in the hall, saying:

"What's the matter with him? What's the matter? Let's call Doctor Slicker!"

My mother *knew* what was the matter with me.

"Now he's going to be all right. Just take it easy. Go back and finish eating. Go on."

She pressed a washrag to the back of my neck. "Now take it easy. I'm not going to say anything. Just be quiet. Take it easy."

Down comes the bottle of Pepto-Bismol and the spoon. "Take this. Stop crying."

But then I *really* started to cry, yelling and blubbering. She was talking low and quiet to me.

"We'll tell him your stomach is upset, that you ate something at school."

The Pepto-Bismol slides down my throat, amid my blubbering. It is now really coming out! I'm scared of Grover Dill again, scared of everything. I'm convinced that I will never grow up to be twenty-one, that I'm going blind!

I'm lying in bed, sobbing, and I finally drifted off to sleep, completely passed out from sheer nervous exhaustion. The soft warm air blew the curtains back and forth as we caught the tail of a breeze from the Great North Woods, the wilderness at the head of the Lake. Both of us slept quietly, me and my little red-eyed, fanged, furry Tasmanian Devil. Both of us slept. For the time being.

Flick chuckled in a somewhat dirty way.

"The next time that bastard comes in here, I'll tell him you're in the phone booth."

All the beer I had drunk had brought upon me a feeling of great peace and magnanimity. I stared dreamily at the gas station down the street. The wind sighed through the high-tension wires somewhere off in the distance.

"Yep. I always was wiry," I said.

"Oh yeah? I remember the time Paswinski chased you up on the garage and you stayed there all Saturday," Flick sneered, stroking old fires.

"I liked it up there! What do you mean, I used to always go up on the garage—I liked it up there."

"Oh sure. Especially when Paswinski was throwing rocks at you."

"Well, I notice *he* never did anything about Grover Dill!"

We both watched silently as across the street a solitary drunk struggled from doorway to doorway. For some reason he carried his hat in his hand, waving it frantically at each passing car. Flick, an old connoisseur of drunks, watched his technique critically as he ricocheted from storefront to storefront.

"They don't make 'em like old Lud Kissel any more." Flick had the sound of a man describing a recognized all-time great.

"Funny thing, Flick. I thought of Lud Kissel in New York, this past Fourth."

"Fourth of what?"

"The Fourth of *July*."

"The Fourth of July? Reminded you of Ludlow Kissel? Old Lud Kissel, the drunk?"

It was my turn to play it expansive. I leaned forward over the bar, sipping my beer meaningfully, milking the moment.

"Flick, do you mean to tell me you don't remember Lud Kissel's Dago bomb?"

"Dago bomb?"

We stared at each other for a long moment and again he lit up like a 60-watt Mazda.

"You mean that big Dago bomb that blew out the . . . ?"

"Yes indeed, Flick, that is the very one I am referring to."

XVI 🐦 LUDLOW KISSEL AND THE DAGO BOMB THAT STRUCK BACK

I threaded my way through the midtown, midday sidewalk traffic that eddied and surged over and around the clutter of Construction paraphernalia. It was desperately hot. My wash-and-wear suit clung to me like some rancid, scratchy extension of my clammy skin. All around me New York was busily, roaringly, endlessly rebuilding itself, like some giant Phoenix arising from still red-hot ashes of its dead self. New York's infamous Edifice Complex blooms mightily in Midsummer.

I scuttled feverishly through shimmering waves of asphalt-scented heat toward the paradise of dark, expensive decadence of my favorite French restaurant, *Les Misérables des Frites*, little realizing that in another split second I was about to enjoy one of the truly secret subterranean pleasures of the human soul. Frantically taking my place in a hunched line of prickly-heated City dwellers doggedly plodding single file over a long, planked gangway, tightly jammed between an enormous excavation and a line of throbbing bright orange engines of construction. Ahead of me a short, stout lady wearing a damp flowered dress, clutching a Bonwit Teller shopping bag in both hands, ducked her head low as she ran interference for me and for those behind me through the wall of ringing sound and sensual heat.

My mind, as is so often the case these days, was totally blank. Sweat trickled in a long, thin, cool line down the knobbles of my backbone and spread out damply along the waistband of my twisted jockey shorts, which were threatening to emasculate me at any moment. My feet moved steadily to the rhythm of a colossal Diesel engine pounding insanely off my port bow. All around us, reaching high into the copper heavens, the stainless steel and aluminum green-glassed cliffs of partly completed and already eroding towers acted as colossal baffles, amplifying the subterranean reverberations of construction almost beyond endurance. New York's Summer Festival was in full swing, and I was a celebrant.

I had reached perhaps the midpoint of the plank ladder, breathing shallowly of the rising clouds of pulverized cement dust and carbon monoxide fumes, a subtle mixture that forms one of the more insidious anesthetics yet devised, dulling the senses and clouding the soul, when it happened. It was more felt, at first, than heard—a long, low gurgling sensation pushing up suddenly from the gut and exploding in the brain like some great comber of some ancient sea, on a lost, forgotten beach:

KAARRROOOMMMMPPHHHHH!

For a split second the great sound hung in mid-air and then, unthinkingly, my ancient GI reflexes working magically and smoothly, I hurled myself to the clapboards, digging in as I landed. The bombardment had begun!

I clung to the earth, waiting for the second round of the bracket, which should come, I hastily calculated, off to my right. Suddenly I became aware of an insistent rapping on the back of my neck as an elderly crane-like citizen behind me croaked:

"Get up, you bum. If you're going to sleep on the sidewalk, at least find a doorway, you soak!"

He stepped over me and sheepishly I regained my feet. Up and down the line I saw other ex-GIs brushing themselves off and once again moving forward in the unending stream of Twentieth Century Man, bound for God knows where. My mind raced as I peered down through the haze of the great canyon of excavation that lay just beyond the barricades. And then I could smell it, an acrid, faint, delicious, familiar, naggingly pleasing scent—Dynamite! The real thing!

Minutes later I sat pensively at a tiny corner table of *Misérables,* waiting for my luncheon date to arrive and vaguely conscious of a difficult-to-define sense of nostalgic pleasure and euphoria. Could it be the Bloody Charlie I was drinking? No, I had barely touched it. As I idly and comfortingly fingered the smooth, sleek surface of my Diners' Club card—my protection against the world—the way a gunfighter of old must have absently fondled his Smith & Wesson Thirty-Eight, I tried to analyze my sudden sense of warmth and well-being. It had started immediately after the blasting operation at the construction site. Could there be a connection? No man wants to admit that he is a secret Atom Bomb fan, so I hastily rejected this transient thought. Yet somehow I could not deny that the tiny whiff of blue smoke had awakened some ancient memory, some long-dormant pleasure. I absently munched one of the new No-Cal composition cashew nuts which are featured at the *boîte* as I raked my memory for a clue. The pleasant sound of diners' voices mingled with the Muzak and the popping of corks. The sizzling of the grill and the hum of air-conditioning lulled me as the Bloody Charlie began its soothing work. Out of the din, voices and sounds of the past emerged, dripping ooze and slime like some ancient creatures unearthed from long-sealed caverns. Dynamite!

Let's admit it. There are few sounds more soul-satisfying, more frightening, more exciting than an explosion. Explosions of one kind or another have always been part of great Folk celebrations from weddings to Wars. I sipped my drink and mused on the first time I had heard that primal roar of exploding black powder. And then it hit me. My God! Tomorrow was the Fourth of July!

The Fourth of July! It had crept up on tiny cats' feet on the scale of the calendar, unnoticed, unsung, unbombarded. It was then that I knew where those pleasant tinglings of mingled regret and exhilaration that we call Nostalgia had come from.

Yes, in just a few hours it would be the Glorious Fourth. And here I was without so much as a sparkler to my name. I ordered another drink and settled down comfortably into my soft eiderdown bed of remembrances of things past. There are times when you just have to let it go.

As I idly mulled the twin olives in my classical Charlie, the Northern Indiana landscape of the late Depression era began to take form, shadowy and persistent, amid the green and gold bottles behind the mirrored bar directly ahead of me. The blackened stumps, snaggle-toothed and primal, of the steel mills and the oil refineries lay etched against the hazy gray-green horizon of the July skies of the Great Lakes. Somewhere off in the distance the construction crew set off another dull, thumping blast that jiggled the silverware on my table, and it all began to come back.

Dynamite, heat, and excitement were all intermingled in that Fourth of July ritual that has long since departed. What is there about a solid, molar-rattling explosion that sets the blood a-tingling and brings the roses to the cheeks? There are muddleheaded souls who will tell you over and over that Man is basically a peaceful and quiet creature, destined ultimately to while away his golden days strumming lutes, penning odes, and watching birds. I have never yet witnessed a turtle preparing to ignite the portentous fuse of a Cherry Bomb. No, it remained for Man to concoct black powder from the innocent elements of the earth and ultimately to split the atom, all in pursuit of that healing balm—the thundering report.

And nowhere was this particular pleasure more honored and indulged than in the mill towns of Northern Indiana. Even today there are countless veterans of those fireworks barrages—hearing partially gone, a high, thin, singing sound in the cranium, sporting stunted, stubbly eyebrows, vaguely jumpy from borderline shellshock—who search in vain for the Fireworks Stand to assuage their deep hunger for the celebrating concussion, the better to honor our glorious American past.

The Fireworks Stand. Even setting the words down stark and simple on the page causes my hand to tremble and my brow to dampen in delicious fear, the sort of fear that only a kid who has lit a Five Incher under a Carnation milk can and has hurled himself prone upon the earth awaiting The End can know. Even the *look* of classical fireworks was magnificent! The Five Incher —hard, cool, rock-like cylinder of sinister jade green, its vicious red fuse aggressive and yet quiet cradled in the palm of the hand —is an experience once known never forgotten.

The Cherry Bomb. Ah, what pristine geometric tensile beauty; a perfect orb, brilliant carmine red, packed chockablock with latent terror and destruction. The Torpedo, an instrument malevolent and yet subtly complex, designed for hand-to-hand celebration. Many a grown man today carries in his shins a peppering of tiny round pebbles buried deep in the flesh from too close familiarity with the roaring Torpedo—a shrapnel victim of the Glorious Fourth. For the uninitiated I at this point must explain that the Torpedo was perhaps an inch high, a half-inch in circumference, symbolically striped in the colors of our country, made to be hurled against a brick wall or a passing Hupmobile, a contact weapon of singular violence that sent its ignitors, tiny rock fragments, showering over an area of fifty yards or more.

The Pinwheel—an expensive device largely used for flamboyant show and yet responsible for some of the major conflagrations of the past. Whole blocks, and indeed in some cases entire towns, disappearing under the roaring flames to the applause of the multitude. I speak with more than average authority on these matters since my father, a genuinely dedicated fireworks maniac, owned and operated a Fireworks Stand every year during my larval stages.

The Depression lay over the land like a great numbing blanket of restlessness and frustration, but on the Fourth the sky would be filled with skyrockets, booming aerial bombs, and hand grenades, because nobody had anything else to do in those days. They could scratch, and make beer, and just stand around. Once in a while they'd go down to the Roundhouse and see if they could pick up an extra day somewhere, but mostly they'd just sit on the porch and chew tobacco and spit. That's what the

Depression was. One of the good things about the Depression, and why a lot of people look back on it with a nutty kind of nostalgia, is because *nobody* made it in the Depression. So nobody had a sense of guilt. Goofing off was just a natural thing to do. In the Depression nobody did anything. It was a license to fool around, and they fooled around in big ways.

I remember guys sitting on their front porch, tossing dynamite —I mean *blasting* dynamite!—out on the streets, just for kicks. Northern Indiana is full of primeval types who've drifted up from the restless hills of Kentucky and the gulches of Tennessee, bringing with them suitcases filled with dynamite saved over from the time Grandpaw blew up the stumps in the Back Forty. And they brought it to the city with them, because you never can tell, and since they never had any money for fireworks there was only one thing to do. And they did it. They would sit on their porch on a quiet, hot, Fourth of July, rocking back and forth in the swing, breaking dynamite sticks, which come about six inches long, into sizes approximating a green Two Incher, like busting off a chunk of a Baby Ruth candy bar. Old Dad, his cigar clamped in his teeth, would Scotch-tape a little fuse on the end, raise it with suitable flourishes to his cigar-butt end— *bbzzzzzzzzz*—hold it aloft for a split second, flip it back by the garage, and dive for the floor.

KKKAAAABBBOOOOOOMM!!

Rufe is celebrating his ancient heritage. Crockery would crash for blocks around, old ladies would be hurled into the snowball bushes, but no one seemed to care. After all, the Fourth is the Fourth. There would be a slight delay as Rufe fused another nuclear bomb, and:

BAAARRROOOOOOOM!

Tin cups would rattle for miles around, windows shatter and smash.

Dynamite was the milk of life to the average hillbilly of the day. He celebrated with it, feuded with it, and fished with it. The Sporting instinct runs strong in the hills. When the fishing season would open, the river would literally be aboil with TNT.

POOOOOOOOOOMMMM!!

An underwater explosion has its own peculiar excitement, a kind of long, drawn-out subterranean gurgle, and then the air for miles around would be filled with catfish, a thundercloud of sunfish drifting over the county for twenty minutes or more, hundreds of the Sporting Elite fielding them in bushel baskets.

The more civilized celebrants, however, on the Fourth, shot their Relief check in one orgy of fireworks buying. Fireworks come in a number of exotically lethal varieties. Among them was the classical Dago Bomb. This was never construed as an anti-Italian name, being more pro than anything else. The Dago Bomb was the *ne plus ultra* of the fireworks world. A true thing of beauty and symmetry, it came in several sizes, four to be exact: the Five Inch, the Eight Inch, the Ten Inch, and the Sure Death. In more effete circles it was known as an Aerial Bomb, but among real Fireworks fans it was most often known as the Dago Heister. It actually looked like those giant non-existent firecrackers that occasionally show up in cartoons, a red, white, and blue tube with a wooden base stained dark green, a long red fuse, and the instructions printed on the bottom:

"Place upright in a clear, unobstructed area. After igniting, stand well back. Not recommended for children. The manufacturer assumes absolutely no responsibility for this device."

Theoretically this infernal machine was to be lit by an expert hand. It would then explode with the first, or minor, explosion, which propelled an aerial charge of pure white TNT into the ambient air, theoretically vertical, for several hundred feet, and then—Devastation!—not once but several times, depending on the size of the Dago Bomb in question. It was not cheap, the smallest going for fifty cents and the largest for around three dollars, which in the days of the Depression was truly a capital investment in destruction.

The legends surrounding this mysterious weapon are countless. The mere sight of one of the larger specimens on the shelves of a Fireworks Stand sent waves of fear and nervous excitement through the Sparkler Buyers. It was truly the Big Time.

It was a Dago Bomb that played a key role in the legend

that was Ludlow Kissel. Mr. Kissel had found his true medium
in the Depression itself. Kissel worked in Idleness the way other
artists worked in clay or marble. God only knows what would
have happened to him were it not for the Depression. He was a
true child of his time. He was also a magnificent Souse. The
word "Alcoholic" had not yet come into common usage, at least
not in the Steel towns of Indiana. Nor were there any lurking
Freudian fears or explanations for the classical appetite for
potage that Kissel nourished. He was a drunk, and knew it. He
just liked the stuff, and glommed onto it whenever the occasion demanded. And if the Store-Boughten variety of Lightning
was not available, he concocted his own, using raisins, apri-
cots, Fleischmann's yeast, molasses, and dead flies.

Nominally, Kissel worked in the roundhouse, and for over
thirty years had been on the Extra Board, being called only in
extreme emergencies, which occurred roughly once every other
month or so. He invariably celebrated a day of work by holing
up in the Bluebird Inn for perhaps a week, and then would return home, propelling himself painfully forward on one foot
and one knee. He was compensating for a tilted horizon. The
sound of Kissel crawling up the gravel driveway next to his
house was a familiar one, and it took him sometimes upwards
of three hours to make it from the street to the back porch. At
3 A.M., lying in my dark bedroom, it was kind of comforting
to hear Mr. Kissel struggling up the steps of his back porch.
Inching painfully step by step.

Thump (One)

Long pause. . . .

Thump (Two)

Longer pause. . . .

Thuuuump (He's made three in a row!)

Split-second pause. . . .

Dump DUNK BUMP K-THUMP!

He's back at the bottom.

Many's the time I've slipped off to sleep with this familiar
sound of human endeavor battling over overwhelming odds—
Kissel trying to make the kitchen door. And then the voice of

Mrs. Kissel, a large flower-print aproned lady who read *True Romances* voraciously, would call out:

"Watch the steps, Lud. They're tricky."

She loved him.

Kissel, one Fourth of July, played a leading role in a patriotic tableau which is even today spoken of in hushed, reverential tones in the area. It was a particularly steamy, yeasty, hellish July. The houseflies clung to the screen doors and the mosquitoes hummed in great whirling clouds in the poplar trees. It was in such weather that Mr. Kissel reached his apogee. He was not a Winter Souse. There was something about the birds and the bees and the hot sun that set off a spark in Mr. Kissel's blood and stoked an insatiable thirst for the healing grape. His stocky, overalled figure reeling through the twilight, leaving a wake of flickering fireflies, was as much a part of the Summer landscape as the full golden moon. Parishioners sprinkling their lawns and snowball bushes would nod familiarly to him as he wove through the fine spray of their brass nozzles.

The Fourth in question dawned hot and jungle-like, with an overhang of black, lacy storm clouds. In fact, a few warm immense drops sprinkled down through the dawn haze. I know, because I was up and ready for action. Few kids slept late on the Fourth. Even as the stars were disappearing and the sun was edging over the Lake, the first Cherry Bombs cracked the stillness and the first old ladies dialed the police. Carbide cannons which had gathered dust in basements for a year roared out, greeting the dawn. And by 7 A.M. the first dozen pairs of eyebrows were blackened and singed, and already the wounded were being buttered with Unguentine and sent back into the fray. Long lines of overheated Willys Knights, Essexes, and Pierce Arrows inched toward the beaches. Babies cried, mothers wept, and husbands swore. Parades fitfully broke out, and the White Sox prepared to battle it out in the big Fourth of July doubleheader with the St. Louis Browns, Futility meeting Hopelessness head on. The sun rose higher and higher and at its zenith blazed down with an intensity of purpose and effectiveness equal to its best work in Equatorial Africa. The asphalt simmered quietly and stuck to the tires and the tennis shoes of the passing parade. Lilac bushes drooped fragrantly and the cicadas screamed from the cottonwoods. Through it all the steady, rolling barrage of exploding black powder in one form or another paid homage to our War of Independence.

As the day wore on, this barrage grew in intensity, because all true fireworks nuts learned from infanthood the art of rationing and husbanding the ammunition for the crucial moment, which came always after dark.

Kissel had not made his appearance throughout the long morning and early afternoon. He was undoubtedly stoking his private furnace in preparation for his *gala*, which, when it came, was worth waiting for. Shortly after noon a few drops of rain sprinkled down, just enough to dampen the shirt and the rose-bushes, but not the spirits. Little did we realize that we were shortly to be the observers of a scene that would be discussed and recounted through the long Winter months of years to come. The event became known simply as Kissel's Dago Bomb.

The White Sox and the Brownies had painfully worked their way into the top of the Third of the first game, a scoreless tie, when Kissel appeared on the shimmering horizon, weaving spectacularly and carrying a large paper bag as carefully as a totally committed drunk can. Kissel was about to celebrate the founding of our nation, the nation which had provided such a bounteous life for him and his.

At first no one paid much attention to the struggling figure as it inched its way from lamppost to lamppost and fireplug to fireplug. Little girls burned sparklers on porches, and I was carefully de-pleating a string of Chinese ladyfingers. These are tiny firecrackers with pleated fuses, all woven together, and designed for the rich and profligate to fire off simultaneously by simply lighting the main fuse. No kid in his right mind ever did *that*, but instead we carefully disengaged, fuse by fuse, the ladyfingers and fired them off one by one, under garbage cans, on porches, and behind dogs. My mother, at regular intervals, called from the kitchen window the Fourth of July watch cry of all mothers:

"Be careful! You're going to lose an eye if you're not careful!"

This was, of course, purely ritualistic, and was only a minor annoyance. Flick had already suffered a flesh wound of a routine nature, his right hand was swathed in grease-soaked gauze, the result of demonstrating that he could hold a Three Incher in his hand when it went off, and still survive. He was now back on the scene, working as a lefty. In short, it was a Fourth like all other Fourths, up to the moment that Kissel took his stance.

He had disappeared into his house to prepare for his massive statement of Patriotism. Shortly afterward he reappeared on the front porch and stumbled down the steps, carrying in his right hand the largest Dago Bomb that had ever been seen in the neighborhood. It was a Dago Heister of truly awesome stature, being fully a foot and a half high and a good three inches in diameter, and was the first all-black Dago Bomb anyone had ever seen. This point has been argued over many a cold Wintry afternoon. Some reports have it that Kissel's Dago Bomb was not a Dago Bomb at all, but some sort of mortar shell. Others maintain that it was indeed a Dago Bomb, but of a foreign make, possibly Chinese, as the somber menacing color was highly unorthodox. Suffice it to say that no one ever really determined just where Kissel obtained the weapon, or its true nature, as Kissel himself was hazy on most details of his life, and this was no exception. His only comment later, which was never disputed, was:

"I sure got one!"

When Kissel emerged from his front door and came down the steps carrying his work of the Devil, the neighborhood almost magically knew that something big was about to happen. Sparklers flickered out; kids ran through vacant lots and over driveways; heads appeared at windows. The crowd gathered. Kissel, with that peculiar deliberateness of the perpetually fogbound, laboriously prepared to detonate the black beauty. He placed it dead in the center of the concrete roadway and stood back to survey the scene, weaving slightly as he worked. The crowd drew back and watched, silently, excitement hanging over the multitude in a thin blue haze. Fireworks of that magnitude rarely were seen and commanded instant respect. The ebony monster stood bolt upright, silently, with a cool quality of the truly lethal; understated but potent.

Shimmering waves of heat caused the scene to take on a strange unreal, flickering quality. The neighborhood fell silent, and only the dull mutterings of distant fire barrages broke the stillness. A few errant drops of tepid rain sprinkled the concrete as we waited. The skies overhead were gray and threatening, with ragged edges of black cloud shimmering in the July heat.

Kissel, at Center Stage, struggled to find a match the way drunks invariably do, going through pocket after pocket after pocket; fumblingly, maddeningly, and finding only pencil stubs and brass keys. It seemed to go on forever until finally someone —this point later was also much in dispute; no one quite knew who actually handed him the book of matches—solved the problem. Kissel took the book of matches in hand, paused for a moment, and belched, a deep, round, satisfying, shuddering burp of the sort that can only come from a vast internal lake of green beer. The crowd applauded and shifted impatiently, all eyes riveted on the dull black menace that stood with such dignity in the center of the concrete roadway.

Finally Kissel struck a match, which instantly went out. He struck another. It too flickered and died. Another and another. There was, I might add, a slight breeze which puffed fitfully from the Northwest. The audience grew restive, but no one dared leave. In fact, more viewers of this historic event were arriving by the minute. Kissel, as is so often the case with the massive drunk, seemed totally unaware of the drama he was creating and with maniacal intensity struggled with his matchbook, lighting match after match. Suddenly, out of the crowd, a kid darted, an experienced detonator of high explosives of all sorts, who shoved into Kissel's palsied hand a stick of briskly smoldering punk. The kid, according to witnesses who testified later, uttered one word: "Here," then turned, and scurried back into the throng and into the pages of local Folk history forever.

Kissel, thinking at first he had been given a cigar, gazed at it numbly for a moment or two and then dimly perceived that here was the means of lighting the fuse of the colossal black Dago Bomb.

The fuse on this type of insanity is of the coated variety, and in this case was about three inches long, a black, stiff, powder-impregnated length of fiber. It doesn't take much to light them, and once lit, the die is cast. Kissel shuffled forward, punk in hand, and made several futile passes at the fuse, the magnificent bomb remaining aloof and cool throughout. With each pass the crowd retreated, and then, with the inevitability of Greek drama, in the muttering silence the telltale hiss sounded forth clear and unmistakable. The fuse was lit!

Immediately the assemblage rolled back in a mighty wave, turned and waited while Kissel continued to attempt to light the fuse, totally unaware that time was growing short. Someone called out:

"Kissel! Hey Kissel, for God's sake, it's lit!"

Kissel raised his head questioningly and said:

"What's lit?"

The ominous hiss continued and then, suddenly and without warning, stopped. Occasionally these fuses are tricky, and extremely dangerous. They have been known to lie dormant like this for hours, seemingly extinguished for no good cause. Obviously this black menace was one of the treacherous.

Kissel returned to his fight, again touching punk to fuse. And this time the fuse, in its unpredictable way, hissed frantically. Kissel, at last seeing that his monster *was* lit, attempted his getaway. He reeled in a half-circle, befuddled, trailing punk smoke behind him and then, staggering forward, knocked the black monster over on its side—hissing fiercely with only seconds remaining!

The crowd, seeing this catastrophe unreeling before its eyes, to a man hit the dirt. Those on the fringes dove into snowball bushes; others simply moaned piteously and dug in. It was good training, as events turned out, for later years.

The Dago Bomb lay on its side, its ugly snout pointing toward the houses which lay across the lawns 200 feet or so away. Cooler members of the mob shouted to those in the houses. "Look out, it's coming! Close your windows!" The fuse sputtered on.

Kissel himself, now aware of the nature of the rapidly approaching catastrophe, made a futile but certainly courageous attempt to right the bomb. Someone yelled:

"Get down, Kissel, you'll get killed!"

Kissel fell over backward and lay flattened out on the concrete, waiting for the call of his Maker.

Then it happened. There are events which lend themselves readily to the descriptive phrase; the words of pen or tongue, and then there are things which happen that cannot be adequately communicated. The incident of Kissel's Dago Bomb must be classified as one of the truly indescribable. Suffice it to say that the bomb was well made and of an order of efficiency that fireworks manufacturers rarely achieve. With a definite clipped, stinging report the aerial bomb, lying horizontally on its side, propelled its deadly cartridge of dynamite out along the earth, skipping, humming, singing in an instantaneous trajectory that struck terror into the very marrow of the bones of those fortunate enough to be on the scene. This Dago Bomb was obviously designed to send its aerial charge at least 500 feet into the air. For an instant or so we were not aware of what sort of aerial charge it was prepared to deliver. We soon found out.

The cartridge, which seemed abnormally large as it emerged from the black maw of Kissel's Folly, skimmed over the sidewalk, parting the spectators like the Red Sea. Over the lawn and the driveway, and with a sharp, audible "click" and whistling sizzle, under Kissel's front porch. And for a long, pendulous moment the universe stood still. Fingernails clawed the earth, heads burrowed into hedges.

KAA-ROOOM!

The first thunderous explosion rocked the neighborhood. The slats of Kissel's porch bellowed outward; the floor tilted instantly downward. A great yellow, swirling cloud of dust rose over the lilac bushes. A second or two passed as an eternity, and then another, and louder, detonation thundered over the landscape:

KA-KAA-BAA-ROOOM!

This time it caved in the rose trellis of the house next door to Kissel's. The crowd heaved and dug deeper as two more giant explosions—KAA-RAAA-BOOM! BOOM!—sounded almost as one, these two under Mr. Strickland's Pontiac.

A heavy cloud of dust swirled for a moment and all was still, except for the pattering of the quiet raindrops.

Kissel slowly pulled himself to his knees and made his statement, which is even today part of that great legend.

"My God, what a doozy!"

Kissel had said it for all of us. As the crowd slowly got to its feet amid the quiet tinkling of glass and the heavy, sensual smell of oxidized dynamite, they were aware that they had been witness to History.

I idly stirred my third Bloody Charlie as off in the middle distance another muffled blast bloomphed and jiggled the bottles behind the bar. Kissel faded back into his landscape and I pensively chewed a cashew nut as I vainly struggled to return to the Here and Now. After all, fireworks, we all know, are dangerous and childish playthings that have no place in the hard-hitting, On-The-Go Male's life of today. A passing cab sent a reflected shaft of light across the mirror behind the bar. It broke into a thousand colors amid the bottles, and subtly I was reminded of yet another historic moment in the annals of the Fourth of July celebrations. Those colored lights reminded me irresistibly of my father and the time the Roman Candle struck back.

The Roman Candle is a truly noble and inspired piece of the pyrotechnician's art, being a long slender wand that spews forth colored, flaming balls that arch high into the midnight sky, one after the other, with magnificent effect. It is held in the hand, and is one of the few pieces of fireworks that bring out talent and skill on the part of the operator. The Roman Candle is graded according to the number of fireballs it can discharge, ranging from eight to, in some cases, as high as two dozen, but these are very rare and expensive. There are few experiences that rival for sheer ecstatic pleasure and total, unadulterated joy the feel of a Roman Candle in full bloom, sending its fireballs up into the dark heavens with that distinctive——Plock —sssssssss—Plock—sssssssssPlock——sound, and the slight but sensual recoil as each colored light arches heavenward. My father was unquestionably one of the great Roman Candle men of his time. That is, until that awful night when he met a Roman Candle that was fully his match, if not more.

He was so irresistibly drawn to Fireworks that, as I have mentioned, he became the proprietor of a Fireworks Stand early in my youth, and this made him a marked man in the neighborhood. A Fireworks Stand is a unique commercial establishment that has, like the May fly, a short but very merry life. For those who have never seen a Fireworks Stand a brief description would not be too far amiss. They were usually wooden stands, ex-fruit dispensaries, or what-have-you, covered with red, white, and blue bunting, over which a large red-on-white sign simply stated FIREWORKS. The interior of these stands was usually a blazing inferno because the July sun knows no mercy. They were dusty and hot, but the shelves were lined with the greatest assortment of bliss and ecstasy this side of the Biltmore bar. Space does not allow a full description of all these magnificent creations. The Mount Vesuvius, for example, a silver cone that when lit and placed on the ground spewed forth a great shower of gold, blue, and white sparks high into the air, emulating the eruption of its namesake. The racks of slender, sinuous Roman Candles, of several calibers, and the lordly monarch of them all, the Skyrocket. Skyrockets were available in a wide variety of potency and weight, just as the rocketry of our Space program of today. The tiny twenty-five-center hardly larger than a Five Incher, wired to a yellow pine stick topped with a red nose cone, was made to be launched from an upright, empty quart milk bottle, and on up the scale to the big Five Dollar Rocket that stood a full four feet and was launched from a special angle-iron and handled with extreme care, it being possible to bring down a passing DC-3 with the proper hand on the sights.

The Pinwheels also came in many sizes and colors and could,

if misused, be spectacularly disastrous. I personally saw one Pinwheel climb right up the side of a garage, over the roof, and spin a block and a half down the alley before it finally burnt itself out, and then only after burning down 300 feet of fence and two chicken coops.

There were many other forms of fireworks of a lesser nature, such as Red Devils, which were a particularly nasty piece of business, being red paper-covered tablets designed to be scratched on the pavement and ground under heel to a sputtering, hissing, general nastiness. They did not explode; merely hissed and burned and gave stupendous hotfeet to anyone who happened to step on them. Of course there were the more prosaic Firecrackers and Cherry Bombs of all sizes and varying degrees of destructiveness, and the odds and ends for grandmothers, girls, and smaller kids; the Sparklers, the Cap Guns, and the strange little white tablets, aspirin-size, that when lit produced a long, sinuously climbing white ash and were called "Snakes." All of these and more my father dispensed over the counter from his Fireworks Stand out on the state highway, where the heat waves rose and fell and the Big Time Spenders bought the stuff by the bags full for their blondes and their egos.

I was considered unbelievably lucky that my Old Man not only owned a Fireworks Stand with all that great stuff on the shelves, but that I actually was allowed to slave away my life in it. Some of my golden moments were spent dispensing Torpedoes and Cherry Bombs and black powder Five Inchers to various slope-browed delinquents of all ages on long, hot, late June and early July afternoons when other kids were out hitting out flies and fistfighting.

As the actual Fourth drew closer, our stock of fireworks slowly dwindled until the actual day of the Fourth itself, our peak moment. Fireworks Stands work strictly on speculation and my father ordered his stuff from the General Motors of the fireworks world, an outfit called the Excelsior Fireworks Corporation. They did not take any unsold material back, which meant that as the Fourth drew to a close what was on the shelves was ours to shoot, to explode, to detonate, to revel in, to memorialize America's struggle for Independence.

It was the Depression, of course, and few families had more than a couple of dollars or so to spend on gunpowder, and our entire neighborhood would wait for our return near midnight from the closed stand on the last moments of the Fourth of July. About 11:30 P.M., the sky above filled with bursting aerial bombs and Skyrockets, and off in the distance the rattle of Cherry Bombs and Musketry thrumming darkly, my father would say: "Let's close up," and immediately begin to load what was left of our stock into the Oldsmobile. Usually we had left a few of the greatest, heaviest, and most expensive pieces as well as several pounds of torpedoes and Sons O'Guns, a few huge rockets, and a couple dozen big Pinwheels and a rack or two of heavy-caliber Roman Candles.

My Old Man, eyes gleaming, cheeks flushed, would hurl us homeward through the dark, on his way to the most glorious moment of his entire year. He was in the saddle and was prepared to split the skies with a shower of sparks and fireballs and the eardrums of the neighbors with giant Dago Bombs. Every year the neighbors waited for this great moment, and the Old Man knew it. He was a magnificent sight, surrounded by boxes of ammunition as he singlehandedly bombarded the heavens on behalf of Freedom and the Stars And Stripes. He was a true artist of pyrotechnics, and rose to his absolute fullness of artistic power when clutching a Roman Candle, his body swaying sinuously with the innate rhythm of the born Roman Candle Shooter as he sent ball after ball arcing higher and higher into the midnight skies, to the roar of the crowd.

Fourth of July was almost always a day of intense, ragged excitement for everyone, usually skirting danger on one side and ecstatic celebration on the other. It caused a kind of homicidal recklessness to set in to the Individual, and certainly the Mass. The night my father encountered his devilish, avenging Roman Candle was no exception. All day cars had carried off great loads of our wares, but now it was over, and the neighborhood was about to witness my father's annual debauch. They stood on

porches and in driveways and watched from windows as in the
vacant lot on the corner my father hauled out his boxes of
surplus fireworks.

He programmed his displays like a true showman, starting
off with a few nondescript Pinwheels and Mount Vesuviuses,
gradually working up through the lesser Skyrockets and Aerial
Bombs to his final statement, a brace of great Roman Candles,
twenty-four-ball beauties fully five feet in length and two inches
in diameter; spectacular examples of the ancient art of fireworks.

I stood in the darkness with my brother and the other assembled urchins of the neighborhood, watching my father in his
finest hour. He was ten feet tall, at least, the biggest father in
miles around, until that incredible moment the Roman Candle
struck back.

The applause had grown from stage to stage, through the
Skyrockets, and now he stood in the center of the arena, the
flickering lights of distant aerial displays outlining him against
the night sky as he took his last two magnificent Roman Candles
that he had saved purposely for the last, the largest and most
powerful of the lot. He was one of the few Roman Candle men
who ever dared to use both hands simultaneously, timing each
ball to rotate one with the other, thereby achieving an almost
continuous display of spectacular Roman Candle artistry.

It was now no more than a minute or two before midnight,
and another Fourth of July would be history. He was a stickler
for time, and the dramatic effect. Carefully, and of course
theatrically milking the moment for all it was worth, he lit
both Roman Candles, held his elbows sharply out from his
body as they hissed briefly. The crowd surged forward, waiting
for his usual masterful display. They knew this was his Grand
Finale.

The first ball—PLOCK—arched green and sparkling from the
left hand, high up over the telephone wires and toward a distant
cloud. PLOCK—the right hand spit a golden comet. My father,
his left hand spinning simultaneously, sent it even higher than
the first. His timing was magnificent! PLOCK—the left hand
shot a scarlet streak upward even higher. PLOCK—again the

right hand. PLOCK—now they were coming faster and faster as my Old Man picked up the beat, and the crowd sensed a performance in progress that was to become classical in its execution.

On the far horizon the steel mills caught the reflected light of the flickering lightning of a gathering summer storm. PLOCK —my father sent another ball blazing white into the northern skies. PLOCK—a blue one, this time toward the Big Dipper. PLOCK—a green arrow darted toward the moon. The audience swayed in unison as my father, both arms weaving magically, the beat and the pulse of his synchronized Roman Candles paid homage to General Washington and the Continental Congress; the Boston Tea Party and the Minutemen. It was almost midnight now and my father, instinctively showing the great finesse and technique of a born Roman Candle Beethoven, knew that he was down to the last two balls.

PLOCK—the right hand sent a yellow star into the firmament. PLOCK—the left. And then something was wrong. The left-hand Roman Candle faltered. A few tiny sparks sizzled briefly. He spun the tube out and upward again; down, out and upward, meanwhile the right-hand weapon—PLOCK—sent its pellet upward. Suddenly, without warning an alien sound:

K-tunk!

And from the south end of the left-hand Roman Candle a large red ball emerged. From the wrong end! He leaped high, but it was too late. The ball skittered along his forearm, striking his elbow sharply, and disappeared into the short sleeve of his Pongee sport shirt!

The crowd gasped. A few women screamed. Children suddenly cried aloud as my father, showing the presence of mind of a great actor in the midst of catastrophe, shot his final ball from his right hand toward the North Star, as simultaneously the red ball reappeared from between his shoulder blades, his Pongee shirt bursting into spectacular flames. With a bellow he raced up the sidewalk, over the lawn, and trailing smoke and flames he disappeared into the house. A brief second of silence, and the sound of the shower could be heard roaring full blast from the darkened home.

Stunned for an instant the crowd remained silent, but then loosed a great roar of applause. They knew they had witnessed the finest performance of a great artist. Midnight tolled, and the Fourth was over.

"Would you care to order, sir?"

I was jerked back into the present by the waiter, who had shoved a huge menu in front of me.

"I guess so," I answered, "it looks like my date is not going to show."

It was just as well. Outside in the clanging street the blasting continued, and here in *Les Misérables des Frites* the bottles rattled. I sat quietly for a moment and watched the heat shimmer on the taxicabs outside, and then, raising what remained of my Charlie, I said to myself:

"Well, here's to the Fourth," and began to read the menu. It was time to eat.

XVII ॐ I SHOW OFF

Flick looked puzzled.

"A Bloody Charlie? How the hell do you make a Bloody Charlie?"

"You mean you don't serve Bloody Charlies here?"

Flick rummaged under the bar and finally found his *Bartender's Guide*.

"Forget it. You will not find it listed in that rag."

I could see that Flick's professional curiosity was piqued.

"Do you mean a Bloody *Mary?*"

"No, I said a Bloody Charlie. Charlie, as in Charlie Company. If I recall rightly, Flick, you were in the Artillery. 'C' for Charlie."

"Well, all right, how do you make a Bloody Charlie?" He sounded skeptical.

"Okay. If you have the makings, I'll be glad to whip us up a couple."

"This I have to see."

"Okay. I will need vodka, which I see you have, tomato juice, Worcestershire sauce, and perhaps a bit of salt. And one other special ingredient."

Flick set the tomato juice, the vodka, the Worcestershire,

and a salt shaker on the bar next to two tall glasses. I waited for him to bite.

"Now I suppose you're gonna tell me I need one a them fancy French liqueurs, or something."

"Not exactly. Do you have any olives?"

"Olives! I got plenty a olives."

"I will need four. Two for your drink and two for mine."

"Why two?"

"It is important that you use only *two* per drink. No more, no less."

I poured a jigger of vodka into each glass, filling them with the ice-cold tomato juice, a dash of Worcestershire in each, a pinch of salt; then very precisely I dropped two olives into each drink. A few quick swirls of a red plastic swizzle stick, and then:

"Cheers, Flick. Enjoy. Here are two classical Bloody Charlies."

"They look like Bloody Marys to me."

I sipped mine appreciatively, smacking my lips loudly, ostentatiously.

"No, Flick, there is a crucial diffcrence. These are Bloody Marys with *balls*. I have invented it. I call it a Bloody Charlie."

Flick sipped his for a moment and said:

"You always *did* have a dirty mind."

I set my drink down precisely on the bar, saying as I did so:

"No, that is not exactly true. In fact, I well remember when I could not even understand the simplest, most basic obscenity. My innocence led me into considerable difficulty."

XVIII 🦢 UNCLE BEN AND THE SIDE-SPLITTING KNEE-
SLAPPER, *or* SOME WORDS ARE LOADED

Every family has a Joke Teller, and he is usually bad news.
That's right, bad news. But the kind of bad news that sneaks
up on you and gets you before you know what's happened.

Joke Tellers are not to be confused with Storytellers. The difference is not only a matter of technqiue, but of degree of
desperation.

Uncle Ben was our family Joke Teller, and he was so far
out on the fringes of the family solar system that nobody ever
mentioned him, even in passing. Uncle Ben would show up at
about every third or fourth family affair. He would arrive about
one-third Bagged, as is the case with most Joke Tellers. He was
not the Drinking Uncle, because he didn't really drink. He just
absorbed the stuff. He didn't really knock it down, like Uncle
Carl, who would fall down and holler and try to climb up the
coal chute and all that kind of stuff. Uncle Ben just quietly
drank. He just had a red nose, and sat, and he always looked
like . . . well, have you ever seen a brass lamp? Uncle Ben had
a kind of Brass-Lamp look. He'd just sit there and glow, and
like most Joke Tellers was indecisively fat. And all he would do
at any party was tell jokes. Not funny stories—Jokes. And I
mean the worst kind. I mean the kind of jokes that should be
fumigated before they are allowed in the house.

Joke Tellers rarely have even a barely perceptible sense of humor. Uncle Ben was no exception. It is very hard to know how to listen to a Joke Teller. What kind of look do you put on your face when he is telling a joke, and hitting you on the arm at the same time? Do you smile in preparation for the punch line? Or do you look sad, which is the way you feel? Or just uncomfortable?

Joke Tellers can be dangerous. I'm about seven years old, and I'm in the sun parlor of Aunt Glenn's apartment. Uncle Ben is over, and one wing of the family is having an Afternoon.

Uncle Ben was the kind who would always sit in another room. When all of the family's having a big thing, he would sit out in another room, drinking beer, coming out only to draw another stein and tell a joke. And then, finally, when the pinochle game was organized, he would play. Badly. In true Joke Teller fashion, everything he did seemed to have some comic or violent overtones. Whenever he played pinochle he would slam his hand down on the table with:

"That's it!"

BANG!

"Seven spades! That's it!"

POW!

He also was a great one for trick shuffles.

On the day in question, Uncle Ben and the men are playing double-deck pinochle. My kid brother and I are out in the sun parlor, knee-deep in ferns. Uncle Ben starts telling jokes, in his Joke Teller's voice. One of the men says:

"Hey, you know the kids are here."

And Uncle Ben says:

"Ah, they're old enough to hear this. And if they're not old enough to hear it, it won't make any difference anyway. Ha-haha."

And he plows ahead:

"And so the bartender says to the guy. . . ."

Of course, my ears are like two giant cabbages hanging out of the side there, because I know I am Hearing Something. And boy, did I!

Well, it went like that for about twenty minutes. Ben is telling them the story. Of course, one thing about a family Joke Teller—it's downhill all the way. It rarely is uphill, because these guys, being notably non-talented, do not know how to pace themselves. They usually pad their stories too much, and often tell the punch line before they get to the end of the story.

He's struggling away with his act. What happens with a Joke Teller is that when they don't get a big laugh, they immediately leap in with a longer story, instead of a shorter one. They pour it on with a longer one. And then they try their dialects. This is always the last resort of a scoundrel, using the Jewish and the Irish dialect in a story. This is almost invariably the stamp of the non-talented but desperate Joke Teller.

Uncle Ben is pouring it out. I'm listening to the stories—the Jokes. And soaking them up like a two-dollar sponge. Remember, I'm seven, and my knowledge of the Seven Deadly Sins was somewhat hazy. In the ensuing years this has cleared up somewhat, but not much.

About four days later I'm out in the backyard with good old Casmir. Casmir came from a very good, basic, wonderful, totally antiseptic Polish Catholic family. I mean the kind that had drapes on top of their drapes. Every third or fourth day his mother would wash down the whole neighborhood, on her hands and knees, wearing a shawl over her head. Go all the way down the street, wash the sidewalks, sweep up the curb, hose down the fences, and brush off all the kids. She was that sort of a Polish lady. She spoke no English at all, discernible. This was Casmir's family. His father wore round black hats and black suits, and for some reason always buttoned his white shirts clear to the top, but wore no tie. Except on Sundays.

Casmir and I are playing by the fence. We are fooling around and hitting things, and just messing around, when I suddenly remember Uncle Ben's great joke. Which I proceed to tell to Casmir, including all the words I could remember, and the Irish dialect that the bartender had.

I had only a vague inkling of what it was about. All of these words meant nothing to me. In fact, I thought one of them had something to do with Hockey.

So I told Casmir the joke, and Casmir laughed because he knew it was supposed to be a funny joke. Both of us are laughing up a storm, and hitting each other on the back, and cackling lasciviously. We mess around some more, and it is time now to go home. It is about four in the afternoon.

The following traumatic experience slowly began to unfold. About five in the afternoon, my mother is out on the back porch, and she rarely spent much time *on* the back porch. She is talking to Mrs. Wocznowski. They rarely talked much together because Casmir's mother spoke no English, discernible, and my mother spoke no Polish. But the two of them are jabbering away out there. I am paying no attention, because I am inside listening to the radio.

Suddenly my mother comes whamming through the back screen door, and let me tell you, there was blood in her eye. Blood! I mean BLOOD! There was smoke coming out of her ears.

"I want to talk to you."

I knew it! You know when there's disaster.

"What?"

"I want to talk to you. Come into the bedroom. I don't want your brother to hear this."

Uh oh. This is the big one. You know when the jig is up——

"I don't want your brother. . . ."

We have both been sitting there listening to *Steve Canyon* or something, and the instant this fatal line came out, it goes off inside of me. I start to break up. I'm crying and hollering like mad.

She drags me into the bedroom and closes the door. There was a silence that went on for, I'd say, about a year and a half. I didn't know anything then about what is commonly known as a "pregnant pause." I wouldn't have known what *that* word meant, but this silence is really hanging there, like big ripe grapes. Containing seeds. Finally:

"Were you just out with Casmir? By the fence?"

"Yah . . . yeah, we were playing, we didn't do nothing!" I said.

"Now wait a minute. Do you know what this word means?" And she says this word, which, by the way, to this day I have never again heard my mother use.

"Yeah, yeah, I know . . . ah. . . ." Long pause.

"What does it mean?"

"Ah . . . well, it's about a Hockey thing there!"

"Oh. I see." And there is another long pause.

"Go back out and listen to the radio, will you."

Well, I went out and sat on the ottoman next to my kid brother. The radio is playing. He knows something has gone wrong, and I know something has gone wrong, but I can't figure it out. I had no idea what it was about. Both of us are sitting there, and it's going back and forth between us.

My mother goes back out in the kitchen, and she's stirring away at the red cabbage. The hamburger is on. Supper is being made.

About half an hour later I hear her out in the back, talking over the fence to Mrs. Wocznowski. And I am frantically trying to hear what she is saying. I'm out in the kitchen, next to the icebox. This is terrible, because I know I have done something awful, and yet I don't really *know*. You know what I mean? You don't really know, you just know that what you have done is unspeakable. Unspeakable! You not only feel that it was unspeakable, you feel untouchable. I mean, you're just really *rotten!* To the core. You are never going to make it up the ladder of human virtues. You are never again going to be accepted into the race. Ever. You know that sickening feeling? It takes a hundred years to grow out of that one, if ever!

So I am crouched next to the icebox, sweating. And listening. I catch one line, and it came winging through the screen door like a shot.

"I don't think either of them know what it means."

Mrs. Wocznowski is struggling in broken Polish, and she has been crying. My mother is struggling along in broken South Chicago-ese, and she has not been crying; she has been laughing. Which is the difference between the types of family, and the whole Ethnic business that they both came from. I did not know 'til some time later that my mother was a retired Flapper.

Between the two of them they somehow got it all straightened out. All I know is that Casmir had trouble sitting down for a month. Apparently he had gone home and told Uncle Ben's story to *his* kid brother. Loudly.

We're sitting around the supper table that night when it began to dawn on me the enormity of what I had perpetuated. My mother all the while has not said anything to me. I have not been given the business, I have not been hollered at. I would have felt better somehow if I *had* been given the treatment. So, naturally, I can't eat.

One of my great favorite delicacies at the time was mashed potatoes thoroughly mixed with red cabbage. Oh boy! It looks terrible, I have to warn you. It looks like the worst glop, but it's great. Tonight, however, I was just fiddling with my fork.

"Why aren't you eating your red cabbage?"

"Ah . . . I'm not very hungry."

And then, of course, she knew that it was really biting me, down where it counts. She turns to my father and says:

"Look, the next time we see Ben, I want you to talk to him."

When she called Ben "Ben" it was *Ben*. Whenever she thought he was all right, she called him "Uncle Ben." Now it was just straight Ben.

"I want you to talk to Ben."

My father looks up from the Sport page.

"What about?"

"You know what about. You know very well what about."

My Old Man started to laugh, and she says:

"Yeah. Him. Today. Casmir."

"Well, what did he say?"

"Ouyay owknay utway."

"Oh no!"

They're both laughing, and that made it even worse. I had

no conception, and that made it even worse, to have two grownups laughing at something I did. I mean, they're really *laughing*. All I knew was that it had something to do with Uncle Ben's joke. And Hockey.

XIX ᘓᕽ WE HAVE TWO SMALL VISITORS

"You know, this isn't a bad drink," said Flick.

"Indeed it isn't. You maybe could sell a few here."

"The only thing is, we might have trouble with the ladies around here if I told 'em why I put the olives in it."

Flick, I could see, was Public Relations conscious. He fished with his swizzle stick for one of the olives; speared it neatly.

"That reminds me, Ralph, of the time my mother made a cake for the PTA, and she squeezed the icing out of one a them squeezers, making roses and all that stuff on the PTA cake. And my Old Man snuck in and squeezed something else on it, only she didn't know it until Miss Shields opened it up at school and they put it out in front of all the ladies at the Penny Supper."

"I presume it was a well-known four-letter word." Flick chuckled at the memory of what his father had written on the cake.

"Flick, speaking of food, do you remember the time you rushed into the kitchen in your house when you were hot as hell, when we were playing ball, and grabbed that bottle out of the refrigerator? And you thought it was cider and drank down a quart of vinegar before you knew what hit you?"

"Oh God! I heaved for about an hour!"

"As I recall, all over my new tennis shoes."

Flick laughed. "And Schwartz's knickers."

"Did you ever find out why your mother put the vinegar bottle in the icebox?"

"I was too busy heaving to worry about that!"

All this talk of food had made me acutely aware that I had not had anything to eat all day, since that dinky little toy Airline breakfast of plastic eggs that they had served me on the plane.

"Hey, Flick, you got anything to eat around here? I am willing to pay."

He turned away from the bar and with a casual wave of his hand indicated a couple of cardboard posters carrying cellophane bags of dried peanuts, pork rinds; the usual bar junk.

"That's about it," he said. "We have those electric sandwiches, though. You stick 'em in the infra-red machine and it cooks 'em."

"No, old buddy. I think I'll pass."

I was looking forward to a plate of good old Indiana frogs' legs which I intended to devour later on in the evening.

Two kids trooped in through the front door at this point, letting in a big blast of frigid air and a strong whiff of Refinery gas, an aroma so much part of the everyday life in Hohman that it is called "fresh air." They were wearing heavy skeepskin coats and giant stocking caps. Their noses ran copiously. The larger of the two got right to the point.

"Can we have a glass of water, please?"

Impassively Flick stared down at the scruffy pair.

"I can't serve kids here."

I could see he was putting them on. The smaller of the two started to whimper weakly. Flick drew a large glass of water, handing it over to me. I passed it on to the elder of the pair.

"You kids can split it. And don't tell your mother that you've been hanging around Flick's Tavern, you hear me?"

They silently drank the water, doggedly, finally handing the glass back to me. Without a word they turned and headed for the door. Flick stopped them in their tracks:

"All right, you guys. Whatta you say?"

The smaller one squeaked:

". . . thank you. . . ."

They were gone. Flick rinsed out the glass.

"Boy, all day long they're in and out of here. I'm surprised they don't ask me for a beer."

Outside, in the unfriendly air, the two struggled out of sight, clinging to one another.

"Flick, that little one with the runny nose looked suspiciously like he belonged to your lodge."

Flick snorted:

"That kid ain't no Elk."

"No, that isn't what I mean. I know a Root Beer Barrel Man when I see one. Did you notice that suspicious bulge in his right cheek? I suspect that he was loaded."

Flick sat down heavily on his high stool behind the bar. He rubbed his hands over his white shirt front. I swear his eyes clouded noticeably, although it could very well have been all the beer, as well as the vodka I had put down, not to mention the other stuff.

"You know, Ralph. . . ." he said at long last, ". . . I haven't had a really *good* root beer barrel in a hell of a long time."

"To be honest with you, Flick, I never fully understood just what you saw in root beer barrels."

Flick did not answer, being off in a world by himself. I pushed on:

"As you recall, I, personally, was a Jawbreaker man. And I am proud to say that I have the silver inlays to prove it."

XX ⮾ OLD MAN PULASKI AND THE INFAMOUS JAW-BREAKER BLACKMAIL CAPER

There is a vast, motley mob of Americans, untold millions, who even today, years after the consummation of their original sin, are paying the Piper. Paying in many ways, the most notable of which is sheer, stark, shrill, agonizing, bone-shattering pain which sometimes strikes its debauched victim late at night and sends his shuddering frame into the gray fringes of near-madness. The agony sometimes becomes so poignant that men, strong men, unweeping men, have been known to toy actively with suicide and even worse as the only escape. And in some instances, not as rare as might be thought, have actually taken that final, fatal step, the pain unbearable that made the sharp, crashing impact of a Thirty-Eight slug behind the ear child's play by comparison.

Yes, the sinners are paying, as they have always paid in the end, and will always pay. There is no escape!

These poor, innocent citizens are Victims, and they seldom even know the origin of their ordeal by fire of what has lately become known in some of the more advanced medical text-books as "The JuJu Baby Plague," sometimes termed "The Root Beer Barrel Rot."

Anyone who has ever experienced a first-degree, Big League, card-carrying dedicated toothache in a major molar at 3 A.M. in the quiet solitude of night has stood at the very gates of Hell itself. There are no words in the language that can adequately describe the ebbing and swelling, ebbing and swelling and then rising to even greater heights, then again deceptively receding, only to turn again to the attack; insistent nagging, dragging, thudding, screaking ache of a tooth that has faced more than its share in a hard, rough and tumble lifetime of JuJu Babies, Root Beer Barrels, Jawbreakers, and countless other addictions devoured during the innocent days of childhood. And like all sinners, Orgiasts of all stripes, he looks back upon the very thing that reduced him to a shuddering, denture-ridden, cavity-wracked hulk with bleary-eyed, teary nostalgia. Everywhere, daily, dentists—cackling fiendishly—reap the harvests sown years ago in Penny Candy stores across the land.

Well I remember the Pusher that sent me on that long rocky road that finally led to $765 worth of silver alloy and various plastic compounds which I now carry in my skull as a mute reminder of past, fleeting pleasures. The fillings are not permanent, but the cavities are!

In the throes of a toothache, all men are one. It is the one affliction known to Man that is truly the Great Leveler. Kings and commoners, Generals and simple peasants of the field all bow to this basic, somehow singularly humiliating curse that has been known and endured as long as there has been Man on earth. George Washington became a Revolutionist because of a bad set of incisors. And no wonder!

Recently there was a dispatch from Burma that told of a rampaging tiger that in a single night, without warning, killed twenty-eight Burmese in a quick dash down the main street of a jungle village. The native hunter who later bagged him simply said:

"He had bad teeth."

One afternoon recently, while staring bleakly out of a waiting-room window, having tired of the ancient *National Geographics* and the Currier & Ives prints, attempting to blot out of my consciousness the sound of muffled moans and occasional sharp yelps of pain which were mingling with the Muzak, my tortured mind—perhaps out of some deep-hidden well of sub-merged masochism—plucked out of my vast file of sinister Life Experiences and dredged to the surface Old Man Pulaski and the great Jawbreaker Tie-In Sale. While waiting my turn on the Rack, I began to piece together the whole sordid tale.

Pulaski, a blue-eyed, blue-jowled native of the Midwest, operated a mercantile establishment that was the Steel-town Indiana version of The Candy Store. Nobody ever called it by that name. It was just "Pulaski's." On the side of his red brick, two-story store there was an enormous Bull Durham sign that showed this great, dark red, arrogant, fully equipped bull looking out into the middle distance toward Chicago, with the simple inscription "Her Hero."

It was under this sign that Pulaski dispensed JuJu Babies, licorice cigars, Mary Janes, Jawbreakers, Navy Cut Chewing Tobacco, Mule Twist, Apple Plug, Eight-Hour Day Rough Cut, Mail Pouch, Copenhagen Snuff, and summer sausage, sliced thin.

Penny Candy is just about the very first purchase that any kid actually makes himself. That very first buy which launches all of us on a lifelong career as Consumers, leading finally to God knows where. Kids take to buying the way fleas take to Beagle hounds. It's just natural. You don't have to learn; some-how you know.

It doesn't take long for Penny Candy buyers to begin that great weeding-out process of the Slobs versus the Anti-Slobs. It is here that it starts. A discriminating Penny Candy connois-seur knew what he was after, while the rest merely settled for anything that was big, lumpy, sticky, and sweet. The JuJu Baby connoisseur today buys Porsches and fine wines while his slack-jawed erstwhile friend continues to dig large, lumpy, sticky-sweet automobiles and syrupy beer that comes in six-packs with self-open tops. I pride myself, perhaps overly so, on having de-veloped an exceedingly discriminating palate for the various vin-tages and *châteaux* of Penny Candy.

The genuine American Penny Candy store bears no relation-ship to the present chi-chi Ladies' Magazine reproductions that are popping up in Greenwich Village, the hipper sections of San Francisco, and Old Town in Chicago. They were invariably dark, with windows filled with cardboard placards advertising Dutch Cleanser, Kayo the magic chocolate drink, Campbell's Pork & Beans, and the Hohman PTA Penny Supper.

The candy itself was displayed in a high, oak-framed case with a curved glass front and sliding glass doors well out of reach of the sneakier purchasers. In the case were rows of metal trays containing The Stuff.

Penny Candy was bought in lots of from two to four cents, and in extreme emergencies one penny, but that was rare. Pulaski, bending high over the case, would peer down at us, looking unconcerned and bored while we made our decisions.

"Fer Chrissake, I haven't got all day! D'y want a licorice pipe or not!?"

And the battle was on. Glaring down at the huddled band of well-heeled investors, many of whom were in well-advanced stages of the Sour Ball Shakes, Pulaski played his cards coolly and well. He knew that he had all the trump as well as the only neighborhood supply of licorice whips and wax false teeth. He was the Man; the Connection. It was a Seller's market.

The wax false teeth, by the way, played a part in a great second-grade drama when suddenly and without warning wax false teeth became a maniacal fad that swept over Harding School like a tidal wave. I remember one historic afternoon when every last male member of my second-grade class showed up with a large set of wax false dentures clamped in his jaw to face Miss Shields and Arithmetic. Little did we realize at the time that the wax false teeth were a foreshadow of things to come for many in that benighted academy of lower learning.

Miss Shields stood for a long electric moment beside her desk and then silently reached out her claw, palm upward, and said simply:

"Give 'em to me."

One by one she de-toothed us, putting the booty in her lower left-hand drawer along with sixty-seven rubber daggers, 922 competition yoyos, seventeen small well-thumbed, smudgy volumes of comic books relating clandestine adventures of Maggie & Jiggs, thirty-six bird whistles, a round dozen Throw-UR-Voice ventriloquist gadgets purchased by mail from Johnson & Smith, two wax mice on a string, and a giant arsenal of water pistols, cap guns, and carbide cannons. Miss Shields had seen a lot, and wax false teeth were just another wave in a giant sea of surrealistic nuttiness that she had fought all of her life.

"Give 'em to me."

And we gave.

Another specialty of wax that had a certain illicit air about it was a small wax bottle filled with a colored, sickeningly sweet syrup, usually green in color, and a sure-fire appetite killer. These bottles had a vaguely illegal quality to them since they had the unmistakable hint of Jug-Hitting, and there was plenty of that on Saturday nights in our neighborhood. The bottles were *not* shaped in the form of milk containers. The kids were practicing up to be grownups even then.

The wax itself was invariably chewed after the bottle had been drained or the teeth had lost their charm, and had a distinctive, vaguely fragrant taste which even now I detect from time to time in coffee containers at ball games. An old Wax Eater never forgets.

I should say at the outset that the wax teeth were larger than life, true pink gum color—gums suffering from a rare case of advanced pyorrhea. The teeth proper were large, horsy, and obscene, and a nine-year-old kid coming out of the gloom of half twilight grinning from ear to ear with a set of Pulaski's teeth gleaming like nightmare fangs undoubtedly sent many a Friday-night Blast-Furnace worker directly to the Salvation Army to take the pledge. We did not, however, frighten Miss Shields.

Just before suppertime Pulaski's would be packed with a jostling throng of customers. Guys from the Open Hearth wearing tin hats, buying next week's supply of Beech Nut "as sweet as a nut," Old Virginia Licorice Twist, Honest Plug Tobacco, Dago cigars known as Guinea Stinkers, and Peach Blossom Chewing Snuff. Short fat ladies haggling over soup meat, and kids making the Big Choice.

At this point perhaps I should describe the variety of Penny

Candy that has become a classic substrata of Americana. No other country I know of has anything remotely like it.

JuJu Babies were exactly what they sound like; small, rubbery, symbolic figures of different colors—black, red, yellow— molded in the form of a Prehistoric ritual baby. Sexless, the JuJu Baby sort of represented all Mankind, to be devoured by Man himself. The JuJu Baby had a habit of getting stuck in the back teeth, and I remember a transparent yellow one that remained jammed between two molars for the better part of a Summer. It was perhaps there that my first step in the direction of Advanced Dentistry took place.

There was the Root Beer Barrel, beloved of kids of slightly more advanced and subtle taste. A small, compact item molded in the form of a tiny barrel, sprinkled over with sugar grains and tasting roughly like a fine blend of stale rootbeer and cake icing. The Root Beer Barrel had the extra advantage of being cheap. Since few kids bought them, they were roughly five to seven for a cent. Demand always controls price; never quality.

For more frivolous eating, or particularly Girl-types, there was a tin pie plate about the size of a half dollar filled with a semi-solid paste usually pink, yellow, or chocolate in color that was to be spooned up with a tiny tin spoon. Many a tongue was split from end to end with the razor-like edge of this lethal instrument. The taste of the "pie" is not easy to define, since it had none other than a kind of electric, incisor-tingling sweetness. There was no other flavor.

Occasionally Pulaski would import a rarer item for his regular customers, exactly like the pie-tin and spoon combination except that the paste was in the shape of a tiny, tasteless but somehow interesting and subtle fried egg. I frankly admit I was a sucker for these fried eggs and even had developed a full technique for eating them that I still follow today with the real article. Using my spoon to scoop out the brilliant orange "yolk," I then would attack by quadrant the white and finally, licking the pan, would throw it at the back of Kissel's head.

Licorice came in many forms and several distinct textures. There were, of course, the traditional smooth, shiny whips, red and black, and the only time I ever was cursed with these was when Aunt Min, who to this day believes I am a nut on licorice, would bring a bag of them home. The licorice pipe, made of a crumbly, bitter licorice, was more my style. A curving stem and upswept bowl of the classical calabash shape of the Old World made licorice barely palatable. Many an evening on my paper route, licorice pipe clamped in my square jaw, Root Beer Barrel tucked next to the second to the left molar on the right, Jawbreaker to the left, I sucked dextrose energy into the marrow of my bones while rotting the roots of my second teeth beyond repair.

The Jawbreaker requires and actually deserves a whole special treatise which, of course, space does not permit here. The virgin, or untouched Jawbreaker in its natural state was roughly a full inch in diameter and as hard and unyielding as obsidian. There were two basic Jawbreakers which actually were divergent types of the same majestic, classic Bicuspid Buster. They were simply know as "Red" and "Black," the Red being coated on the outside with a brilliant, flaming, gleaming, smooth enamel of pure carmine; the Black stark, austere, and yet somehow dignified with its glistening, pristine ebony shell has not yet been improved upon as a study of sheer geometric and aesthetic unity. Here was and is truly a masterwork in the Penny-Candy genre of creativity. Structurally, both Jawbreakers were identical, but both represented opposing sides of the nature of Man and his universe. Ying and Yang. The Red Jawbreaker man rarely touched the Black and the Black Jawbreaker adherent knew what he wanted and would accept nothing else.

The Jawbreaker was *never* chewed, but sucked over long periods of time, allowed to soak in the salival juices, the lining of the mouth puckering and retreating as the succulent elixirs of layer upon layer of Jawbreaker forever established a whole range of attitudes of gustatorial appreciation. The Jawbreaker revealed its endless subtleties layer by layer, holding back, suggesting, stating, until finally, the inner core, the pit, the Mother Lode was finally reached.

Each layer of a Jawbreaker was slightly and subtly a different shade of coloration from the one that preceded it, after the initial black or red coating had been sucked off, had disappeared, the Breaker would emerge dead white and then a few moments later it changed imperceptibly to a dull, mottled brown with overtones of green, followed by a rich brick-red vein. Next, perhaps, a mocking, impudent onion-yellow. White again! And then a somber, morose purplish-gray, and on down, layer after layer, color after color, until finally, at about the size of a tiny French pea, it would crumble and reward the *aficionado* with a minute seed which crunched and then disappeared. The Jawbreaker, a fitting parable of life itself, infinitely varied, sweet, and always receding until finally only the seed.

The Black Jawbreaker unquestionably was one of the major influences in the formative years, the Silly Putty years, the cellophane-transparent malleable days of my budding youth. It was a Black Jawbreaker that taught me a major lesson of Man's Inhumanity to Man.

There were other, lesser Penny Candies; the strips of white paper dotted with geometric rows of yellow, white, blue, and red pellets of sugar, fit only for cretins and two-year-olds, the banana-oil flavored, peanut-shaped obscenities beloved of elderly ladies, and girls, the jelly orange slices, and others.

There were a few minor works that bear mention. The Spearmint leaves, for instance, too subtle for ten-year-olds, which must be grown into. The flat, coconut-flavored watermelon slices; blood red, green-rinded, black seeded, sprinkled with sugar and fly spots. Oh yes, and the candy ice cream cones with pink and white marshmallow "ice cream" covered with sugar and a marshmallow cone that briefly caught me before I knew better. The tiny red peppermint hearts that old Pulaski sold by the scooping of a minute wooden barrel; hotter than Hell and arrogantly unpleasant.

But it is the Jawbreaker, when all is said and done, that represents the absolute pinnacle of the world of Penny Candy, lost and gone, but festering on in countless root canals wherever Dental appointments are made and broken on long American afternoons.

Sudden likes and dislikes, inexplicable fads, swept the Penny Candy buying world at Pulaski's like crosscurrents in a riptide. Suddenly and without warning everyone bought nothing but Mary Janes. Then there would be a total shift to Tootsie Rolls or Root Beer Barrels, and the trays of pie-tins and spoons, marshmallow ice cream cones, and JuJu Babies would be untouched. This bugged Pulaski.

But one summer I discovered the only completely satisfying and genuine experience that I really wanted. The Black Jawbreaker. They got ahold of me the way Hashish gets a stranglehold on a Lebanese rug merchant in a Middle Eastern den of vice and degradation. Day after day, with every last cent I could scrape up, it was nothing but Black Jawbreakers. I became an evangelist, convincing others—Schwartz, Flick, Kissel—until one day the inevitable finally happened.

The store was full of steelworkers and kids. Pulaski's screen door was banging continually. The flies were flying in great formations around the light bulbs and clinging like tiny clusters of dead grapes to the spirals of flypaper that hung from the ceiling.

Pulaski was back of the hand-operated lunch-meat slicer and a short, angry lady was leaning over the Toledo scale, fixing him with a beady eye. Pulaski was alone in the store that day, and the tide was coming in. For at least forty-five minutes he battled the salami buyers and the guys who wanted the work gloves. The flies hummed; the heat came in puffs through the screen door.

At least eight of us milled around the glass case, the Jawbreaker Fever hot on our brows. Pulaski ignored us as long as he could, until finally he dashed over behind the case and opened negotiations.

"All right, what do you want? Quick!"

Flick led off: "Gimme some Root Beer Barrels."

"How many do you want!"

Flick: "Gimme four and one Mary Jane."

Pulaski rushed back to the meat-market counter, filled a container with a mess of sauerkraut, weighed it up, shoved it across the counter to Mrs. Rutkowski, said:

"I'll be right back," and rushed back into battle.

"They're six for a penny. Mary Janes are two for a penny. D'y want Mary Janes or Root Beer Barrels?"

"Gimme four barrels and one Mary Jane."

"Fer Chrissake!!"

Nine Tin-Mill workers came in in a covey, hollering for beer. Mrs. Rutkowski, in broken English, said something about pickled pigs' feet. Pulaski retreated and started handing out bottles of beer and Polish pickles. Flick hollered out:

"I only want four barrels."

Pulaski, for the sixty-third time that day, weighed his left thumb, the heaviest in Northern Indiana, along with a couple of pork chops. Everything was on credit anyway, so it really didn't make much difference. The Depression was like that.

The place was getting crowded. The flies hummed on and the screen door banged. Mrs. Rutkowski angrily yelled something that could have been Lithuanian, and Pulaski rushed back to the candy counter. Looking right at me and completely ignoring Flick, he said:

"Awright, what do *you* want?"

He knew what I wanted very well, and before I could even open my mouth he belted me with this thunderclap:

"No more Black Jawbreakers unless ya take one Red one for every Black."

They were two for a penny. I *hated* Red Jawbreakers!

"I am getting stuck with too many Red Jawbreakers."

This was the first time that the laws of Economics and Human Chicanery had impinged on our tumbleweed, windblown lives. For a second we said nothing, stunned.

"What?"

"I said no Jawbreakers unless you buy Red *and* Black."

There wasn't a Red Jawbreaker man in the crowd.

"Make up your mind. D'ya want 'em or not?"

We looked in through the curving glass case and saw that beautiful tray of magnificent Jawbreakers, almost all Red, the few remaining Blacks spotted here and there like diamonds in a bank of blue South African clay. Flick said:

"*Red* Jawbreakers!"

Schwartz said:

"I'd rather have some rotten Tootsie Rolls!"

I thought it over. For as long as I had remembered, Jaw-breakers were two for a penny. *Black* Jawbreakers. Two for a penny, and now, in effect, the price had doubled. I thought about it. Finally Pulaski's face loomed over the counter, looking down at all of us. I don't think he ever saw an individual kid. They were always just that jostling little mob in front of the case, with the hot, sweaty pennies.

"Awright, you guys. I don't have any more time to mess around. You want Black Jawbreakers or not?"

The only other Jawbreaker salesman in town was a good twelve blocks away, and still I couldn't say it.

"Gimme a penny's worth of Jawbreakers."

Pulaski reached into the case, carefully taking one Red Jaw-breaker and one Black Jawbreaker, and handed them over to me, picking up my penny from the glass top of the case. One after the other we gave in, until finally there was only Flick.

"Awright, what do *you* want?"

"Four Root Beer Barrels and a Mary Jane."

"Fer Chrissake, all right!"

Pulaski grabbed a handful of Root Beer Barrels and a Mary Jane and shoved them in Flick's fist. Mrs. Rutkowski seemed to be asking for spareribs, or something, in broken Croatian. More steelworkers surged through the door. The screen door slammed. Pulaski clanked the sliding panels of his candy counter shut, turned his back on us, and hurried back behind the meat counter.

It was the first Jawbreaker Tie-In Sale. To get the gold you must also take the dross. The Jawbreaker remained true to its spirit, a pure distillation of Life itself; give and take.

Out on the street I stuck my black beauty far back on the right side, right where my wisdom teeth would be eventually impacted. I shoved the red monster into the pocket of my Levis. I'll give it to my kid brother, I figured. The great Jaw-breaker pushed my cheek walls out until the proper tension was reached and the first soul-satisfying taste of that dark, rich, ebony masterpiece began to sink into my veins. It was worth the exorbitant price.

I stood at the window, looking out over the vast, crowded metropolitan traffic-jammed street, the burning coals of my aching tooth subsiding somewhat in the tepid bath of recollection and nostalgia. Only a steady, dull, thumping, subterranean pulse remained. I was still paying Pulaski.

A high thin whine of the steel burr as it bit into the marrow of another victim's left upper canine wound its way into my consciousness. It stopped. There was a moment of silence and then that white Archangel of Pain, the blonde, crisp, Shirley Temple-ish dentist's assistant, touched me on the elbow.

"The doctor's ready."

I turned.

"So am I, Miss."

Together we moved forward toward the Rack.

XXI ᒾᕈ ENTER FRIENDLY FRED

Flick sucked noisily at a hollow tooth as I stood up stiffly to get the kinks out of my legs. Bar stools are not good for the knees. Not only that, but my conscience was beginning to bother me. Here I was, frittering away an afternoon chewing the fat with Flick, when I should have been out filling up my blue-lined notebook with acute observations on the evolving life of the Industrial Midwest, not to mention the impact of Automation on the day-to-day life of the solitary citizen. Also, I was on an expense account, and there wasn't much to squander it on in Flick's. I enjoy living to the full.

I stalked to the end of the bar, flexing my shoulder muscles and jiggling my feet. This is known in Indiana tavern circles as "Shaking Down The Suds." Flick moodily changed his apron. It was getting late in the afternoon now, and the big rush of steelworkers was due shortly after four when the shift at the mill changed.

Again the entranceway swung open with a puff of frigid air. This time a tall, thin, natty customer displaying a formidable set of store teeth and a dour piercing gaze strode resolutely to the bar. Flick glanced up and, without a word passing between the two, took a bottle of bourbon down off the mirrored shelf behind the bar and poured a double. Neat. The man quickly

tossed it off, threw a dollar down on the bar, said: "Be seein'
you," and was gone. Flick rang up the buck as I returned to
my stool.

"Well?" I asked.

"Oh, him? That's Fred. Friendly Fred. He runs the Used-Car
lot across the street."

I looked over at the lot. A touch of twilight gloom was
beginning to dull the surfaces of the shiny fenders and grinning
grilles. The banners fluttered jauntily, snapping and cracking in
the breeze.

"He sure has some great-looking junkers over there," I re-
marked, dredging an expression out of my misty past.

"Yep. Sure has."

Next to bowling, automobiles are probably the single most
important fact of a Midwesterner's life, after his job, of
course. The family heap, the weekly paycheck, and a decent
bowling average are all they ask of Life.

"What are y' driving these days, Flick?"

"Olds 88."

"How's she do on gas?"

"Oh, seventeen, around town. Maybe nineteen, twenty on
the road," Flick lied.

"Can't ask for more than that."

I found myself sinking into the laconic conversation that I
had almost forgotten existed. I had become completely ac-
climated to the martini-drenched, impassioned, self-pitying
monologues of the French restaurants and expensive bars of
New York. Here, the Ego—if it existed at all—was barely discernible. They had never even heard of the word "Career."
Job, yes. Career, no.

"Olds 88. Hydromatic?"

"Yep."

"Four-door?"

"Nope. Hardtop."

"What color is it?"

"Dark blue. 'Bout the same color as that old Graham-Paige
your Old Man used to have."

"The what?"

"The four-door Graham. With the V-grille."

Now I remembered. Of course! The Graham-Paige. In Hohman, cars were never forgotten, any more than old love affairs are ever really erased in other cultures. Family histories are measured in terms of cars, such as: "Clarence got the whooping cough when we had the Willys-Knight," or, "Alex ran away with the Ledbetter girl right after we got the Hupmobile."

"You know, Flick, there's something I never told you about that Graham-Paige," I said.

"Well, if you're gonna tell me about the bad clutch it had, forget it. I know about that."

Flick was showing off again.

"No, Flick, there's something that's been on my conscience for a long time. It has to do with that Graham-Paige."

XXII ﾊﾟ THE PERFECT CRIME

My father loved used cars even more than he loved the White Sox, if possible. A Used-Car Nut is even more dedicated than the ordinary car worshiper. A true zealot never thinks in terms of a *new* model. His entire frame of reference and system of values is based on acquiring someone else's troubles. It is a dangerous game, and the uncertainty of it appeals to the true Used-Car *aficionado* the same way that Three Card Faro draws on the profligate.

My father, in company with other Used-Car fanatics, loved to spend long Saturday afternoons roaming the Used-Car lots on the South Side of Chicago, beating the bushes for hypothetical great buys and spectacular deals in Willys-Knights, Essexes, and Hudson Terraplanes. And when the Used-Car type actually tracked his car down and made the buy, it was a total commitment. All the way. And if the car turned out to be actually functional, his love for it far transcended the love and involvement of the lesser men who simply went to a dealer and bought a new car.

Anybody can buy a new car and expect to get a fairly operative machine, but it takes guts, knowledge, and a reckless sense of deadly abandon to come home with, say, a Lafayette Six previously owned by other shadowy drivers that had gone through God knows what hells, and to feel confident of victory. A used car, therefore, is a far more powerful love object than a new one. And my father played this deadly game to the hilt. Each succeeding used car was loved and babied, petted and honored in its turn.

Some of the great emotional scenes of his life occurred on Used-Car lots when he was deserting the Pontiac Eight for the "new" DeSoto. He would even go back day after day to see if they were treating the Pontiac well, and then would get moody and morose when it finally disappeared forever off the lot.

The new DeSoto—he always referred to each used car as "new" —at first would seem strange and formal to us, vaguely unfriendly, like living in someone else's apartment. On Saturdays, when we cleaned the car, we'd find foreign hairpins and other people's lost papers under the seats. But gradually the DeSoto or the Pontiac or the Hupmobile would become Ours.

Of course, at that time cars had distinctive personalities and characteristics in themselves and did not all come stamped out of the same mold, painted with the same paint, and advertised by the same agency. A Terraplane man was a completely different breed than, say, a Buick type. John Dillinger drove a Terraplane, which said a lot for the Terraplane type—an angry, rakish, wild machine. It was not a matter of Status then, but of attitude and personality, and the Used-Car man had the fiercest loyalties of all. He was usually not only dedicated to certain makes of cars but to specific years within the breeds. I remember spending long afternoons with my father, hunting for a particular Graham-Paige that reputedly was of the finest of vintage years.

The day we found that beautiful midnight blue four-door Graham, with its stark Gothic radiator grille, was one of the true Festival days of that epoch. She sat bracketed between an elderly Plymouth and a stodgy LaSalle, glowing darkly with a sort of prim, contained politeness—a true aristocrat unaccountably cast in with the rabble. She had more than a few years on her, but was spotless and ageless.

The old man lit up like a Christmas tree and immediately went into his cagey Used-Car Buyer's cool, calculating bargaining character. It was exciting, in several ways. The contest between Father and *his* Friendly Fred, the imminent loss of the trusty old Pontiac—did the Graham have a sponge-rubber transmission? The lurking reefs of disaster were always there.

Later, the first time he wheeled the midnight blue Graham up the driveway and around the back, was just the beginning of it—the week-long Festival of Love for the new Graham.

At the time I was just below the legal minimum age limit for driving. And I used to sit in the back seat and watch my father shift gear, casually make left turns, back into parking spots, and wheel the Graham around like a second skin.

In the Midwest driving is like breathing. Kids living on the Maine coast learn to sail at a certain age. They all do. In the Midwest, driving is simply part of life, and they are serious about it. Afternoons, when the car was parked in back, I would sit in the front seat and practice shifting gears, working the clutch, and mentally whistling down US 41 in the center lane. And once in a very great while, when we would be out for a drive on a Sunday, my father would maybe let me back the car out of the driveway, or on the *really* great days he'd say:

"You want to take over?"

Do I want to take over! What a question!

He'd sit next to me:

"Easy on the clutch now."

I'd ease the clutch out.

"Wait now, don't shift to Second yet. There, get it moving. All right, into Second now. Well, for crying out loud, push the clutch all the way IN before you shift! YOU'RE GONNA STRIP THE GEARS! Here, lemme do it!"

Next thing I know I'm sitting in the back with my kid brother. Flubbed it again!

I was always trying to curry favor with both the Graham and my father by surprising him, especially on Sundays. The surprise consisted of washing the Graham or polishing the chrome with some pink stuff that my father used.

I was in the garage, working on the front bumper. It was Sunday. The family was going out that night, and I was about to surprise everybody with a spectacular job on the chrome. I polished the rims on the headlights, and it's a tough job. My knuckles were scraped, my fingernails torn, the pink stuff soaking into my skin, but the grille was beautiful, just beautiful. And then I decided to back the car out of the garage by myself, to really surprise them. So that when they came out on the back porch they would see this blinding vision flashing chrome. In my mind's eye I could hear them say:

"Why, what has happened to the Graham-Paige? It looks better than new!"

And I would just stand proudly, modestly by and wait for the praise and the honor that would be due me.

I finally finished the job. The Graham was glistening. I scrunched down in the driver's seat and started the engine. What a sense of Power! I checked the ammeter. It was flickering slightly on the "Charge" side. Gas gauge—quarter full. Oil pressure—forty pounds. Normal.

I eased the clutch in and gently moved the gearshift lever into "Reverse." Already I was a master of gear-shifting. "Ease out on the clutch gently," and I began to roll backward out of the garage.

Screeeeeeaaaa. . . .

I slammed on the brake and the clutch and hung in midair for a split second.

My God! I had scraped the left rear fender on the garage door! I put her in First and tried to roll forward.

Eeeeaawwwrrrrr.

It was stuck! The fender was dragging against the door. My God! I was sweating. And sick with fear. I had *really* done it this time, all the way!

I quickly scrunched over to the other side of the seat, and out. I was going to push the car into the garage. I couldn't move it. It was really stuck! I had to drive it in again.

I got behind the wheel and put it into First. I was going to do it real slowly. Reeeal sloww. . . .

EEEEEEEAAARRRRHHHHHH. BOING!

I could hear the door scrunching and ripping. I got out again and looked. I could just see the edge of a huge scrape mark on that beautiful midnight blue fender. The paint was peeling off in long curls. It was jammed, and I didn't know what to do. I knew that if I moved any further I'd strip off more paint. I had to do it!

I eased out on the clutch.

RRRRRRRR

It was stuck!

I could hear people moving in the house, doors slamming. Any minute now somebody was going to come out! I just knew it. My father! He was going to come out in the backyard to look in the trunk, or to pick up a football or something.

The screen door slammed open, and it was my kid brother. My God! I head him off.

"Hey Ran, hey. Would you go down in the basement? See if you can find my old . . . ah . . . my . . . remember that old skyrocket I had? See if you can find my old skyrocket, will you, Ran? Go on, Ran, see if you can find it for me."

He looked at me and then went back in the house and down in the basement.

I didn't want anyone to know what I had done, and time was running out!

I leaped in the car. Any minute now my Old Man was going to come out. I knew it. I slammed it in gear.

EEEEEEeeeuuuunk!

It was free!

I turned the key off and got out. There it was! The back fender neatly peeled, a long scratch the entire width of the fender and then some. What was I going to do!?

I knew what to do. Nothing! Absolutely nothing!

Five minutes later I was two blocks away, knocking out fly balls and pretending I had never seen a car in my life.

That night we were all dressed up and in the Graham. I was in the back seat, and worried sick. Nobody had even noticed that the back fender was scraped. I was keeping my mouth shut, and I was sweating: a thirteen-year-old Rascolnikov sizzling with guilt, fighting against the urge to blurt out:

"Stop the car! Look at the left rear fender! I did it! I am guilty! I am unworthy to exist in the bosom of such a wonderful, innocent group on its way to see Fred Astaire and Ginger Rogers! I am guilty and despicable!! Rotten to the core!!"

But what did I do? The same thing that modern man always does. Plays it cool. At least as cool as it is possible to be while shuddering under wave after wave of fear and guilt.

We parked the car and went into the movie. I was still safe. Darkness had obscured the raw wounds of my crime.

I squirmed through the movie in a cold sweat, barely able to concentrate on my taffy apple. All I remember was that this guy Astaire kept wearing a high silk hat—like Jiggs—and hopping around on the tops of pianos.

Another crucial moment came when we approached the Graham in the parking lot. I hung back, waiting for the thunderclap.

It did not come. The Chief merely got in the front seat and said:

"Pile in. Let's go."

I scrunched down in the back seat and in my relief and nervousness talked a blue streak all the way home.

But later, in bed, the old icy sweat came back. He would *have* to see it tomorrow, and he would know! There was no escape! I squirmed and sweated for half an hour or so, and then developed a gigantic gut-heaving stomach ache. My mother dragged me into the john, limp and wan, and hung my head over the bowl. Taffy apples of years past squirted out of my nose, my ears. . . .

"That'll teach you to listen to me about all that junk you always eat."

I finally fell asleep out of sheer exhaustion.

The next morning for a few brief rapturous minutes I had completely forgotten that I was a doomed man. And then, halfway through my Wheaties, it all came back. My spoon hung in midair. The sun streamed through the kitchen windows.

My mother's Chinese-red chenille bathrobe hunched over the stove, making coffee. All the old familiar things of my former carefree life lay about me. The cracked plastic radio on top of the refrigerator, the old kitchen table, my Little Orphan Annie shake-up mug, the blue glass Shirley Temple sugar and cream set which meant so much to my mother, all part of a Better Time.

After school that day I went through the motions of ballplaying, a wizened, care-bent figure at second base, knowing full well that retribution was inevitably drawing nigh. It *had* to come tonight!

My father usually got home from work about six, just in time for supper. We were expected to be in the house no later than five-thirty, washed up, and ready to eat. Tonight I lagged in the gloom, trying to forestall the inevitable. My fellow ballplayers had long since melted off into the twilight. In the distance I could hear my mother shouting for me through the kitchen door, and finally, painfully, I dragged myself home.

Staring out at me from the bathroom mirror—hollow eyed, lined death's head of a face, covered with Lifebuoy suds.

And then it came. A great angry roar of flying cinders, the Graham-Paige booming up the driveway, roaring around the back angrily, and then—silence.

The water trickled feebly in the sink. My kid brother blabbed somewhere off in the distance. I clung weakly to the towel rack, waiting for the fatal blow.

The kitchen screen door slammed. There was now no escape! A brief thought of drinking iodine passed through my tortured cranium. They'd feel sorry then! But would they? They would probably welcome it, after what I had done!

I hear my mother's voice from the kitchen:

"What's the matter?"

And then a bellow of inchoate rage. I knew any minute thunderous footsteps would head for the bathroom. Already I could feel the sobs welling to the surface.

And then my father's voice, booming in rage:

"Those bastards down at the parking lot! They banged up the fender on the Graham and the bastards *deny* it!!"

I clung to the sink, bells ringing in my skull. I had been witness to an actual miracle. I would never again be an Unbeliever!

The voice angrily continued:

"I drove it in that lot absolutely perfect! Not a scratch on it!! Come on out and look at it!"

Again the door slammed and silence reigned. I tottered into the kitchen, weak and shuddering with relief. I peeked out of the back window and I could see my mother and father angrily stalking back and forth around the rear fender. They came up the back porch, with my mother saying:

"That's terrible. Isn't there something you can do with the Better Business Bureau? Why don't you call the Better Business Bureau? Don't let them get away with it. You're just too easy on people."

"WHAT DO YOU MEAN 'EASY'!? I HOLLERED FOR TWENTY MINUTES! The guy says that car wasn't touched! The lying bastard!!"

"Well, I'm going to call them myself. I'm going to call them."

She sweeps past me into the dining room to the phone. My father plumps down at the kitchen table, white with rage. Off in the living room, the sound of my kid brother crying could be heard. He always did this when there was trouble.

I did nothing, just looked innocent. My mother slammed back into the kitchen.

"You're going to get satisfaction now. I really told them. It's that lot across from the Real Estate office, right? Across from the Real Estate office?"

"Yeah."

Never in my life, before or since, have I enjoyed meat loaf so much. Mashed potatoes and peas and carrots—a magnificent repast!

The next day my father came home from work beaming, radiating victory from every pore.

"They paid off, the bastards. Ten bucks for a repaint job! The guy said he'd paint it himself. I said 'No.' In a pig's ear. I want the dough. I'll get it fixed myself. I've got to admit you were right. They called up that phony and really burned his ear. He paid up!"

Once again I felt at home at the kitchen table. I belonged in this well-ordered, virtuous environment. Justice had been done, and I could proceed again along the great highway of Life, sun shining, birds singing, with a clean windshield and a full tank of Phillips 66.

XXIII 🦢 FLICK BAITS THE HOOK

"You remember the time I stripped the second gear in my Old Man's Pontiac? He kicked me three times around Harding School without stopping."

"Yep, we've all been through it, Flick."

He reached behind him and flipped a switch. An orange-red neon sign hanging in the window flickered and sputtered into life:

BEER

Flick was baiting his trap for the Swing-Shift crowd who probably already were nursing a fierce thirst. A pair of the vanguard had just clumped in, their safety shoes thumping the floor loudly. They had settled into one of the booths. Life in Flick's Tavern was picking up.

Flick took a couple of schooners over to them. They laughed together for a few moments, and he returned, wiping his hands on his clean apron. The phone behind the bar rang. He picked up the receiver.

"Hello, Jake? You'll handle the bar yourself tonight. Yeah. I'm going to the game tonight. Okay, Jake. I'll see you later."

He hung up. He explained to me:

"That was Jake."

"So I heard."

"Going to the game tonight."

The Game, of course, meant Basketball, which in Indiana is far more a mystique than an athletic contest. Basketball has been responsible for suicides, divorces, and even a few near-lynchings. I well remember one coach who left the county heavily disguised in dark glasses, beard, and the trappings of a Talmudic scholar after a disaster in a Sectional tournament. In recent years I had not kept up with the Basketball fortunes of our mutual high school.

"Who are they playing?"

"La Porte Slicers. It's a breather."

"La Porte? Do you remember the time we went to the Marching-Band contest at La Porte? And we took First Place in the Class A Division?"

"Your spit valve stuck halfway through the "National Emblem" and you damn near drowned when your sousaphone backed up on you."

I chuckled:

"And Duckworth told you what you could do with your trombone after you screwed up on a countermarch and knocked over three clarinet players. He damn near did it *for* you!"

"It wasn't my fault. Schwartz swung left. He faked me out."

"You know, Flick, some nights even in New York, when I wake up at three in the morning, I can still hear Duckworth's whistle. It scares me."

"You're not the only one!"

"Flick, there's no doubt about it. Duckworth was a genuine, absolute, gold-plated Gasser!"

"In spades!" Flick capped me.

XXIV ⧽ WILBUR DUCKWORTH AND HIS MAGIC BATON

When the bitter winds of dead winter howl out of the frozen North, making the ice-coated telephone wires creak and sigh like suffering live things, many an ex-Bb sousaphone player feels an old familiar dull ache in his muscle-bound left shoulder, a pain never quite lost as the years spin on. Old aching numbnesses of the lips, permanently implanted by frozen German silver mouthpieces of the past. An instinctive hunching forward into the wind, tacking obliquely the better to keep that giant burnished Conn bell heading always into the waves. A lonely man, carrying unsharable wounds and memories to his grave. The butt of low, ribald humor; gaucheries beyond description, unapplauded by music lovers, the sousaphone player is among the loneliest of men. His dedication is almost monklike in its fanaticism and solitude.

He is never asked to perform at parties. His fame is minute, even among fellow band members, being limited almost exclusively to fellow carriers of the Great Horn. Hence, his devotion is pure. When pressed for an explanation as to why he took up the difficult study and discipline of sousaphone playing, few can give a rational answer, usually mumbling something very much like the famed retort of the climbers of Mount Everest.

There is no Sousaphone category in the renowned jazz polls.
It would be inconceivable to imagine an LP entitled:

HARRY SCHWARTZ AND HIS GOLDEN SOUSAPHONE BLOW

COLE PORTER

IN STEREO

And yet every sousaphone player, in his heart, knows that no
instrument is more suited to Cole Porter than his beloved
four-valver. Its rich, verdant mellowness, its loving, somber blues
and grays in tonality are among the most sensual and thrilling
of sounds to be heard in a man's time.

But it will never be. Forever and by definition those brave
marchers under the flashing bells are irrevocably assigned to
the rear rank.

Few men know the Facts of Life more truly than a player
of this noble instrument. Twenty minutes in a good marching
band teaches a kid more about How Things Really Are than
five years at Mother's granite knee.

There are many misconceptions which at the outset must be
cleared up before we proceed much further. Great confusion
exists among the unwashed as to just what a sousaphone *is*.
Few things are more continually irritating to a genuine sousaphone man than to have his instrument constantly called a
"tuba." A tuba is a weak, puny thing fit only for mewling,
puking babes and Guy Lombardo—the better to harass balding,
middle-aged dancers. An upright instrument of startling ugliness
and mooing, flatulent tone, the tuba has none of the grandeur,
the scope or sweep of its massive, gentle, distant relation.

The sousaphone is worn proudly curled about the body, over
the left shoulder, and mounting above the head is that brilliant,
golden, gleaming disk—rivaling the sun in its glory. Its graceful
curves clasp the body in a warm and crushing embrace, the
right hand in position over its four massive mother-of-pearl
capped valves. It is an instrument a man can literally get his
teeth into, and often does. A sudden collision with another
bell has, in many instances, produced interesting dental mal-
formations which have provided oral surgeons with some of their
happier moments.

A sousaphone is a worthy adversary which must be watched like a hawk and truly mastered 'ere it master *you*. Dangerous, unpredictable, difficult to play, it yet offers rich rewards. Each sousaphone individually, since it is such a massive creation, assumes a character of its own. There are bad-tempered instruments and there are friendly sousaphones; sousaphones that literally lead their players back and forth through beautiful countermarches on countless football fields. Then there are the treacherous, which buck and fight and must be held in tight rein 'ere disaster strike. Like horses or women, no two sousaphones are alike. Nor, like horses or women, will Man ever fully understand them.

Among other imponderables, a player must have as profound a knowledge of winds and weather as the skipper of a racing yawl. A cleanly aligned sousaphone section marching into the teeth of a spanking crosswind with mounting gusts, booming out the second chorus of *"Semper Fidelis,"* is a study of courage and control under difficult conditions. I myself once, in my Rookie days, got caught in a counter-clockwise wind with a clockwise instrument and spun violently for five minutes before I regained control, all the while playing one of the finest obbligatos that I ever blew on the "National Emblem March."

Sometimes, in a high wind a sousaphone will start playing *you*. It literally blows back, developing enough back pressure to produce a thin chorus of "Dixie" out of both ears of the unwary sousaphonist.

The high school marching band that I performed in was led by a maniacal zealot who had whipped us into a fine state of tune rivaling a crack unit of the Prussian Guards. We won prizes, cups, ribbons, and huzzahs wherever we performed; wheeling, countermarching, spinning; knees high, and all the while we played. "On the Mall," "The Double Eagle," "El Capitan," "The NC-4 March," *"Semper Fidelis"*—we had mastered all the classics.

Our 180-beat-to-the-minute cadence snapped and cracked and rolled on like the steady beating of an incessant surf. Sharp in itchy uniforms and high-peaked caps, we learned the bitter facts of life while working our spit valves and bringing pageantry and pomp into the world of the Blast Furnace and the Open Hearth, under the leaden wintry skies of the Indiana prairie land.

The central figure of the scene was our Drum Major. Ours was a Spartan organization. We had no Majorettes, Pom-Pom girls, or other such decadent signposts on the roadway of a declining civilization. In fact, it was an all-Male band that had no room for such grotesqueries as thin, flat-chested, broad-bottomed female trombone players and billowy-bosomed clarinetists. A compact sixty-six man company of flat-stomached, hard-jawed Nehi drinkers, led by a solitary, heroic, high-kneed, arrogant baton twirler.

Drum majors are a peculiarly American institution, and Wilbur Duckworth was cast in the classic mold. Imperious, egotistical beyond belief, he was hated and feared by all of us down to the last lowly cymbal banger. Most drum majors of my acquaintance are not All-American boys in the Jack Armstrong tradition. In fact, they lean more in the general direction of Captain Queeg, somehow tainted by the vanity of a Broadway musical dancer, plus the additional factor of High School Hero.

In spite of legend, many drum majors are notably unsuccessful with women. Wilbur was no exception, and his lonely frustration in this most essential of human pursuits had led him to incredible heights in Baton Twirling. He concentrated and practiced hour upon hour until he became a Ted Williams among the wearers of the Shako. His arched back, swinging shoulders, lightning-like chrome wands; the sharp, imperious bite of his whistled commands were legendary wherever bandsmen rested to swap tales over a Nehi orange. At a full, rolling, 180-beat-per-minute tempo, Duckworth's knees snapped as high as most men's shoulders. He would spin, marching backward, baton held at ready port, eyes gleaming beadily straight ahead in our direction. Two short blasts of his silver whistle, then a longer one, a quick snap up-and-down movement of the wand, and we would crash into "The Thunderer," which opened with a spectacular trombone, trumpet, and sousaphone flourish of vast medieval grandeur. Precisely as the last notes of the flourish ended and "The Thunderer" boomed out, Wilbur spun like a machine and began his act. Over the shoulder like a stiffened silver snake with a life of its own, under both legs, that live metal whip never lost a beat or faltered ever so slightly. Catching the sun, it spun a blur high into the Indiana skies and down again, Wilbur never deigning so much as to watch its flight. He knew where it was; it knew where he was. They were one, a spinning silver bird. Even as we roared into the coda, attacking the sixteenth notes crisply, with bite, we were always conscious of the steady swish of that baton, cutting the air like a blade, a hissing obbligato to John Philip Sousa.

Like all champion Drum Majors—and Wilbur had more medals at seventeen than General Patton garnered over a lifetime of combat—Wilbur's act was carefully programmed. Almost in the same way that an Olympic skater performs the classical School figures, Wilbur had mastered years before the basic baton maneuvers, the classical flips and spins, and performed them with razor-sharp, glittering precision. He would begin with a quick over-the-back roll, a comparatively simple basic move, and then, moment by moment, his work would grow increasingly complex as variation upon variation of spinning steel wove itself through the Winter air. And then finally, just as his audience, nervously awaiting disaster, to a man believed there was nothing more that could be done with a baton, Wilbur, pausing slightly to fake them out, making them believe his repertoire was over, would give them the Capper.

Every great baton twirler has one thing that he alone can perform, since he alone has created and honed and shaped his final statement. Midway in his repertoire, Wilbur would whip a second baton from a sheath held by a great brass clip to his wide white uniform belt. Using the dual batons, he worked upward and upward until the final eerie moment. As the last notes of "The Thunderer" died out, a drummer, on cue, beat out the rhythm of our march, using a single stick on the rim of his snare.

Tic tic tic tic tic tic tic

As we marched silently forward, Wilbur then, with great deliberation, holding both batons out before him, began to spin them in opposite directions.

Synchronized! Like the blades of a twin-engine plane, twin propellers interleaved before him, gaining speed. Faster and faster and faster, until the batons had all but disappeared into a faint silver film, the only sound the "tic tic tic" of Ray Janowski's snare and the steady, in-step beat of feet hitting the pavement.

His back arched taut as a bow, knees snapping waist-high, at the agonizingly right instant, with two imperceptible flips of the wrist, Wilbur would launch his twin rapiers straight up into the icy air, still in synchronization. Like some strange science fiction bat, some glittering metal bird, the batons, gaining momentum as they rose, would soar thirty or forty feet above the band. Then, gracefully, at the apex of the arc, spinning slower and slower, they would come floating down; Wilbur never even for an instant glancing upward, the band eyes-front. Down would come the batons, dropping faster and faster, and still Wilbur marched on. And then, incredibly, at the very last instant, just as they were about to crash into the street, in perfect rhythm both hands dart out and the batons, together, leap into life and become silver blurs. It was Duckworth's Capper!

The instant his batons picked up momentum and spun back to life, Janowski "tic'd" twice and the drum section rolled out our basic cadence, as the crowd roared. Unconcerned, unseeing, we marched on.

Wilbur rarely used the Capper more than once or twice in any given parade or performance. Like all great artists, Wilbur gave of his best sparingly. None of us realized that Duckworth had not yet shown us his greatest Capper.

The high point of our marching year traditionally came on the Thanksgiving Day Parade. And that fateful Thursday dawned dark and gloomy, full of evil portent. The last bleak week in November had been literally polar in its savagery. For weeks a bitter Canadian wind had droned steadily off Lake

Michigan, blowing the blast-furnace dust into long rivers and eddies of red grime on the gray ice that bordered the curbs and coated the bus stops and rutted the streets. These are days that try a sousaphonist's soul to the utmost. That giant chunk of inert brass gathers cold into it like a thermic vacuum cleaner. Valves freeze at half-mast, mouthpieces stick to the tongue and lips in the way iron railings trap children, and the blown note itself seems thin and weak and lost in the knife-like air.

The assembly point for the parade was well out of the main section of town, back of Harrison Park. Any veteran parade marcher knows the scene, a sort of shambling, weaving confusion. The Croatian-American float, the Friends of Italy, the Moose, the Ladies of The Moose, the Children of The Moose, the Queen of The Moose, the Oddfellows' Whistling Brigade, the Red Men Of America (in full headdress and buckskin), the Owls, the Eagles, the Wolves, the Imperial Katfish Klan, the Shriners (complete with Pasha and red fezzes), the A. F. of L., the C.I.O., Steelworkers Local 1010, all gathered to snake their way through the ambient Indiana-Sinclair Refinery air, for glory and to thank God that there is an America. Or maybe just to Parade, which seems to be a basic human urge.

This gathering point is always known as a "rendezvous" in parade-ese. On the bulletin board the week before, the usual notice:

THE BAND WILL RENDEZVOUS AT 0800 ON HOHMAN AVENUE OPPOSITE HARRISON PARK. EACH UNIT WILL BE NUMBERED. LOOK FOR THE NUMBER PAINTED ON THE CURB—TWELVE. WE WILL STEP OFF *PROMPTLY* AND SMARTLY AT 0915.

Of course by twelve-thirty we are still milling around, noses running, and way off in the distance, always, the sound of some band or other playing something, and still we stood. The thin trickle of glockenspiel music came back to us through the frozen trees and bushes as the Musicians' Local Marching Band tuned up. Megaphones bellowing, cars racing back and forth over the disorganized line of march, until finally, slowly and painfully, we moved off. Wilbur Duckworth shot us aggressively into our assigned march position, and we were under way.

Rumors had gone from band to band, from drummer to drummer, that the Mayor up ahead on the reviewing stand was drunk, that we were delayed while they sobered him up, that he had chased a lady high school principal around the lectern. But these are just Parade rumors.

The Thanksgiving Day Parade is really a Christmas rite. Behind us on a huge white float rode Santa Claus, throwing confetti at the crowd as we moved through town.

It's hard to tell from a Marcher's standpoint just what Parade Watchers think, if anything. As we got closer to the center of town, the crowd grew thicker; muffled, hooded, mittened, earmuffed, gray staring faces of sheet metalworkers, iron puddlers; just standing in the dead zero air. This is where you begin to learn about Humanity. Their eyes look like old oysters. They just look. Once in a while you see a guy smoking a cigar; he spits, and from time to time a kid throws a penny or a Mary Jane or a Cherry Bomb into the bell of your sousaphone.

All the bands, of course, are marching to their own cadence. Up ahead the Ladies' Auxiliary of the Whales shuffles on. In the cold winter of the Midwest you can hear a girdle squeak for three blocks.

We march past the assembled multitude, Duckworth never glancing to right or left, straight ahead, brow high, paper-thin black kid gloves worn on his baton hands. Up ahead the flags and banners of all kinds are fluttering in the icy-cold breeze.

LITHUANIAN-AMERICAN CLUB. HOORAY FOR AMERICA! GOD BLESS ALL OF US

The steelworkers just stand there silently, looking. From somewhere far behind a glockenspiel in the German-American Band tinkles briefly and stops, and all around the steady drumbeats roll. We were on the march.

Strung overhead from lamppost to lamppost across the main

street were strings of red and green Christmas lights. Green plastic holly wreaths with imitation red berries hung from every other lamppost.

We are now right in the middle of town. This is the big moment. It's like Times Square in Hohman, Indiana. The crossroads. A streetcar line ran right down the middle of the main street, and I am straddling a track, trying to keep up the 180-beat-per-minute cadence; blow our own special version of "Jingle Bells" on my frozen sousaphone. Bitter frozen, sliding along the tracks with the ice packed in hard. I have lost all feeling. My ears, my nose, my horn are frozen; my hands are frozen.

We moved haltingly ahead. Slowly, slowly. We'd bump into the Italian ladies ahead, and the German plumbers behind would bump into us. Somewhere the Moose would swear, and the Eagles would yell. And then we were right at Ground Zero, the reviewing stand to our right, the assembled multitude cheering the National Champions on to further heights.

Wilbur spun and faced us with his old familiar stare, and suddenly the cold was forgotten. We were On! Two sharp rips of the whistle, a sustained, long, rising note, baton at port; two quick flips of the wrist, and our great fanfare boomed out. The parade had come alive. The Champs were on the scene. The American Legion Junior Fife and Drum Corps faded into oblivion. The Firemen's Scottish Bagpipe Company disappeared into limbo. Wilbur Duckworth was in command.

Ray Janowski's beat was never sharper, leading his drum section to heights that rivaled our best performances. Duckworth about-faced and went into action. His great shako reaching up like a giant shaving brush with plume into the sullen gray sky. A magnificent figure, his gold epaulets glinting as we wove at half-tempo over the hard-caked ice, little realizing we were about to participate in an historic moment that has since become part of the folksongs and fireside legends of Northern Indiana.

"The Thunderer" echoed in that narrow street like a cannon volley being fired in a cave. Blowing a sousaphone at such a moment gives one a sense of power that is only rivaled, perhaps, by the feel of a Ferrari cockpit at Le Mans.

Spitzer, our bass drummer, six feet nine inches tall, caught fire. His sticks spinning into the air, his drum quivering, the worn gold and purple lettering on its head:

NATIONAL PRECISION MARCHING CHAMPIONS CLASS A

The crowd is subdued into a kind of tense silence. They were viewing greatness; the panoply of tradition and pomp, and they knew it. The fourteen-inch merchant mill and the cold-strip pickling department at the steel mill rarely see such glory. Children stopped crying; noses ceased to run, eyes sparkled, and blue plumes of exhaled breath hung like smoke wreaths in the air as we slammed into the coda.

Already I was beginning to wonder whether Duckworth would dare try his Capper on such a dangerously cold day as this, with those sneaky November crosswinds, and numbed fingers. His ramrod back gave no hint. One thing was sure, and everybody in the band knew it. Wilbur had never been sharper, cleaner, more dynamic.

By now he was three-quarters through his act. His figure eight and double-eagle had been spectacular. The trombones just ahead of me, usually a lethargic section, were blowing clean and hard. Wilbur's twin batons were alive. His timing was spectacular.

We arrived at the dead center of the intersection precisely as the last note of "The Thunderer" echoed from the plate-glass windows of the big department store and died out against the gray, dirty façade of the drugstore on the opposite corner. For a moment the air rang with the kind of explosive silence that follows a train wreck, or the last note of "The Thunderer" played by a band with blood in its veins and juice in its glands. And then it began. Janowski "tic'd" his solitary beat. We marched forward almost marking time in place. The crowd sensed something was about to happen.

Duckworth towered ahead of us, weaving slightly left, right, left, right, as his twin batons, in uncanny synchronization, began to spin faster and faster.

Sound carries in cuttingly cold air, and even the Mayor up on the reviewing stand could hear the sound of those spinning chromium slivers:

zzzzzzzssssssstt zzzzsssssssssssst zzzzzzzssssttt

Wilbur held it longer than any of us had ever seen him do before, stretching the dramatic tension to the breaking point and beyond. Beside me, Dunker muttered:

"What's the hell's he doing?"

Wilbur spun on. Janowski "tic'd" off the rhythm.

Tic tic tic tic tic . . .

We marched imperceptibly, like some great glacier, across the intersection. And then, like two interlocked birds of prey, Duckworth's batons rose majestically in the hard November gloom.

Higher and higher they spun, faster than even the day that Wilbur had won the National Championship. It was unquestionably his supreme effort. He was a senior, and knew that this was his last full-scale public appearance before the hometown rabble. His last majestic Capper.

Every eye in the band staring straight ahead followed the climbing arc of those two beautiful interleaved disks as they climbed smartly higher and higher above the street. Wilbur, true to his style, stared coldly ahead, knees snapping upward like pistons. He knew his trade and was at the peak of his powers.

And then it happened. Instinctively, every member of the Bass section scrunched lower in his sousaphone at the awesome sight.

Running parallel with our path and directly above Wilbur's shako, high over the street, hung a thin, curving copper band of wire. The streetcar high-tension line. Slightly below it and to the left was another thin wire of some nondescript origin. The two disks magically, in a single synchronous action, seemed to cut the high-tension wire in half as they rose above it, without so much as touching a single bit of copper. Then, ten or twelve feet above the high-tension wire, they reached their apex and in a style cleaner and more spectacular than any of us ever had suspected was in Duckworth, they slowed and began their downward swoop. We watched, the crowd watched, and Wilbur marched on, eyes straight ahead. My God, what a moment!

The Mayor leaned forward slightly on the reviewing stand and even the children sensed that History was about to be made.

For a fleeting instant it appeared as though the two batons would repeat their remarkable interleaving, dodging, weaving avoidance of that lethal wire on their way down. In fact, the one on the right did. But the left baton hovered for just an instant, spinning slower and slower above the copper band, and then, with a metallic "ting," it just ticked, barely *kissed* the current carrier with its chrome-silver ball. The other end fell across the other nondescript wire, gently. And for a split second nothing happened.

Janowski "tic tic tic'd" bravely on. Our cadence never varied as our feet sounded as one on that spiteful, filthy ice.

Then an eerie transparent, cerulean blue nimbus, a kind of expanding halo rippled outward from the suspended baton and from some far-off distant place, beyond the freight yards, past the Grasselli Chemical Plant, an inhuman, painful quickening shudder grew closer and closer, as though a wave were about to break over all of us.

BOOM BOOM BOOM!

Hanging over the intersection was a gigantic, unimaginably immense Fourth of July sparkler that threw a Vesuvius, a screaming shower of flame in a giant pinwheel down to the street and into the sky, over the crowd and onto the band. The air was alive with ozone. It seemed to flash with great thunderbolts, on and on. Time stood still. It could have been ten seconds, or an eternity. It just hung up there and burned and burned, ionizing before our eyes.

Janowski "tic'd" on. A few muffled screams came from the crowd. Fuses were blowing out over the entire county, as far away as Gary. High-tension poles were toppling somewhere miles away. Steel mills stopped; boats sank on the river. It was as though some ancient, thunderbolt-hurling God had laid one right down in the middle of Hohman on Thanksgiving Day. The ground shuddered. Generators as far south as Indianapolis were screaming. Duckworth had hit the main fuse. It was the greatest Capper of all time!

By now the second baton had descended. Without so much as an upward glance, Duckworth caught it neatly and spun on. The drum section picked up the cadence and we marched smartly through the intersection, leaving behind a scene that forms the core of several epic poems relating the incident.

Duckworth immediately signaled for "El Capitan," and as we attacked the intro the crowd burst into a great fantastic roar of applause and surging emotion. The aroma of burnt rubber, scorched copper, ionized chrome, and frozen ozone trailed us up the street. Santa Claus, in a window, sat mouth agape. Grumpy's hammer was held stiffly at half-mast. The Christmas trees had flickered out, and MERRY XMAS neon signs were dark.

We knew that the baton that had gone up in smoke had been one of Wilbur's awards—his Presentation set of matched wands, won at the State Championships. The other, the survivor, he held lightly in his gloved right hand, his arm shooting high over his head and down diagonally across his body, up and down, up and down. He spun as we finished "El Capitan." Three quick blasts, the signal for "Under the Double Eagle." His eyes as steely as ever; his jaw grim and square.

From all sides we could hear the sound of sirens approaching the scene we were leaving behind us. "Under the Double Eagle" with its massive crescendos, its unmatched sousaphone ob-bligato. As we played this great classic and Duckworth led us on into the gloom, every sousaphone player, every baritone man, the trombones, the clarinets, the piccolos and flutes, the snare drummers and Janowski, all of us thought one thing:

"Did he plan it!?"

You never can tell about Drum Majors. This was not the sort of mistake Wilbur Duckworth would make. Had he calculated this? Practiced, worked for this moment for four long years? Was this gigantic Capper, this unparalleled Capper his final statement to Hohman, Indiana, and the steel mills, the refineries, and the Sheet & Tube Works, those gray oyster eyes, and the Croatian Ladies' Aid Society?

Up ahead Duckworth's arched back, as taut as spring steel, said nothing. His shako reached for the sky, his great plume waved on. He blew a long, single, hanging blast, holding his remaining baton at a high oblique angle over his head. Two short blasts followed, and he smartly commanded a Column Right. The drums thundered as we moved into a side street and headed back toward school. The parade was over. The wind was rising and it seemed to be getting colder. A touch of snow was in the air. Christmas was on its way.

XXV ❧ I RELATE THE STRANGE TALE OF THE HUMAN HYPODERMIC NEEDLE

The retired trombonist stood behind the bar with his shoulders thrown back, an old familiar light blazing in his eyes. He wore the look of a man on the mark; tensed, waiting for the sharp downbeat, lips slightly pursed for the opening blast of "Under the Double Eagle." Gradually he relaxed, as we returned to the warm, moist, sudsy atmosphere of the friendly corner tavern.

"You know, Ralph, I don't tell many people this, but once in a while I go down in the basement when nobody's home, and I play my trombone. The lip is still there."

He drummed his fingers in a rhythmic, quick cadence tempo on the polished mahogany to the pattern of our well-remembered and much envied, by the other bands, of course, March Cadence. It is not generally known outside of the marching band world that each band has great pride in its distinct March Cadence drum pattern. It can be identified by this sound just as surely as a set of fingerprints gives away an axe murderer.

"Well, Flick, there are times when I can feel an old, dull itch in my left shoulder. Especially when I'm watching football games on TV, and they come on with the half-time shows."

"Ah, they got all them girls with them cowboy hats. You don't see many good *marching* bands. Just a lot of bazooms, doing the Frug."

"Times change, Flick." Again the beer was sparking deep philosophical concepts. Flick continued, with a touch of bitterness in his voice:

"Fer Chrissake, there's nothing funnier than a short, fat girl clarinet player wearing a band suit, trying to do a double-time quick countermarch."

"It's Showbiz, Flick. That's what it is." We were getting a bit maudlin.

"It's Showbiz, Flick, it's all Showbiz. They're always doing this stuff like a salute to TV, or a salute to Richard Rodgers, or *My Fair Lady*, for God's sake. Can you imagine what Duckworth woulda said if they had tried to foist off a Major*ette* on him, or what the hell do they call them—a Pom-Pom girl, or a Color Guard?"

"Plenty a bazooms. . . ."

"It's Showbiz, Flick."

We sat together, Flick now perched on his high stool, me on mine, staring grimly out into the middle distance.

"I'm watching one the other day, Flick. They must have had a band of about 30,000 pieces. They came out with more junk hanging on 'em. Horns, whistles, smoke bombs, sirens; these guys had it all, and I'll be goddamned if they don't start making a formation while this announcer on the TV says; 'We are now going to pay a tribute to Doctor Kildare, that famous TV doctor.' And you know what they made, Flick, in a formation while they were playing that theme song from that TV show?"

"A bedpan?" Flick guessed.

I knocked my beer over into my lap and leaped up, brushing the suds off the fine English flannel, the pride of my life. Flick grinned the self-contented grin of a man who knows he's made a funny. He drew me another beer, cackling all the while.

"Hell, no! A bedpan woulda been great. I'd a cheered! What this band did was march around, and they make a big hypodermic needle. 'Covered the whole damn field! And then somebody blows a whistle and the plunger goes in, and the whole Bass section and about thirty-eight trumpets and six guys playing glockenspiels go pouring out through the needle. They're the dope, see, and when they get out of the needle they spell out 'Ouch!,' fer Chrissake. Well, I can see about 500,000 Junkies sitting out there, coming to in the middle of the football game and seeing this giant spike. And thinking all of a sudden they're doing a commercial for Heroin or something. It's a wonder they didn't bust the whole goddamn stadium!"

The phone rang. Flick picked up the receiver.

"Yeah? Now, you know I'm going to the game tonight. (Pause) You can have the car. They won't even know I'm not there. Okay, I promise. I will *not* miss the next meeting; okay? That's a promise."

He hung up.

"The wife. Janis."

I remembered Janis faintly from school as a dark, quiet girl. I hardly knew her. I decided quickly not to pursue the subject any further. You never know.

"What meeting you talking about, Flick?"

"PTA. She drags me to that damn thing every month. They sit around and talk about the Penny Supper. And how to raise more money to buy more World Books."

"You got kids?" I asked.

"You know it!"

A sudden thought hit me. The PTA. Teachers, parents— the old alma mater.

"Do you ever see any of our old teachers? Like Mr. Milton? Or. . . ."

I groped for a few names that were indelibly, forever tattooed on the tough hide of my memory.

"How 'bout ah . . . yeah, old Fatso Appleton?" *He* was a notorious Shop teacher who ran his Shop classes like an actual *Sweat*shop. I guess he figured we better learn early.

"He's tougher than ever," Flick said. "In fact, a couple years ago some kids even tried to start a union, in his Shop, and he imported a bunch of Scab students after they went out on strike. Locked 'em out."

"Too bad we never thought of that when we were around. What a jerk! How 'bout Miss Bryfogel?"

He thought for a long moment and said:

"No . . . I don't see her around any more. She really was something."

I thoughtfully munched a pretzel.

"She certainly was, Flick. I, for one, will never forget her."

XXVI ᢒᡦ MISS BRYFOGEL AND THE FRIGHTENING CASE OF THE SPECKLE-THROATED CUCKOLD

The sticky-sweet, body-warm taste of Pornography lingers in the soul long after the fires have been banked and the shades drawn. Where did it all begin? What ancient caveman drew the first dirty picture on the wall of his dank granite hole and then, cackling fiendishly, scuttled off into the darkness. At what point in time did some lecherous pornographer—his acne itching, his palms sweaty—proclaim his smudgy craft as Art? Thereby giving rise and hope and sustenance to a whole generation, nay, an immense population of beady-eyed, furtive probers in the rank undergrowth of human debauchery.

At long last we have finally solved that age-old problem, that ancient challenge which drove countless philosophers of the past to the verge of madness; of how to change the base metal lead into precious gold. Even as I write this, battalions of hard-working, Serious, dedicated artists, their tongues lolling, their breath coming in short, uneven pants, foreheads sticky with clammy perspiration, their agents impatiently clamoring at the door of their sacred writing chamber, are contriving at immense artistic cost yet another description; evocation, of a basically simple bodily function, or yet another monstrously imagined portion of the human anatomy. Theirs is not an easy task. Pause and consider. There really aren't many four-letter words, and there are just so many ways you can arrange them. Already, perhaps, the end is in sight.

But their task is dwarfed by the legion of ready reviewers whose duty it is to transmute their inchoate lead into magnificent golden works of Art. His arsenal of phrases, like that of the Artist, is also limited, and hence sees repeated use:

"Biting satire. . . ."

"Scathing indictment of our Puritanical sexual mores."

"Brilliant parody—a real thrust at the Victorian ethos."

"Deliciously savage tongue-in-cheek treatment of. . . ."

"Ribald, picaresque, rollicking novel that has a deep undertone of. . . ."

"Ecstatic poetic vision, reminiscent of an enlightened D. H. Lawrence."

I repeat, theirs is not an easy task. Yet willingly, nay, *eagerly*, they sit imprisoned in their digs, eyes bulging, a work of Art clutched in their palsied talons. They suffer great insights for all of us.

What has happened to the old-fashioned Dirty Old Man, not to mention the old-fashioned Dirty Young Man? The answer is obvious. They are now Artists, destined to stand in that great pantheon that stretches back through the mists of time to Euripides, marching forward with Melville and Conrad, Chaucer and Shakespeare. It has been a long, difficult process but we in our time have finally solved the old riddle of the alchemist.

And yet, let us be honest. Deep down in the innermost recesses of our minds there is something that peers out at us with tiny, red-rimmed eyes, its mildewed beak chittering, that reminds us by its lewd cackling that we are scrawling pictures on the walls of our cave. There are times when you can ignore this insistent, omniscient beast, and then there are times when you can't. There are just so many ways to spell "ass."

Not long ago I was subtly and forcibly reminded of that inescapable fact. It was Sunday, a gray, milky, Nothing Sunday in the great tradition. I lounged, coffee cup in hand, in my gilded cell, vaguely conscious of a gnawing and unfamiliar sense of shame and discomfort. Knee-deep in the Sunday papers I sat, futilely warding off those elusive pangs of shame and guilt. I am a Twentieth-Century Man. I should not know these feelings! Then why the vague feverish flush, the clammy palms, the fugitive desire to hide under the daybed? True, I had been in attendance at a monumental debauch the night before and had indulged myself strenuously, but, after all, the Debauch itself is now a recognized art form, and I merely an aspiring, creative performer. Then why this persistent sense of unease? Could it be that I was suffering from an attack of recurrent vestigial conscience? I immediately crossed that out, since, being a representative citizen of our time, I knew that it was an impossibility.

It must be caused, then, by something from without my body and psyche, certainly not from within. But what?

I looked about me. My television set droned on harmlessly in the corner with its endless professional golf match, its perpetual succession of Arnold Palmers, Julius Boros, Gary Players, Jay Heberts, and other heroic figures of our time, hitting little balls with short sticks perpetually over the green hills of TV Land. Surely it could not be *this* innocent vision. I looked about the room again. All was familiar and normally sybaritic.

I sipped nervously at my rich, full-flavored, tepid instant coffee and tried to get my mind back into healthier channels. Forcibly I made myself think of Higher Things. I tried to recall a few of the better scenes from a magnificent 8mm Art film I had seen the week before at the Nouveau Cinematique Realité Festival I had attended. *The Passionate Transvestite*, a superb, delicate, subtly controlled delineation of a sensitive theme, and its attendant feature, *Tilly the Toiler Meets Winnie Winkle*, a wildly robust comedy making light of the Puritanical mores of our day. *Passionate*, as it is known to us cinema *aficionados*, was almost better than *Candy Meets King Kong*, a frank Anti-War statement couched in cuttingly sardonic Voltairean brushstrokes.

It was no use. Something was troubling me. I stirred restlessly, kicking at the drift of newspaper that covered my ankles. Something caught my eye. And held it. Those sinister fugitive pangs of guilt rose to a crescendo. And then I knew! It was unmistakable! Draped over the toe of my Italian ostrich-skin, alligator lounging slipper, provocatively half-opened, was the *Sunday Times Book Review Supplement.*

It held my steady nervous gaze like a hooded cobra about to strike. But this was only the good old familiar *Book Review Supplement,* a trusted friend that had sustained me through many a slippery moment at countless cocktail parties. And yet now, for some unaccountable reason, this friendly, faithful companion had touched off that sinister, faint but insistent sickness of fear and humiliation, deep in my vitals where such things happen.

Ordinarily, on long, timeless Sundays, I save the supplement and the magazine section for last, as a kind of self-indulgent treat, but today, unmistakably, a new and alien note had been sounded. The *Book Review Supplement* had mysteriously stirred some long-dead, or at least sleeping, specter in my soul.

Perhaps my language is a bit overwrought, but there are times when it is not easy to maintain the cool steady eye and the casual hand.

What was there about this innocent fold of paper? I bent forward to look more closely at the cover page. Its familiar staid measured grayness suddenly came into sharp focus. "New Edition of Renaissance Classic"—the heading in bold type, and at center page a black and white woodcut showing a languorous youth lounging under a fairy-tale tree, and over him stood a Florentine lady wearing the flowing gowns of the nunnery. Where had I seen that lad, that spent lad, that lady of the Church before?

And then, eerily, faintly perceptible, a voice drifted out of the bottomless depths of the swamp of my subconscious, the indistinct syllables bursting like bubbles of some loathsome combustible gas generated by the decomposed slime of prehistoric monsters. A feminine voice! What in God's name is she saying to me?

I strained to hear that ghostly caller. It seemed to come somehow from the very grain of the woodcut itself! Somewhere, in some far-off land, Sam Snead was sinking fifteen-foot putts,

Cary Middlecoff was happily birdying, but there was no joy in my soul that day. I hunched even further, deeper into my motor-driven Vibra-Snooze lounging chair, alert, my senses tingling, ready for danger. The voice came nearer and nearer, and then, clearly, distinctly, I sensed it was asking me a question, a question I had been asked before, *aeons* before. My God! It was now impossible to evade!

"Where did you get that book?"

With an inchoate cry I leaped to my feet, sending that rank scorpion, that culture shark the supplement spinning into the corner where it lay for a moment, its pages sinuously fluttering like some ghastly living thing.

Shaken to my underpinnings I stumbled, half-crazed with a terror such as I had not known since my days as a ten-year-old innocent. I rushed to my Inna-Wall sliding teakwood-paneled Danish bar and blindly pressed a button. Seconds later, clutching three fingers of Chevas Regal, I tried to regroup.

But Miss Bryfogel pursued me, asking her question again and again, louder and louder! Miss Bryfogel! And then it all began to come back, the whole sordid, fetid mess.

Shakily easing myself back into the comforting depths of my chair, driven by forces beyond my control, I painfully began to reconstruct that awful moment of my fall from Grace and Purity. I once was as pure as the driven snow, an apple-cheeked lad who delighted in the birds of spring and the soft humming afternoons of summer, and I was insanely, madly, totally in love. With Miss Bryfogel. My commitment was complete.

Miss Bryfogel taught sixth-grade English, and for every fifty-five minute period that I was permitted in her presence I lay prostrate at her feet. Her soft heart-shaped face and dark, liquid eyes haunted me in my every waking hour. She never gave the slightest indication that she, too, was stirred to the depths. But I *knew*.

Miss Bryfogel would read poetry to us, as my classmates, clods to a man, dozed fitfully. But I, love buds a-tingle, eyes misty, wept with her over *Evangeline* and *Old Ironsides*. I had only one way to tell her of my love. To speak to her through our mutual secret language, the one thing other than insane passion we shared together—the Book Report.

Perhaps it is because we are a nation that, almost to the last individual, spent the greater part of its youth sweating over the accursed book report that we have become in our adulthood a nation of book-review readers. What is a book review but merely an overblown book report? And we all half suspect that, like our book reports of our dim past, the book reviewers rarely bother actually to read the books. We instinctively admire their suave fakery, their artful dodging, their expansive self-congratulatory phraseology, their mellifluous padding. We have been through it, too, and we know good trickery when we see it.

Miss Bryfogel placed great importance on our weekly reports. Early in the semester she had issued a mimeographed sheet to us, called the Suggested Reading List, from which we drew our ammunition.

I was never a stylist, but I felt that sincerity and neatness, as well as meticulous spelling and ample margins would get my subtle message through.

As far as my actual reading went, I ran heavily toward *The Outdoor Chums*, which my Aunt Glenn persisted in giving me, *Flash Gordon Meets Ming The Merciless*, and *Popular Mechanics*. And three ancient copies of *G-8 And His Battle Aces*, which I had re-read at least seventy-four times, getting more from their rich mosaic at every reading. However, these were not Reportable.

And so, every week was sheer torture as I phonied and nervously mocked up my Friday report. The books themselves were taken from the public library, and were doled out to us by Miss Easter. Miss Easter was a kindly, thin, ancient lady who had been born wearing a pair of gold-rimmed bifocals and with a full head of blue-gray hair, a true dedicated librarian; an alert protector of the morals of the young. I recall vividly one hellish week trying to read four consecutive words of something called *Ivanhoe* which had been highly recommended by both Miss Easter and my true Heart-Wound.

My reports themselves actually ran to a sort of form. For example:

"*Robinson Crusoe*"

by

DANIEL DEFOE

"*Robinson Crusoe* is about this man who got lost on this island. He made a hat out of a coconut shell and found this foot-print on the beach. His island was named Friday, and they had a goat. This is a very interesting book. It was exciting. I think *Robinson Crusoe* is a good book."

Or,

"*Black Beauty*"

by

ANNA SEWELL

"*Black Beauty* is about this horse that got sold to a very cruel man. He hit Black Beauty and Black Beauty was very unhappy because Black Beauty was a kind horse and didn't hit anybody. I think books about horses are very exciting, and *Black Beauty* is a very exciting book. It has three hundred and two pages, and I think anyone would enjoy reading *Black Beauty*."

I felt strongly that unqualified applause for any book on the Suggested Reading List would convey to Miss Bryfogel my deep feelings about the books she read, and also would net me at least a C.

My love grew from Friday to Friday, and little did I realize that disaster was drawing closer and closer by the hour. Trouble invariably sneaks up behind on little cats' feet; soft and innocent and shadowy. And it quite often results from an attempt to better oneself, to raise the sights, to elevate the standards, to break through into a clearer, brighter world.

Miss Bryfogel continually encouraged something she called "Outside Reading," which meant books not on the official list.

Miss Easter had a vast file of these desirable Non-official Official books at her command. She worked hand in glove with all the Miss Bryfogels at the Warren G. Harding School, ceaselessly striving to push back the frontiers of Barbarism and Ignorance and to raise high the fluttering banners of Culture. And in Hohman, Indiana, that is not an easy task. Amid the dark, swirling mists exhaled by the Blast Furnace, the Coke Plant, and the Oil Refinery, Miss Easter quietly brooded over acres of silent kids hunched over *The Lady of the Lake* and *David Copperfield* in her brightly lit island of fantasy and dreams—her library.

On several occasions I had gone the treacherous route of the Outside Reading. It was dangerous, and usually stupendously boring. But already I had mastered the art of manufacturing an entire book report from two paragraphs selected at random, plus a careful reading of the dust jacket, a system which still earns a tidy living for many a professional reviewer.

However, the library was not the only source of books available to the probing mind. There was home. And in my instance, the bookcase in the dining room, filled to bursting with my father's precious collection of bad books. We did not subscribe to Literary magazines. I doubt whether my father had ever read a book review in his entire life, if he even knew they existed, so hence he read for pure pleasure and ran heavily to *The Claw of Fu Manchu*, *The Canary Murder Case*, *The Riders of the Purple Sage*, and the complete exploits of Philo Vance. At least these were the books that he kept in the dining-room bookcase. I never really associated them with book reports. They were just Stories, and book reports were about Books.

There were other volumes that were kept around the house, were not talked about much, but were just there. Not many, just a few mysterious books kept in my parents' bedroom, or in the closet. No one ever said we shouldn't read them. They were just kept out of our way. For as long as I could remember there had been this thick green-covered, bulky book on the bottom shelf of my mother's end table. It had been there so long and was so much a part of the scenery that it wasn't a book any more; just a Thing. It was always there. I had opened it maybe twice in my entire life—tiny print, incomprehensible; just a book. Until that pivotal day when everything changed.

It was a chill, dark, lowering afternoon. Faint puffs of oily wind bearing the essence of Phillips 66 and the Number-One Open Hearth through the gaunt trees, and under the eaves. I was home alone. And itchy.

These are dangerous conditions, known to us all. Ranging through the empty house, looking for something to do, somewhere to light, chewing a salami sandwich, I homed in inevitably to the Fountain of Evil. I rarely went into my parents' bedroom, because it was somehow off my main beat. Nothing Freudian or Victorian; it just wasn't where my action was. However, as the barometer fell and my itch increased, I drifted in past the brass bed, just looking. Drawn.

The how and why of the exact instant the Book came into my hands I do not clearly recall, and perhaps even that fact is significant. I somehow knew without even being told that it was wrong. I somehow knew that what I was doing was vaguely on the other side of the line. Our instincts run deep.

I dragged the book, my ears acutely alert for footsteps on the porch, into the bathroom and began my descent into iniquity and degradation.

The title of the book meant nothing to me. I had not seen it on Miss Easter's shelves, nor on Miss Bryfogel's Selected lists, but it was thick and had small print, so I figured it must be good. Or at least Official. Not only that, it had a foreign name, and anyone who has ever gone to school knows that any book with a foreign name is Important.

Well, I hadn't read four sentences when I realized that I had in my hands the golden key to Miss Bryfogel's passionate heart. Not only was this book almost totally incomprehensible, it was about friars and abbots, counts and countesses, knight errants, kings and queens, and a lot of Italians. It also had pictures, woodcuts that reminded me of other Important books that Miss Bryfogel spoke highly of. In accordance with my usual practice of book reporting, I looked through the Table of Contents to pick out something specific to read and to quote in case of embarrassing questions.

I had never seen a Table of Contents like this before. It was listed:

"Day The First"
"Day The Second"
"Day The Third"

and under that heading something caught my eye:

"The First Story:
Massetto of Lamporeccio feigneth himself dumb and becometh gardener to a convent of women, who all flock to lie with him."

Well, this was a natural, since I knew what "dumb" meant. There were plenty of dumb kids in my class. And Mrs. Kissel, next door, had a garden. I was on home grounds.

I plowed ahead, and the more I struggled to read the more I realized that this was good for at least a B+. My senses alert to sounds in the driveway, I forged into unknown territory. There was something about that story that drew me on like some gigantic magnet hauling an atom of iron with its unseen, mysterious force field. Does the iron understand magnetism? Did I understand what went on in the convent? As the gardener lieth with the abbess?

I somehow got the idea that an abbess was either a safety patrol lady or some kind of bad tooth. But there was something about it! I could not lay it down. And I began, mysteriously, to sweat, a telltale cold clamminess.

The stories didn't exactly end. Not like *The Outdoor Chums*, where Dan, the bully, shakes his fist at Will, the fun-loving Chum, and, retreating in his cowardly way, surrounded by his toadies, says:

"Will, and all the rest of you Outdoor Chums—I'll get you yet! Just wait and see!" Brandishing his clenched fist in the air while the Outdoor Chums laughed gaily, mounted their electric canoe, and headed for camp. No, these stories didn't exactly end. They just petered out. But I was hooked.

Steamily, itchily, I read on and on and on. And on. The house grew darker and colder, the winds were rising. On the far-off horizon the night shift took over in the vast, sinister steel mills. The skies glowed as the Blast Furnaces and the Bessemer Converters painted the clouds a dull red and orange. My eyes ached throbbingly, my throat was dry and parched. I read of maidens and virgins, nightingales and cuckolds—a small, yellowish, canary-like bird. Finally, palsied with fatigue, a changed man, I carefully replaced the green volume in its regular spot and went into the kitchen to knock together another salami sandwich. It was a good afternoon's work. Wait till Miss Bryfogel sees what great books I'm reading now.

It was one of the very few times I ever looked forward to getting to work on a book report. It was Thurday and next day was of course our day of reckoning.

After supper I scrunched over the kitchen table, my blue-lined tablet with its Indian Chief cover before me, my Wearever fountain pen clutched in my cramped claws. I began my love offering to Miss Bryfogel.

"*The Decameron of Boccaccio*, by Giovanni Boccaccio." I thought carefully, my mind humming like a well-oiled clock, toying with phrases, rejecting, and finally selecting the opening line:

> "This is the best, most interesting book I ever read. It is by a Italian and I think this book is very interesting. It is about these people that tell stories about knights and friars and cuckolds."

(I figured this was a nice touch, since I knew Miss Bryfogel liked birds.) Gathering steam, I went on:

> "There was this one story about a man named Massetto who worked in a garden and he made believe he was dumb and he did a lot of funny things, and there was this lady named

the Abbess who said she would lieth with Massetto because,
I guess, she didn't want to embarrass him because he was
lying. She did, and they were very happy. I liked this story
because I think having a garden is a good thing to have.
There are a lot of other stories I liked in this book. It is
very hard to read because it has small printing, but anyone
who would read this would like it."

I leaned back and re-read my masterpiece. It was good, the
best work I had ever done. My mother, hunched over the sink
in her Chinese-red chenille bathrobe, doing the dishes, was
vaguely humming "When the Blue of the Night Meets the
Gold of the Day." At that time she was deep in her Bing
Crosby period. The kitchen was warm, my stomach was full,
and Life was complete.

Friday dawned bright and clear, a perfect gem of a morning.
I floated to the Warren G. Harding School with that high ex-
hilarated feeling of a man who has his homework in his notebook and the world in his hand. Birds sang, milkmen whistled,
and I could hardly wait for Miss Bryfogel and Six-B English.
Now she would know. She could not mistake my devotion for
a mere passing whim.

Miss Bryfogel that afternoon sat at her desk looking even
more unattainable, elusive, and sultry than ever before. Her
opening remarks followed her classic pattern:

"Pass your book reports up to the front and open your books
to page seventy-eight."

Ahead of me Simonson shoved his smudgy scrap of paper,
bearing the title *Sam, The Young Shortstop*. From behind me
Helen Weathers poked my ear with *Lassie Come Home*, and I,
violins playing pianissimo in my soul, added my magnificent
epistle to their scrubby lot. Miss Bryfogel simply stacked the
book reports together, shoved them in a drawer, and we went to
work on gerunds.

At long last my heavenly tryst with Miss Bryfogel ended.
The bell rang, and caressing her lovingly with my burning,
myopic eyes I drifted out into the hall, knowing that the trap was

set. She had a whole weekend to think about me and our life together. Now that she knows the Higher Things to which I aspire, the pinnacles I have conquered, there can be no stopping us!

Saturday and Sunday flew by on the wings of ecstasy. And then Monday—blessed Monday. It was the first time in the recorded history of education in the state of Indiana that a normal, red-blooded, Male kid ever sprang out of bed at 7 A.M., a full fifteen minutes early, and took off for school without so much as a single whine.

The day dragged endlessly, achingly toward that moment of sublime triumph that I knew must come, and the instant I walked into Miss Bryfogel's classroom I knew I had made the Big Strike. I was not even at my seat when she called me up to her desk. I turned, the way I had seen Clark Gable do it many times. Miss Bryfogel, her voice sounding a little odd—no doubt due to passion—said:

"Ralph, I'd like you to stay a few minutes after class." The Jackpot!

I swaggered back to my seat, a man among children. Fifty-five minutes later I stood before Miss Bryfogel's altar, ready to do her slightest command. She opened:

"Ralph . . . ah . . . about your book report. That was a very well-written book report."

I said:

"Heh, heh, heh. Good."

I was not used to this. Nobody ever talked about my work. I was strictly a C+ man, and C+ men never get praised. Miss Bryfogel was talking in a strange, low voice.

"It was very well written. Did you really . . . *enjoy* the book?"

"Yes. It was a very exciting book."

Then Miss Bryfogel did something I had never seen a teacher do before. The first faint whisper of Danger wafted through my ventilating system. She just sat and looked at me for a long time and finally said, very quietly:

"Ralph, I want you to be very truthful with me."

Truthful! Was Miss Bryfogel laboring under the delusion that I was leading her on, toying with her affections? I said:

"Yes?" I was beginning to sweat up my corduroys a little.

"Did you *read* the book or did you copy that from somewhere?" Well, there is one golden rule of all book reporters: never admit you didn't read the book. That is cardinal.

"Yes . . . I read it."

"Where did you get the book? Did you get it out of the library? Did Miss Easter give you that at the library?"

The Animal in us never sleeps. The dog lying on the hearth, eyes half-closed, senses Evil. His back hair rises out of pure instinct. The acrid scent of TROUBLE, faint but real, filtered in through the chalk dust and the lunchbags. My mind, working like a steel trap, leaped into action:

"Well . . . ah . . . ah . . . a kid gave it to me. Yeah, a kid gave it to me!"

Miss Bryfogel closed in.

"A kid? Anybody from class?"

Uh oh! Look out!

"Ah . . . no! A kid . . . I met on the playground at recess. A big kid."

"A big kid gave you that book? That's a big book, isn't it? A thick book."

"Yes, it's the biggest book I ever read."

"And a kid gave it to you? Does he go to Harding School?"

"Ah . . . I never saw that kid before. No, I don't know where he's from. A big kid . . . by the candy store."

Miss Bryfogel swiveled her chair and stared off at the Venetian blinds for what seemed like two years. Slowly she turned back to me.

"A big kid by the candy store . . . gave you Boccaccio's *Decameron?*"

". . . . . yeah."

"Did he say anything to you?"

". . . yeah. Yeah, he said . . . 'Here's a book!' "

"He said 'Here's a book?' And he gave you *that* book?"

". . . . . yeah!"

"By the candy store? Would you recognize him if you saw him again?"

"Well, it . . . it was dark!"

"It was *dark*?"

"Yeah! It was dark! It was . . . ah . . . raining! It was dark!"

Miss Bryfogel took some paper clips out of her top drawer and straightened them up for a while and then said, even more quietly than before:

"Are you telling me the truth?"

". . . . . yeah!"

"WHERE DID YOU GET THAT BOOK!?"

". . . . . home!"

"At home? Do they know that you read this book, at home? Does your mother know?"

". . . . . yeah!"

"Are you sure?"

"Ah . . . . yeah."

Miss Bryfogel picked up her pen and took a sheet of paper out of her desk drawer, and looked at me in a way that Jean Harlow never looked at Clark Gable.

"I'm going to give you a note. You are going to take it home to your mother, and in one hour I will call her to see that she got it."

My socks began to itch. I had been through this note business before!

". . . . . okay."

"Are you telling me the truth?"

"NO!"

This moment, this very instant in time, this millisecond was one of the great turning points in my life, and even then I knew it. Miss Bryfogel leaned back in her swivel chair. She was soft and warm again.

"Ah. Where *did* you get the book?"

"My father's room."

"Oh? Did he know you took it?"

"No."

"You know that you did something wrong, don't you?"

". . . . . . . yeah."

"Did you like the book?"

Somehow I knew that this was a loaded question, a key question.

". . . . . . . yeah."

"I see. It was pretty funny, wasn't it?"

". . . . . . no!"

I was telling the truth. It seemed like for the first time in two years I was telling the truth. I hadn't gotten a single boff from the book. Funny! The only thing that I liked about it was castles and knights. There wasn't a single laugh in it!

"Are you sure you didn't find it funny anywhere?"

"No!"

She knew I was telling the truth.

"Well, that's good. That's much better. Now, will you promise me one thing—that you will not sneak into your parents' room and get books any more, if I promise not to send a note home?"

". . . . . . okay!"

"You can go now."

A great crashing wave of relief roared over me, and, bobbing in the surf, I paddled frantically toward the door. Just before I was through it and out safely:

"Oh, Ralph?"

"What?"—Figuring she is about to welsh on the deal.

"I'm curious. Did you read *all* of it?"

"Yes."

"Well, that's very good. I like to see stick-to-itiveness. Now go out and play."

I sipped my warm Scotch thoughtfully as Miss Bryfogel's voice faded off into the darkness of my memory forever. Arnold Palmer was coming into the 18th three under par, Julius Boros was lining up a putt. My knees were stiff; my soul was sick. Outside somewhere, far off, a siren droned into the distance. Wading through the papers I retrieved the *Book Review Sup-*

plement. Yes, there he was, my old friend, the languorous youth, reclining provocatively. The nun looked down upon him as she had for all these centuries, and somewhere off in the fairy-tale background the cuckolds sang sweetly as they busily built their nests.

XXVII 🦢 POLKA TIME

"I don't get it," Flick said.

"Get what?"

"All that stuff about a cuckold. Isn't that one of them yellow birds they put in clocks?"

I was saved at this point by the sudden entrance of three large, pink-faced youths wearing work jackets and plaid corduroy caps who clattered noisily up to the bar.

"Man, were you hot last week! Boy, was you on!" One shouted at Flick with a noticeable, very familiar Polish accent.

"I throw a *working* ball, Stosh," Flick shot back.

There followed a quick flurry of shouting between all four, regarding bowling, the Game, and a waitress called Ellie. I will spare you that. Finally, one of the men threw a twenty-dollar bill on the bar and bellowed:

"KEEP THEM BEERS COMIN', FLICK, UNTIL WE HOLLER!"

They clumped over into a booth, after priming the jukebox, which immediately boomed out a deafening polka. Flick came back, after delivering the suds.

"That was Stosh and Joe and Yahkey. They're good boys. They work in the Sheet Mill over at Youngstown."

Inwardly I shuddered, realizing how narrowly I had missed being one of the boys myself, forever doomed to the Sheet

Mill where I had once spent a few harrowing centuries one summer.

"They sure throw their dough around, don't they?"

Flick polished a glass as he said:

"The mills are workin'. They get plenty of Tonnage these days."

"Yeah, I can see that."

"Well, they work their ass off for it." Flick defended them.

"Don't I know it! Flick, my back still aches from my days in the mill!"

Flick went on in his Wise Old Bartender manner:

"Once you been there, you never forget it."

The change from the twenty, fives and singles and silver, lay spread out on the bar in a pool of beer. I idly shoved a half-dollar around with my forefinger, making larger and larger concentric circles.

"This dough means a lot of sweat," I said reflectively. "Flick, do you ever get nervous when you look at cash? Like you figure it's going to all of a sudden disappear?"

I smoothed out a beer-soaked five. He leaned forward confidentially and spoke in a low voice to me:

"Don't tell anybody. It is."

"You got that same fear, too?"

There was no doubt that we were now getting close to Home Base. Flick was no longer a Bowler. My credit card had dissolved in my pocket; my English flannel had magically somehow become worn denim; my well-cut sport coat a zippered canvas work jacket. I spoke in a low, tense voice:

"I wonder what those three guys would say if we told 'em about the Kissels?"

The jukebox roared into another polka disk; the three open-faced Simple Toilers in the booth downed their beer merrily as they told their dirty jokes. Flick looked over his shoulder at them in a long, piercing way, turned back to me, and, leaning even closer to my ear, said in a flat voice:

"Not one of 'em would believe it. They'd think we made it up."

XXVIII 🦢 "NEVERMORE," QUOTH THE ASSESSOR, "NEVERMORE. . . ."

Mister Poe's sinister, beady-eyed raven has always been a figure of great speculation and conjecture among literary analysts. How did Poe come up with such an eerie apparition? What did it mean? What was the source of this evil bird? In what dark, cluttered, moldy recess of Poe's mind did it live? Why?

It said little; just bleakly stared, a hooded angel of death and destruction and God knows what.

Any resident of Northern Indiana, of a certain benighted period in history, could tell you in spades where Poe got his raven. The banshee wind rattling the eaves, murky shapes lurking in the gathering gloom; those gleaming inhuman, all-seeing eyes could only mean one thing. Unquestionably, some-where along the line, Poe must have run afoul of an Indiana Personal Property Tax Assessor.

Even at this remove the very word "assessor" sends thin, jangling squeaks of fear through many a Hoosier nervous system. One sure way to clear the street of random Mankind in an Indiana hamlet is simply to bellow at the top of the voice:

"The Assessor is coming!"

Instantly a palpable wave of chill dread causes doors to slam, windows to darken, and souls to quake.

The Indiana Personal Property Tax was *very* personal. In

theory it was also very basic and simple. All personal property was evaluated and taxed. *All* personal property: footstools, footballs, fielders' mitts, and eggbeaters. Everything. The evaluating was done by a specter called the Assessor, who came to call, like the raven, and stared with bleak unblinking eyes. What was even more deadly was that the Assessor was appointed from among the neighborhood itself. Brother against brother, hand to hand, the eternal war of State versus Man was waged. Every two years or so the lines were drawn.

Very few people actually paid the taxes, and there were always rumors of impending doom. Brown envelopes arrived in mailboxes periodically, throwing panic into murky kitchens, but few actually paid. Nonetheless, the Assessor came, with clipboard and ruthless eye.

Year after year the forms were filled; the arid, flat envelopes hidden away in dresser drawers unopened, while the tiny cancer of fear grew heavier and heavier and then waned as no lightning bolts from the State House appeared and life went on.

The Assessor, however, produced some stark moments of truth. A knock on the door; a hush while my mother crept through the living room to peek between the curtains, a strangled whisper:

"The Assessor! For crying out loud, quick. Unplug the radio! Take it down to the coal bin! Hurry up!"

More than one four-year-old kid was crushed under a refrigerator that was being quickly grappled down the back stairs into the basement.

My mother, after the first shock, hissed:

"Don't open your trap! Don't say a word, either of you! Do you understand? Not a WORD!"

In came the Assessor, scanning our worn Oriental rug as he nodded curtly and began to put a price on our world.

"How old is the rug? How long have you had that umbrella stand made out of the hollowed foot of an elephant? How much did it cost? New, that is. I don't have that bridge lamp on last year's list. New, eh? How much is that Flexible Flyer over there worth?"

All over the house, room after room, closet after closet they went, my mother keeping up a running counterpoint:

"Oh, why that's just an old thing. My sister was going to throw it out and I just thought I'd bring it home. Didn't cost anything. We got that refrigerator at the Salvation Army. It burns out all the time and makes a funny noise. This is the first time in months that it's stopped making that funny noise."

"Sounds pretty good to me. Sounds good."

"I can't understand it. We can't even sleep when it's going. We're thinking of giving it away. It's not worth the four dollars we paid for it. What a gyp!"

"Sounds pretty good."

He made a note on his clipboard, smiled thinly, and moved on. He never even bothered to remove his lumpy gray hat.

We had a prop radio that we showed the Assessor every time he came. Our real radio with the magnificent Gothic Cathedral cabinet was lurking under piles of old tires in the basement. We showed him an old battery set that Uncle Tom had had and that was surplus from the Civil War. It had received some of the very first messages that Marconi had tapped out, using a magnetized railroad spike and Edison jars. My mother extolled its virtues:

"It's a sentimental friend of the family. But it's our radio. It uses dry cells and has a propeller on the side that is wind-driven. Since the creek dried up, the battery doesn't work. We get nothing but whistles. But my husband likes it."

"Hmmmmm. That's a genuine Crosley Bandbox. Beautiful carved cabinet there. Bird's-eye oak. Looks hand-rubbed."

"Look where the mice ate out the back here. See, I stick this Sears Roebuck catalog behind so nobody can see it."

She banged the cabinet hollowly, hoping it would crack. Another enigmatic smile, and then the rug:

"Say, that's not a bad-looking rug you have there. Oriental, isn't it?"

"Now wait a minute. Look, here's the place where the hole was burned, where Uncle Carl dropped his pipe and burnt the hole in there. Where the beer was spilled."

She moved the rickety, moth-eaten overstuffed davenport back to show him the place that she tried to hide from the rest of the world.

"Oh well, they could fix that. A couple of dollars and they'll reweave that like nothing. Oriental, isn't it?"

He plucked at the fringe, fingering it appreciatively like a connoisseur of fine linens and tapestries or an Armenian rug dealer coming across a rare find. My mother's panic rose.

"Say, that's a nice picture up there. Look at that—a sailboat, isn't it? That's a lovely picture. It's an original, isn't it?"

My mother fended off this blow:

"Original my foot! Original Woolworth."

On it went, my mother systematically degrading our lives by simply telling the truth. She invented nothing. Before the Assessor came, we always pretended that the holes in the rug didn't exist and the picture wasn't an original Woolworth; the refrigerator not a crummy piece of tin that soured milk and curdled cream. Here she was, laying it down—the truth. And I am hearing it; a kid. Who loved his home and the things in it.

"No, Ma! Ma, it's our refrigerator! It has great ice cubes! And our great rug! I lay on it and follow the pattern with my eyes! It's a beautiful rug! With gold fringe! Ma, it's not a terrible rug!!"

Finally the Assessor closed his book.

"Well, that's it. You're not doing too bad."

His feet dragged over our threadbare carpet, the worn linoleum, and out into the cold for another two years. The Assessor had come and gone.

A few hours later my father got the full report as he breezed in through the kitchen door, smelling of the outside and the office.

"What's new?"

"The Assessor was here."

"WHAT!"

He stopped in his tracks, his face suddenly white.

"The Assessor was here."

The yellow light bulb grew dimmer. The refrigerator sighed

deeply, going into action with a squeak of the pulley and thump of the compressor. The floor shook. Over the roar my father shouted:

"Who was it?"

"That tall thin man who lives in that brick house on the other side of the Schwartzes. Around the back, over the garage."

"Oh, I've seen him around."

He slowly removed his overcoat and plumped down in the one kitchen chair that was not broken somewhere, somehow.

"Did you get the radio in the coal bin before he got in?"

"Yep."

"D'you think he saw it down there?"

"I don't know. He looked in the coal bin."

There was a terrible fear that somehow somebody would get the impression that we lived like human beings.

"What's for supper?"

"Meat loaf."

Gradually the chill thawed. Finally it faded out completely as the months went by. Then, out of the blue, without so much as a murmur of thunder on the horizon, the hammer fell.

It was a crackling sunny clear-eyed Friday afternoon. Our mosquito swarm of kids slowly worked its way toward home, kicking, hollering, throwing stuff, looking for junk, drifting like rain through the alleys, over fences, under porches, down innumerable shortcuts; Schwartz, Flick, Alex, Junior Kissel, me, and a covey of lesser satellites.

At last we reached the block, ready to rush in to individual houses, grab some Graham crackers or fig newtons and out the back doors to begin whatever game was being played at that moment in time. Throwing rocks was an important way of getting home. Rocks were thrown at a regular established set of targets—Mrs. Schaeffer's birdhouse, Pulaski's Coca-Cola sign, and every telephone pole that got in our way. Our arms were sharp and rubbery and the rocks bounced and clanged. Every night the sparrows, robins, and wrens ducked and dodged, squawking raucously, urging us on, taunting, a barrel-rolling and skittering through the ambient air amid a hail of whizzing clinkers.

Occasionally a lucky shot shattered an insulator high up amid the crisscrossing tangle of telephone wires and then a frenzied roar of flight up the alley, out of the danger zone. Particularly delectable were the posters that festooned fence posts, garages, and telephone poles. Fat-faced seekers of county office were constantly peppered with a steady barrage of anything that could be picked up and hurled.

"Watch me get old Corngrass. In the ear!"

ZZzzzziiiizzzzz . . . THWONK!

"Wowie, what a lucky shot!"

"Lucky! That's the third night in a row I got him. Lucky! Watch THIS!"

ZZZiiizzz K-THONK BONK!

Another blow for Anarchy was struck. Old Corngrass had run for mayor for as long as anyone could remember, each year using the same stolid, toad-like portrait; hair precisely parted with a thin, naked line down the middle of his skull, rimless glasses gleaming dully before beady, staring eyes. He never made it, maybe because he was so easy to hit with rocks.

Now we were on home turf.

"Watch me get that red one."

ZZizzzz—the rock whistled past a new red cardboard poster, small, compact, with no picture.

ZZzzziiizzz

SSSSSiissss

Whooosh

Three projectiles simultaneously bracketed the target. All missed. We drifted idly toward the telephone pole, unaware of the disaster that was about to strike us all.

Flick arched an apple core toward the sign. It splatted on the post a few inches high. Schwartz slanted a bottle cap upward, curving nicely, trailing after a passing bluejay who yawked distainfully and continued on.

I don't know who read it first. Maybe we all did; black print on red poster card.

SHERIFF'S SALE

TO BE SOLD AT AUCTION. TOMORROW AT ELEVEN AM ON THE
PREMISES AT 8745 CLEVELAND STREET THE GOODS AND TOTAL
CHATTELS OF LUDLOW L. KISSEL OF THAT ADDRESS WILL BE
AUCTIONED AT SHERIFF'S SALE. THE SUM REALIZED TO DEFRAY
DEFAULTED PERSONAL PROPERTY TAXES. THE SALE WILL BE
PUBLIC, COMMENCING AT ELEVEN AM. BY ORDER OF THE AS-
SESSOR'S OFFICE.

> BUREAU OF TAXATION,
> STATE OF INDIANA.

That was all. It was enough. None of us had ever seen a sign
like this before, but our instincts, deep and animal-like, told us
that it was serious; a dangerous sign. Other dangerous signs
showed up from time to time on front porches and screen doors.
QUARANTINED—DIPHTHERIA. SCARLET FEVER. SMALLPOX. This was
one of those, but different, somehow worse.

The neighborhood was unusually quiet, we noticed for the
first time. Flick dropped a rock at his feet with a hollow clunk.
Junior Kissel, without a word, turned and ran, cutting across the
street, up the sidewalk, disappearing toward his house. Halfway
down the block another identical sign gleamed in the bright
sunshine. Schwartz, in an odd scared voice, broke the silence:

"What's an auction?"

"I don't know. Some kind of card game or something," Flick
answered.

"Maybe it's like on the radio. That Lucky Strike auctioneer.
. . ." Schwartz said.

"I don't think so," I said.

We broke up and headed for home, through the quiet hushed
neighborhood. My mother was down in the basement, wringing
out the wash in the gray, murky gloom, the concrete floor
around her wet and flecked with patches of dank soapsuds. The
old Thor washing machine muttered as it squeezed the clammy
water from overalls, pillow cases, and housedresses. Her face was
red from the steam and soap as she bent over the basket, twisting each garment for the final drops. Weak sunlight filtered in

through the narrow basement, ground-level windows fading out in the perpetual dark of the basement.

"Ma, what's an auction?"

She straightened up, never missing a beat as she snaked a long, heavy bedsheet through the rubber rollers.

"What's a what?"

"What's an auction?"

"An auction?"

"Yeah, what's an auction?"

"Why?"

She was talking in her half-hearing, hardly listening, working, answering-silly-questions MOTHER voice.

"Well, there's a sign on the telephone pole that says they're going to have an auction at Mr. Kissel's house. The Sheriff is going to be there."

The sheet squished on for what seemed like a long time. Suddenly she reached over quickly, snapping off the washer with a movement she had used for years. The basement was deathly still. She turned and looked right at me. Her voice sounded strange.

"What did you say? What was that? What are you talking about?"

"There's a sign on the telephone post that says they're having an auction at Mr. Kissel's house. With the Sheriff. And it says. . . ." Now I was scared.

She rushed up the basement stairs, wiping her hands on her apron as she went.

"Don't leave the house until I come back."

She was gone, out the back door. I was alone in the kitchen now, looking out the window over at the Kissel's house where she had gone. Another lady, tall, skinny Mrs. Anderson crossed the alley and disappeared into the house. No kids played in the yards. No radios were turned on as they always were. My kid brother came up through the back door into the kitchen where I stood on tiptoes, watching the Kissel house.

"What's wrong?" he asked.

"I don't know. Mom said not to go out."

He said nothing more. Finally, after what seemed like hours, she came into the kitchen and without saying a word began making supper. That night we ate quickly. Almost immediately after the dishes were washed we were sent to bed, and for the first time in a long while did not cause the usual protesting uproar.

Late that night I could hear my mother and father talking in low tones in the living room, through the closed door, until I fell asleep.

Somehow the sun always shines on Saturdays in Indiana. Outside the bedroom window a yelling crowd of spatsies, the generic Kid name for sparrows, argued, swore, made clattering love. Out in the kitchen water ran and pots banged.

At first when the full delicious impact swept over me that it was Saturday—no school today—blessed, fantastic Saturday and that this afternoon Flick and Junior and I would ride the range with Roy Rogers and Trigger at the Orpheum, I reached over in ecstasy, belting my brother in the ribs, ready for action. He groaned almost at the same time that I remembered something funny was going to happen today.

I got up and padded into the kitchen where breakfast was already on the table. The Old Man, dressed in his Saturday clothes, was halfway through his eggs. Drifting through the kitchen window from somewhere outside came the roar of a truck motor backing and shifting. My mother, over near the sink, looked out.

"They're here."

My father dropped his fork, circled the table, and peered from the other window. I stood on tiptoes.

At an angle, almost filling the whole of their sandy, weedy backyard stood a tall, gray official-looking truck, behind the Kissel's house. Men in overalls moved in and out the back door, carrying boxes and barrels. Already piled high in the sunlight, warped, cracked, and stained with the chewing of the years, stood the Kissel furniture. The men struggled under loads of nondescript junk, back and forth, from the basement to the attic, from the garage to the kitchen.

The sheriff drove up in a black Ford with a white star on the door and got out. He didn't look like a movie sheriff at all, being fat and wearing a long, grayish overcoat. He really looked more like a dentist than a sheriff. He had two men with him; one a tall, thin, red-faced man with eyes that popped, who began making a list in a notebook. The other set up a kind of platform behind the back porch. It folded, and looked as though it had been used. One of the workmen brought out a microphone and hooked up a leatherette-covered speaker on the ground near the truck. We watched from behind the geraniums.

From behind geraniums all over the neighborhood other eyes watched. Strange people began arriving in dented blue cars, panel trucks; some just wallking, carrying baskets and bags. They were the first Auction Followers we had ever seen. There is a race of Human Vulture that lives off the disaster and defeat of others, picking the bones clean. They perform a necessary function, just as any scavenger does. Those on the scene early were rummaging through the piles of coffee pots, old tires, potted ferns, and Mr. Kissel's toolbox which he carried to the roundhouse on the few days he worked every month.

"There's Mr. Kissel's bottle-capper," I said, breaking the silence in the kitchen.

"Yeah," my father answered, continuing to stare into the bright sunshine.

Mr. Kissel made Home Brew and when we played in Junior Kissel's basement we always fooled around with his bottle-capper, capping bottles of water, pretending we were bootleggers. Now the bottle-capper lay in the yard next to Mrs. Kissel's old Hoover vacuum cleaner.

Old furniture under the light of a bright sky seems more tired and worn than anything else I know. In an eerie way more human, too. The crowd was getting bigger by the minute. Some carried lunches; others babies. They were excited and anxious for the action to begin. None of the neighbors showed up. At least they weren't in the crowd that pushed and waited around the platform. They were strangers. It doesn't pay for vultures to make friends.

My kid brother wanted to go out and join in the fun, but the Old Man said:

"We'll go out and play Catch after the people go. You stay here until they leave."

He was a dedicated Catch player. Any time he announced that we were going to play Catch kids listened, and hunted for their mitts. His slider was the best I've ever seen outside of Comiskey Park.

The sheriff got up on the platform to begin the proceedings, his voice echoing hollowly among the sagging garage doors, the drooping clothespoles, and the limp wetwash. The auctioneer began with a brass table lamp, the one we used to see through their dining-room window, with the green shade. It was quickly bought. The crowd moved in excitement as the auctioneer went into high gear. Mrs. Kissel's enamel kitchen table went for seventy cents.

Once my father turned to my mother and said:

"I guess they're not home. I don't see them anywhere."

She didn't answer, but I knew that Junior Kissel wasn't around.

Someone bought Grandpa Kissel's World War I helmet which Mr. Kissel had hung on the inside of the basement door. It was a great thing to play with. I guess someone bought it for their kid. No one wanted the mattress, a lumpy, yellow-stained, bluestriped heirloom that had come down from Mrs. Kissel's parents and had seen the raising of ten kids. It lay under the truck bed, shoved out of the way while the more valuable items were bartered off.

Rusty saws, an old single-barreled 12-gauge shotgun that brought four dollars, a spectacular oil tablecloth with red ornamental lettering: A CENTURY OF PROGRESS. CHICAGO WORLD'S FAIR, with a gold picture of the Hall of Science. The bidding for this one was sharp and bitter.

Finally it was over. It didn't last long, maybe forty-five minutes or so, but when it was over the end was definite. The sheriff got up and announced that the auction was now officially completed. He mentioned an address where another was scheduled in a day or two, on the west side of town. The people got back into their cars, trucks, station wagons and left as quickly as they had come, loaded down with their loot.

Without confusion or hesitation the men and the sheriff packed away their gear like a well-practiced team, and were gone. All that remained in the backyard was a jumble of lunch bags, pop bottles, chicken bones, crushed cartons, empty barrels, and the mattress.

By now it was almost lunchtime and I was already getting hungry. My mother, watching the final truck disappear, said:

"Oh well."

The Old Man went down into the basement to get his glove for the game of Catch.

Later that afternoon someone said that the Kissels had gone to Lowell, a town a few miles away, to spend the weekend with Mrs. Kissel's brother-in-law and sister. They never came back. Somewhere along about the middle of the next week a FOR RENT sign appeared on the Kissels' front door. Not long afterward a new family moved in. We never saw Junior Kissel again.

XXIX › THE POSSE RIDES AGAIN

I glanced at my stainless-steel Rolex, noting that it was getting along toward 4:00, Shift-Change time. I could see that Flick was showing the tenseness of a man about to swing into action.

"I'll tell you one thing," Flick said, "I keep up with the bills. I don't owe nobody. Just a minute; I'll be right back."

He moved on down the bar, checking his ammunition for the first wave of serious drinkers, which would arrive within the half hour. I looked again at my Rolex. For some reason I didn't quite recognize it at first as belonging to *my* arm, and to be honest I wasn't sure that it *was* even my arm. Somehow that sleeve and that watch all belonged in New York. Another world. Back there they probably would not even believe there *was* such a man as Flick. Or Stosh, or Kissel, or Yahkey. They'd probably figure I made 'em all up.

I fleetingly thought, Maybe I should try to tell Flick about *Les Misérables des Frites*, and Henri, the lascivious head-waiter. How could I tell him about the expense account, and how hardly anybody I knew ever paid for anything, ever, and that the vast Gravy Train they were on considered cash itself to be vaguely insulting and out of date. I figured it was no use.

In the booth, the three Sheet-Metal men began hollering at Flick, who looked up from his inventory and yelled back:

"HOLD YER WATER, FER CHRISSAKE! I GOT BETTER THINGS
TO DO THAN FEED YOU BASTARDS ALL DAY!"

The red-faced one wearing an orange safety helmet shouted:
"TURN ONNA TV, FLICK! WHAT THE HELL YOU GOT IT FOR?"

This exchange took place at full voice, since the jukebox was
shaking the floor.

"I'LL TURN IT ON WHEN I'M DAMN GOOD AND READY!"

I wondered briefly how Flick would get along with Henri, the
effete and painfully elegant headwaiter who controlled the entire
East Side of New York.

Flick finally reached up and snapped on the switch of the
monster color TV set that hung high over the bar mirror. It
seemed to warm up instantly. A thundering herd of posse riders
roared across the screen. Mister Clean appeared briefly, and disappeared. Again the posse thundered, this time in the opposite
direction, their guns roaring above the booming polka. Obviously
conversation was out of the question, or at least it had become
somewhat hazardous.

There is something about TV sets in bars that makes even
sane people look at them. I sipped what seemed to be at least
my thirtieth beer of the afternoon, staring upward at a moon-
faced cowboy strumming a guitar. Behind him I could see old
familiar country that I knew like the back of my hand. Those
Hollywood back lots were as familiar as my own backyard, when
I was a kid.

Flick finished his bottle-checking, armed himself with a clean
bar rag, and stood briefly looking up at another posse, this time
roaring directly at us, the puffs of their guns, their square jaws,
the flying hoofs blending well with the eternal jukebox. We both
watched for a long moment.

"I seen it."

"So have I. If I remember correctly, Flick, that fat guy on
the left is going to get shot. He. . . ."

Just as I said it, the fat guy spun into the air, dying
spectacularly as cowboy extras always do, clutching at the clouds,
slipping into the sagebrush, milking his scene as far as he could
under union rules.

"Yep. I seen it."

Flick turned back from the set with the air of a man adding a period at the end of a sentence.

I, however, continued to stare at the set. It seemed one of those eerie coincidences that happen once in a while, and that cause ladies who wear tennis shoes to believe in ESP, flying saucers, and swamis. I was not sure whether I should bring it up, else Flick suspect that I had had at least one beer too many. I could see he was the kind of bartender who did not serve drunks, but probably tossed them by the scruff of their neck out into the gale.

"Flick, I have seen that picture, too."

"Yep. I seen it," Flick said.

"You know, I have a feeling that I saw it with *you*."

He looked back up at the set again for a long moment, as though to check his memory. The posse thundered down a ravine, diagonally this time, from left to right. Finally he said reflectively:

"By God, I think you're right. It played with *Rhythm on the Prairie*, with Dick Foran. And they had Bob Steele, in person."

We both disappeared briefly into our own dream world, eventually broken by Flick, who said:

"That was the day Schwartz threw up in the drinking fountain in the lobby."

"Correct! That's right."

We returned to the posse for a bit, and finally I had to ask a question that was on my mind ever since the first gunshot.

"Flick, did Doppler ever show his face around here again?" He turned back to me, his expression as grim as any of those hard-faced men riding in that eternal posse, pursuing endless Badguys through the wilds of MGM Land.

"Doppler?"

His voice snapped like Ken Maynard biting out the name of a sheep rustler.

"He wouldn't *dare* show up around here. They'd string him up in a minute."

XXX &⤳ LEOPOLD DOPPLER AND THE GREAT ORPHEUM GRAVY BOAT RIOT

Five thousand years from now, when future archaeologists are picking and scraping among the shards and the midden heaps, attempting to put together the mosaic of the rich, full life led by twentieth-century man, they will come across many a mystery that is impenetrable even to those who lived through it. A cracked fragment of a Little Orphan Annie Ovaltine Shake-Up Mug, a Shirley Temple Cream Pitcher, a heavily corroded Tom Mix Lucky Horse-Shoe Nail Ring, an incomplete set of Gilbert Roland/Pola Negri/Thomas Meighan Movie Star Sterling Silver Teaspoons with Embossed Autographs will undoubtedly be key items in files marked:

INEXPLICABLE ABORTIVE RELIGIOUS OBJECTS FOUND IN GREAT NUMBERS, YET WITH NO SEEMING DIRECT CONNECTION WITH THE GREATER PHILOSOPHICAL CURRENTS OF THE TIME

But we will know, won't we?

Not long ago, in a shabby motel in New England, I sat down on a cold, rainy dawn to a bowl of soggy Wheaties and found myself suddenly, and for no reason, thinking of Rochelle Hudson. Rochelle Hudson! She had not entered my conscious musings since the age of eight. The sound of traffic roaring by on the Maine Turnpike reminded me that Reality was only a hundred yards away. As I spooned up more of the cereal that Jack Armstrong ate and that Hudson High won its football games for, I hurled Rochelle Hudson from my mind. Instantly she was replaced by Warner Oland, the original and definitive Charlie Chan. He grinned at me from under his Homburg, enigmatically, and disappeared. There stood Judge Hardy, about to have a man-to-man talk with either me or Mickey Rooney. The thump of a football, and roly-poly Jack Oakie, wearing a white sweater with a big block C, picked up his megaphone and started a Locomotive as Tom Brown, his arm in a sling, June Preiser clinging to his jersey, trotted out on the gridiron—Center College six points behind and only four seconds left in the game! The crowd roared, blending with the sound of a huge Diesel bellowing by on its way to Augusta.

I was yanked back to the Now momentarily as a plate of toast was clanked down next to my coffee. But I could not fight it. Without reason or rhyme the film unwound in my subconscious, picking up the tempo of the thundering traffic on the great turnpike, as Jimmy Cagney, his Maserati in flames, roared past the immense grandstands at Indianapolis, the mob screaming for blood, his oil line broken, his faithful mechanic—Frank McHugh—dying of burns in the cockpit next to him. The checkered flag fell as Jimmy, his goggles misted from streaming gasoline, a thin, ironical smile on his lips, swerved into the pits. Out stepped Alan Hale, rugged, silver-haired, beaming, in the full-dress uniform of the Royal Canadian Mounted. With him, riding easy in the saddle, was Dick Foran. And a string of broad-chested Malemute dogs howled as they headed into the great forest after another Fugitive from Justice.

With an enormous conscious wrench of will power I struggled to break this ridiculous montage of fantasies that continued to crowd irresistibly in upon me. I could not get my mind off these shifting, kaleidoscopic images. I tried to concentrate on my road map as I finished the Wheaties, and the harder I stared at the red lines the more they seemed to resemble Pat O'Brien, in the uniform of a Navy Chief, barking out orders to Wallace Beery.

What the hell is this!? I am a grownup, hard-hitting, *H*ip contemporary man, and I have no time for such transient, imbecilic time wasters.

I swished my plastic spoon around the bottom of the bowl to scoop up the last few spongy flakes, and it was at that instant that I *knew*. It was the bowl *itself* that had caused Rochelle Hudson to make an unscheduled guest appearance!

I stared hard at it. It was unmistakable, a bowl of remarkably aggressive ugliness, made of a distinctive type of dark green glass, embossed with swollen lumps and sworls representing the fruits of the vine and the abundance of Nature. A bowl that had but one meaning. I peered at it long and hard. Yes, there was no mistake. It was genuine—a mint-condition, vintage Movie Dish Night Premium Gift Bowl.

I glanced the length of the lunch counter at the proprietor who lounged listlessly next to the coffee urn, watching the rain fall outside on his gravel driveway. We were alone. I could not resist it.

"Excuse me, but what kind of bowl is this?" I asked.

He looked up.

"What do you mean what kind of bowl? Glass."

"Yeah. I *know* it's glass. But where did you get it?"

"Whattaya mean. . . . are you an Inspector?"

I never knew there were Cereal Bowl Inspectors working the Maine Turnpike.

"No. It's just that you don't see bowls like this very often."

He looked back out at the rain and I knew that our conversation was at an end. I stirred my coffee and examined the green-glass monstrosity lovingly as I faintly heard Myrna Loy's mocking voice twitting William Powell through the sounds of the radio in the kitchen, which was playing a Beatle record.

Yes, in attics and cellars and kitchen cupboards throughout the length and breadth of America there are still remnants, bits and pieces of Movie Dish Night DeLuxe Dinnerware Sets, some green glass, others blood red, a few a strange, pearlescent orange, but all united in universal ugliness. Ugliness unfettered, unrestrained by effete taste, as direct and uncluttered as a Johnny Weissmuller scenario. The kind of ugliness so pure and distilled that it shines with the golden, radiant light of the Pure in Heart and the Simple of Mind; ugliness so stark and clean that it becomes beautiful in its clarity. And the sellers of beauty have never had it easy in this, or any other, age. Mr. Doppler was no exception.

Mr. Doppler! My God, I even remembered his name. But then, how could I forget it? I gazed mistily into the cloudy depths of the glass receptacle and the images of that fateful night began to emerge from the milky film that lined the bottom. Mr. Doppler and the Great Gravy Boat Riot! Eerily, faintly, the radio in the kitchen began to play Artie Shaw's "Begin the Beguine," and the story slowly all came back to me.

Mr. Doppler operated the Orpheum Theater, a tiny bastion of dreams and fantasies, a fragile light of human aspiration in the howling darkness of the great American Midwest where I festered and grew as a youth. Even now the word "Orpheum" sends tiny shivers of anticipation and excitement up the ventilation pipes of my soul. And Mr. Doppler, like some mythical God, reigned over his magnetic palace of dreams, fighting the good fight alone and uncheered. He was rarely seen in person. His name, however, always stood at the head of the program throwaways that landed on the porch every Monday afternoon, outlining the Orpheum's schedule of mirages for the following week. In Roman letters surrounded by cherubs blowing trumpets and a kind of Egyptian architectural arch, festooned with grapes and tiny cornucopias and presided over by a pair of blurred Greco-Zanuck Tragedy-Comedy masks, would appear the proclamation:

LEOPOLD DOPPLER PRESENTS

This smudgy, dog-eared schedule was kept next to every icebox in the county, for ready reference and to settle arguments of a Theological nature.

Mr. Doppler was in direct communion with Dennis Morgan, and he, personally, had a hand in Roy Rogers' affairs. Hollywood was a mysterious thing in those days, even more so than today, and for good reason. It *was* more mysterious, and it was the time of the Great Depression. People read *Photoplay* and *Screen Romances* and other dream journals as seriously as today they digest the *New Republic, Time,* the *Realist:* contemporary fantasy almanacs. One time my Aunt Clara lapped the entire field at Christmas by giving my grandmother a two-year subscription to *Real Screen Tales.*

So night after night the Faithful would gather, bearing sacks of Butterfinger bars and salami sandwiches, to huddle together in the darkness, cradled in Mr. Doppler's gum-encrusted seats, staring with eyes wide with longing and lit with the pure light of total belief at the flickering image of Ginger Rogers, dressed in a long, flowing, sequin-covered gown, swirling endlessly atop a piano with wasp-waisted Fred Astaire, flicking an ivory cane carelessly and spinning his tall silk hat as he sang, in a high, squeaky voice, "The Carioca." In the darkness the sound of girdles creaking in desire and the cracking of Wrigley's Spearmint in excitement provided a soft but subtle counterpoint to Sam Goldwyn's hissing sound track.

Outside those sacred doors crouched the pale gray wolf of Reality and the Depression. On the skyline the dark, sullen hulk of the steel mills lay silent and smokeless, like some ancient volcano that had burnt itself out, while the natives roamed the empty streets and told wondrous tales of the time when the skies were lit by the fires of the steel crucibles. And there was something that occupied them all, called Work. Even the word "Work" itself had an almost religious, mythological tone.

On Saturdays the congregation consisted entirely of kids. At least during the daylight hours. The carved Moorish doors of the Orpheum were flung wide from 10 A.M. on to the moiling rabble who came to spend the entire day, and weekend if possible. Three cowboy pictures, featuring such luminaries as Roy Rogers, Bob Steele, and Ken Maynard galloping endlessly over the back lots of dusty Los Angeles real estate, firing countless rounds of black-smoke blank cartridges, the sound track turned up to deafening volume, the thunder of movie horses, the screams and

grunts of the wounded and dying mingled with the steady uproar of the popcorn machine and the occasional outbreak of a
fistfight in the balcony and an incessant two-way traffic up and
down the aisles to the plumbing facilities. The muffled curses
of the ushers clubbing the more violent into submission
provided those of us who were there with a great and accurate
foretaste of life to come. More than one kid, caught up in the
inchoate intricacies of a Republic picture Cowboy plot, found
himself torn between answering an urgent call of Nature or missing the final defeat of the treacherous sheep ranchers, and had
to make a bitter and crucial decision. It almost invariably went
one way. Many a kid had to skulk damply down back alleys on
the way home in total darkness to avoid public humiliation, his
corduroy knickers squishing limply as he crept from garage to
garage, from chicken house to chicken house, hoping against
hope that the spanking breeze from the lake would dehydrate
him in time.

Clamped in his seat from 10 A.M. to well past 7 P.M., or just
before the Greasy Love Stuff came on, a kid swirled in a mael-
strom of excitement and convulsive passion that has left a last-
ing mark on all who sat in attendance. There are countless men
today, and not a few women, who have what they euphemisti-
cally call "bad knees," resulting from a malady just recently
diagnosed as Triple Feature Paralysis, a knee permanently as-
suming a lambent *L* shape with concomitant bruises and con-
tusions resulting from action in the seat ahead, accompanied by
a quick, snapping cramp of the upper buttocks. Its symptoms
are unmistakable.

Strategically spaced between the Cowboy epics were episodes
of Flash Gordon and Superman serials to quell the troops between rounds of gunfire and volleys of guitar-playing. Outright
anger rolled in waves from the audience invariably the instant
Gene Autry took up his Sears Roebuck melody box to sing "Red
River Valley" through his noble Roman nose. It was a distinctly
Anti-Sentimental crowd. Luckily Autry worked in the pre-
Switchblade era, but there were other means to vent aggression
on a beaded screen. As the first notes of the steel guitar rolled

out over the throng, a shower of bottle caps and chocolate-covered raisins arched through the hazy, flickering beam of light that cut the darkness above our heads. The ushers leaped forward at the ready, but by then the gunfire had reasserted itself and blessed Violence stilled the mob. It was early TV, but with far more audience participation.

A colossal high point came along about the third running of *Thunder on the Prairie* starring Johnny Mack Brown. The lights would go up in the house illuminating a scene of carnage and juvenile debauchery unrivaled in the most decadent day of the Roman downfall. Knee-deep in Baby Ruth wrappers, sated with popcorn, jaws aching from a six-hour session of bubble-gum chewing, we sat holding our Ticket Stub, waiting for the fateful drawing. On stage was wheeled a chicken-wire drum, filled with torn tickets, and behind a silver, bullet-shaped microphone appeared the slight but commanding black-clad, balding figure of the great, legendary Mr. Doppler himself. In person. Behind him was piled the Loot for that day: Chicago roller bearing roller skates, Hack Wilson model fielders' mitts, Benjamin air rifles, and, of course, the Grand Prize—a Columbia bicycle with balloon tires and two-tone iridescent paint job.

Mr. Doppler grabbed his audience hard and fast with his opening line, the instinct of a sure-born Showman blazing through:

"Shut up in the balcony!"

To a kid we scrunched forward in our teetery seats, Hershey bars clasped frozen in midair, dripping between unheeding fingers. Ticket stub held at ready, we waited expectantly for our number to be called.

Two ushers on stage spun the drum and a volunteer, usually a wiry, pimply-faced lout from the first two or three rows, pulled the tickets while Mr. Doppler, milking each drawn number for all it was worth, built the drama of expectancy and chance as surely and skillfully as only a true Dramatist can.

At long last, the Grand Prize. The house lights dimmed and went out. Wheeled center stage in the brilliant blue-white vaudeville spot, it stood alone and coldly inaccessible. A vast hush fell on the huddled throng, broken only by the soft, muted squishing of Mary Janes being ground to bits by loose milk teeth. All things hung suspended as the drum spun and slowed and finally stopped. Doppler raised his hand imperiously in the way that Mighty Casey must have, quelling the multitude as the crucial moment approached. Absolute silence as the volunteer's grubby claw fished among the ticket stubs, searching for his own, no doubt, finally drawing from the chicken-wire cage a tiny orange fleck of torn paper. He solemnly handed it to the usher, who ceremoniously presented it to Mr. Doppler. The sun stood still in the firmament.

Mr. Doppler gazed for a moment at the stub and then looked meaningfully out over the audience and back again to the stub.

His voice, ringing with feedback, intoned:

"The winning number is . . . *D*. . . ."

A pregnant pause. We hunched forward as one man, seats creaking in unison. *All* our tickets began with *D!*

"*D* . . . Seven. . . ."

Muffled groans, anguished outcries, seats slammed angrily in isolated spots. Doppler raised his eyes menacingly. Again silence.

"*D* . . . Seven . . . Oh. . . ."

More screams and thumps. My palm itched sweatily. I was still in the running. This could be the week!

Mr. Doppler continued, pretending to have difficulty in reading the number.

"*D* . . . Seven . . . Oh . . . let's see. This is *D*-Seven-Oh-*Three*. . . ."

On a rising inflection, the audience now in a state of frenzy, scattered wails of lament and thuds of bodies falling amid popcorn cartons as Doppler closed with a smashing finish, his voice rising to a crescendo.

"*D*-Seven-Oh-Three-EIGHT!"

I sank back into my seat as a high thin squeak came from somewhere near the EXIT sign to the left of the popcorn stand. A great roar arose among the defeated as a tiny, limp figure, carried down the aisle by jubilant companions, rushed toward the stage, yipping as they came. My God! It was a girl!

Muttered obscenities in the darkness. The mob was now in an angry mood at this unexpected turn of events. A girl! Flick, next to me, half-rose in his cockpit, his meat hook poised to hurl the remains of a taffy apple onstage as a statement of defiance. The sharp bark of an usher in the aisle catching him in midair: "Siddown!"

The flashlight beam caught him, taffy apple cocked, jaw set. He sat, sheepishly.

Onstage it was all anti-climax, and Mr. Doppler knew it. Quickly wrapping up the scene, he hurried the bicycle, kids, and ushers offstage and darkness fell. As we prepared for the first volley of the fourth feature of the afternoon. It was again the beating surf of crackling paper wrappings, the steady crunch crunch crunch of mastication picked up in tempo and blended into the fanfare of bugles superimposed on the opening credits and the great classic line:

REPUBLIC PICTURES PRESENTS

As the Longest Day wore on, time completely obliterated, the Outside World non-existent, no day, no night, just the thunder of the Pursued and the Pursuers and the crunch of fist meeting jaw and the crash of bottle hurled through barroom mirror roared ever onward. Life was complete. Occasionally a menacing form roamed up and down the aisles, searching for a huddled fugitive from supper. A sharp outcry in the darkness and a kid would be dragged, kicking and screaming, protestingly toward the EXIT sign and back into life.

Then, finally, three quick Mighty Mouse cartoons in succession as a capper for the road, and it was all over for another week. Back out in the real world at last splinter bands of bloated, sticky, Tootsie Roll-filled kids drifted homeward, recounting in absolute detail every labyrinthine twist and turn of each feature, reliving each fistfight and walkdown, each ambush and thunderous escape in the embattled stagecoach as the ideological arguments began. The Ken Maynard faction snorting derisively at the lesser Bob Steele contingent. An occasional Roy Rogers nut would sing nostalgically, nasally, "On The Streets Of Laredo." A few holdouts for Tim Holt, outnumbered but game, all united finally in UNIVERSAL distain for the effete Dick Foran and Gene Autry.

The great day was almost over. We all had to face the ordeal of trying to stuff down baked beans and spare ribs at supper, which was not easy on top of four Milky Ways and a rich compost heap of other assorted indigestibles drifting like some great glacier down through our digestive systems.

The uproar on Saturday afternoons at the Orpheum was as nothing compared to the constant hoopla and razzmatazz of the rest of the week, when Mr. Doppler's Orpheum would rise to a fever pitch of excitement. Very little of it had anything to do with actual movies, although the Orpheum pretended that it was in the Film business and so did the customers.

Monday night, immediately after supper, the Faithful—or at least one contingent of them—would scurry through the darkening streets toward the sacred temple to play Screeno. I have heard that in other movie houses this was called Keeno, but Mr. Doppler was a Fundamentalist. As the Judy Canova fans pushed through the turnstiles, they would be handed a crude sheet of cardboard ruled off in squares, with the great black letters:

SCREENO! EVERYBODY HAS A CHANCE TO WIN! WATCH YOUR NUMBERS!

Next to the door was a wastebasket filled with corn kernels. Each lover of the Cinematic Art would grab a handful on his way in to the humid arena of the Fun Palace, slide down in his seat, and wait for the action.

About 7 P.M. on would come the Movietone News, with the bathing beauties and the horse races, funny goose-stepping comic soldiers wearing scuttle helmets marching in phalanxes to the sound of *"Deutschland Über Alles,"* Westbrook Van Vorhees and the Voice of Doom. Ten minutes of previews of coming attractions, featuring music by the Coming Attractions Band, and the first feature would begin, with Ben Blue chasing Judy Canova around a haystack as the mob rustled their cards and crunched on corn kernels in keen anticipation of the delights that were to follow.

By the time Judy had deafened the multitude and the eighth reel spun out, the moment of exultation arrived. The house lights would go on; the popcorn bags stashed, and there would be a moment of suspended animation while the real reason all were there was getting under way. On stage the great white screen stood empty. Mr. Doppler could be heard—himself!—testing the PA system, his rich, dynamic voice:

"Hello, test. Hello, test. One-Two-Three-Four. Can you hear me up in the booth, Fred?"

And then, silence. Next on screen a great blue and red numbered wheel appeared, with an enormous yellow pointer, and Mr. Doppler would get right down to business.

"All right, folks, it's time once again to play the Fun game, Screeno. Anyone filling out a diagonal or horizontal line with corn kernels wins a magnificent grocery prize. Yell out 'Screeno.' Be sure to check your numbers. And now, here we go!"

A spectacular fanfare would wow into the sound system, since Doppler really believed in Production all the way, and the evening would start. On the screen the pointer, a yellow blur, spun as band music played softly behind. Everyone leaned forward in their seats, their cards held at ready as they waited for the call of Fate and Riches to lay its golden breath on their fevered, movie-loving brows. The pointer slowed, and stopped, and Doppler's voice intoned:

"The first number is B Twelve."

Rustlings, creaking of seats, muttering. Some steel-mill wit up in the gloom hollers:

"Screeno!"

The crowd titters and the pointer spins again. A constant obbligato of dropping, rolling, and scrunching corn kernels and excited mumblings played like a soft flame under the great pot of edible gold that all pursued. Finally someone inevitably shouted:

"SCREENO!"

And the first prize of the evening was snagged. Doppler, his voice trembling with emotion:

"And now the first Screeno gift of the evening, a five-dollar bag of groceries from the Piggely-Wiggely store on Calumet Avenue, Credit Extended, Superb Meats and Groceries; We Cash Checks. This five-dollar bag of superb vittles goes to. . . ."

The usher would hurry down the aisle with the winner's Screeno card and his name, the audience shifting restlessly, distractedly waiting for the next game to begin, and somewhere off in the middle distance the sound of celebration as the winning party, already tasting the Piggely-Wiggely bacon, celebrated the great coup.

The pointer whirled; the action roared on. The kids, not eligible to participate under the strict International rules of Classical Screeno, spent most of the time throwing corn kernels at the balcony and the silver screen.

To the right of the stage glowed a magnificent smoked ham and all the other grocery gifts for the Screeno crowd. During the Depression a seven-pound ham was good for at least four months in the average family, not including 800 gallons of rich, vibrant pea soup, so Screeno was a very serious game. Rising above the usual Orpheum aroma, a rich mixture of calcified gum, Popcorn, hot leatherette seats, steamy socks, and Woolworth Radio Girl perfume and hair oil, was the maddening scent of smoked bacon, fresh pickles, and crushed corn kernels.

Screeno was played for at least forty-five minutes, until the last can of Van Camp's Pork & Beans had been won. The excitement rising upward until the final great moment, the Grand Award—a year's supply of Silvercup Bread, provided by the local A & P store. Bread truly was the staff of life to a dedicated Screeno addict. A year's supply of bread! The very bread that the Lone Ranger lived on and that Tonto used to make the French toast and to sop up the gravy of the Lone Ranger's solitary chuck wagon beans.

Immediately after the Grand Award, which of course Doppler masterfully squeezed for every last drop of dramatic tension, the lights would go out and on would come somebody with a rich Bavarian accent saying:

"Munngeys iss der cwaziest peebles."

And once again Culture marched on into the next feature. There was never a recorded instance of a Single Feature playing the Orpheum.

And so went Monday. Tuesday was known as Bank Night. Bank Night was for the really Big Time movie fans, and that crowd usually avoided Screeno like the plague. Every week the Bank Night jackpot rose by hundred-dollar jumps, and every week Tuesday night at Zero Hour, amid a deep hush, the spotlight on stage, the sinister cage containing the Bank Night registration slips was spun as the world perceptibly slowed in its orbital flight around the sun. Mr. Doppler, standing solemn and straight—no razzle-dazzle on Bank Night—waited beside his silver microphone as a shimmering white card was drawn by one of the audience. A moment of agonizing hesitation and in a quiet voice Mr. Doppler would say:

"Tonight's Bank Night registration drawing for *seventeen hundred* dollars. . . ."

A pregnant pause at this point to let the 1700 bucks sink even deeper into the souls of the harpooned congregation, most of whom hadn't seen a whole ten-dollar bill for five years running.

Seventeen *hundred* dollars! Everyone in the house had followed the progression of Bank Night from the first 100 dollars to its present astronomical height, and each week Mr. Doppler would change the great red figures on the marquee, and all week —seven long days—the feverish Bank Night dreamers passing back and forth on their aimless errands were constantly reminded. Seventeen hundred dollars! And next week—*eighteen* hundred dollars!

As each week rolled into history, the sweat, the nervousness, the fear that someone else would strike it big grabbed at the very vitals of each registrant. He scrabbled and scraped week after week to scratch up the price of a ticket, until finally, at the 1700 mark, it had become almost a compulsive nightmare.

The movies shown on Bank Night unreeled before uncomprehending, glazed eyes, their pupils contracted to pinpoints glowing in the darkness, their breath coming in the telltale short pants of the near-hysteric. Seventeen hundred dollars meant the difference between actual Life and gnawing, grubbing, penny-scrabbling, bare Existence. On Bank Night there were *no* friends, only solitary sparks of human protoplasm—alone—plotting, scheming, hoping against hope that no one else would win.

". . . is Number Two-Two-Nine-*Five!*"

Silence. A stunned, watchful, waiting, *fearful* silence. Will the $1700 be claimed? Is Two-Two-Nine-Five here? A single thought in each Depression-ridden mind. Judy Canova, Jack Oakie, and even Clark Gable drowned in a dark, swirling sea of anxiety.

"Is the holder of that card in the house?"

Silence.

"I repeat, Number Two-Two-Nine-Five. Is the holder of that card in the house? Once."

An usher on the right of the stage, in a blue spotlight, raised a padded mallet and struck a gong.

BOOOONNGGG

The clangorous boom rolled out over the multitude like some cataclysmic death knell, echoing and re-echoing from Coke machine to gilded cherubim, high above the arched stage and down into the depths of the hearer's subconscious, a sound that must be something like the one that will be heard on Judgment Day before the great trumpets blow and Gabriel rises to summon the Faithful from their graves.

"Once."

A dramatic pause.

"Twice."

BOING!

Another dramatic pause.

"TWO-TWO-NINE-FIVE. Three times and *out.*"

BOING!

A deep collective sigh of relief, blessed, numbed, tremulous relief rose from the darkness. The audience settled back into their seats. Already plans were under way in fevered minds on how to grub together next Tuesday's admission.

Somewhere, someplace, in some dark mortgaged hut, Number Two-Two-Nine-Five, who had decided to stay home this one night in order to save the forty cents' price, tossed uneasily in his sleep, unknowing, as the great ship of Fortune sailed by him, unseen, unheard, into the darkness forever. The bedsprings creaked as he shifted in his sleep. He slept on.

Mr. Doppler played on the vast organ of human emotions like a master musician, twittering on the Acquisitiveness stop as one possessed of an evil genius.

Wednesday night was Amateur Night. Between features a long file of banjo players, mouth-organ virtuosi, clog dancers, Bing Crosby imitators, and other Talented out-of-work steelworkers would engage in mortal artistic combat for another list of Grand Awards, including a free, all-expenses paid two-day trip to Chicago, a full thirty miles away, ten vocal lessons at the Bluebird Music School—Accordion Our Specialty—and fifty dollars top prize, as determined by the applause of the audience. At least that's what the poster in the lobby called it—applause. Applause is not exactly the word that described the pandemonium, acrimony, catcalls, distain, obscene noises of enormous variety and general commotion that accompanied each act as claque battled claque. It set the earth to jiggling so that the vibrations alone could be felt over a radius of thirty miles.

The Orpheum on Amateur Night gave many of us who were fortunate enough to be in attendance at these cabalistic rituals a glimpse of Life that left us with a vague understanding of that thing, that stuff of which riots and great historical movements are made.

One night stands out in particular. A bulky bricklayer clumped onstage. In the pit the piano player began a flower intro to "Neapolitan Nights." The bricklayer pursed his lips wetly and began to whistle in a high, thin, bird-like trill, his hairy chest perspiring, cheeks popping, eyes bulging. An instant wave of pseudo-feminine whoops rolled out from the audience and

crashed like a riptide of derision around the Hod Carrier. He
stopped in mid-trill.

"Awright, ya bastards! Who's the smart ass?"

His fists were like two giant clubs at his side. Another great
roar, more of a snort actually, from the audience en masse. The
sweat gleamed on his forehead as he dredged his visceral depths
with a quivering, snorting hawk, and the offended artist let fly
a large silver oyster into the void. To a man, cut to the quick,
the outraged critics arose and rushed over, under, around, and
beside the seats, thousands of kids cheering and bird-whistling,
goading the battlers on. It was the first time that Mr. Doppler
called the police in order to get the second feature under way.
It was not to be the last.

Thursday was Sing Along Night, and it was the one night of
the week that Mr. Doppler was forced to book a real movie.
It was on Thursdays that Bob Hope and Bing Crosby traveled
their eternal Road, panting and leering after Dorothy Lamour.
It was on Thursday that Gary Cooper sat tall in his dusty, worn
saddle. It was on Thursday that Andy Hardy, better known as
Mickey Rooney, and Judy Garland decided to put on a show to
buy the serum for the Widow's boy, dying of a strange, un-
named Hollywood disease while Donald O'Connor, the wise-
guy freshman, made passes at Andy's girl in the gym between
tap dances. Thursday was Serious Picture Night, and in keeping
with the solemn occasion Mr. Doppler also presented the
Orpheum Sing Along.

As Bob and Bing rode their camel off into the sunset and
the Paramount mountain shimmered hotly on the beaded
screen, rising from the cavernous darkness of the pit, electric
motors humming, the mighty Orpheum Wurlitzer rose, sparkling and glowing, sequins shimmering and catching the light.
A massive, brilliant white, multi-tiered instrument, it rose like
some specter, and seated before the impressive, arching key-
board, golden, wavy hair shimmering, white tuxedo coat spotless,
sat the famous Orpheum organist, booming out "Chiribiribim"
as on screen a slide appeared with a scene of gypsies caught in
mid-fandango, tambourines raised, eyes flashing hotly, in eye-

searing Technicolor. The organist spun on his twirling seat, unveiling a grinning set of dentures that made anything that Liberace was to do later along the same lines pale to insignificance. The slide changed:

"Follow the bouncing ball and sing along with the world-famous Orpheum Wurlitzer."

A beautiful moonlit scene appeared, sailboat in the middle foreground, two silhouetted couples mooning against the sky, and above.

"Red Sails in the Sunset. . . ."

The white ball bounced from word to word as the audience, conditioned by countless hours of Kate Smith, Harry Horlich and the A & P Gypsies, Jessica Dragonette and the Silver Masked Tenor, belted it out. A Depression audience did not mess around. When that bouncing ball bounced, they belted!

Beside me in the darkness my mother giggled self-consciously but sang on, curlers rattling, eyes shining as the mighty Orpheum organ bellowed. The empty coal bin and next month's rent forgotten as slide after slide marched across Mr. Doppler's Sing-Along screen. The only time I ever heard my Old Man sing was when the mighty Wurlitzer, like some demonic pipe of Pan, drove him on.

"Betty Coed has lips of red for Harvard,
"Betty Coed has eyes of Yale's deep blue,
"Betty Coed. . . ."*

And on screen a cheerleader in white sweater and white ice-cream pants, with big block Y, held his megaphone high as a golden-haired coed, Betty herself, tilted her perky profile toward an orange sky, as the ball bounced.

So went Thursday. And after Thursday, inevitably, Friday, and it was Friday that finally proved to be Mr. Doppler's Armageddon.

For years theater owners everywhere had struggled bravely

---

* Lines from "Betty Coed" by Paul Fogarty and Rudy Vallee, copyright 1930 by Carl Fischer, Inc., New York. Copyright renewed. Reprinted by permission.

to keep the seats filled. Not that people didn't want to go to the movies. They did, even more maniacally than now. But cold cash was hard to come by, especially cash to be used for Fred MacMurray Viewing and Mickey Mouse Ogling. A movie-goer had to have a real *excuse* for buying a ticket; an investment in Reality, a utilitarian expense. And one historic night Mr. Doppler came up with his master stroke.

A spectacular display in a gleaming glass case appeared without warning in the Neo-Mosque lobby of the beloved Orpheum. For extra dramatic effect the lobby had been especially darkened, with strategically placed baby pink, blue, and amber spots focused on the cause of the eventual downfall of Mr. Doppler and the Orpheum, too. Above the case in fuchsia-tinseled letters the simple, stark, meaningful word blazed forth:

FREE!!

The motley throng who gathered in stunned silence on that fateful night stood slack-jawed and bedazzled by the incredible riches displayed before them, and it was all to be theirs, free, just for coming to the movies!

Artistic sights are rare in hamlets of the Midwest, slumbering quietly in the shade of the steel mills, caught in the tangled spider web of endless railroad tracks and groaning under the weight of vast acres of junkyards, but when they do appear the natives respond with voracity. Starving travelers in a wasteland of an artistic desert, they devour each scrap of beauty with a relish that warms the cockles. Tonight was no exception. The Three Stooges forgotten, they stood clogging up the lobby in dark silent clumps of humanity, eyes shining, unbelieving.

Row on row of radiant, magnificent works of pure beauty lay displayed before them, cushioned on dark, blood-red velvet and setting each observer's soul on fire with instant desire. They stood, silent, almost afraid to believe the evidence before their very eyes. A simple, tasteful placard spelled it out unmistakably so that even the dimmest wit could comprehend:

FREE! FREE!
Beginning next Friday, one piece of this magnificent set
of Artistic DeLuxe Pearleen Tableware, the Dinner Service

of the Stars, will be presented FREE to each adult woman in attendance. The moviegoer will be able to complete this one hundred and twelve piece set of magnificent dinnerware and enjoy at the same time the finest of movie entertainment.

Signed by the Management: Mr. Leopold Doppler

The amber spot played sinuously and enticingly over cascading ledge upon ledge of pearlescent, sparkling, grape and floral encrusted tureens and platters, saucers and gravy boats, celery holders and soup bowls. It was a display potent enough to bring moisture to the eye of a Middle Eastern caliph.

It would probably have been difficult to knock together a complete set of *any* kind of dinnerware from among the entire audience of that night. My mother stood gazing at the artistic opulence, her breath coming in short pants, her eyes glowing like coals. Our cupboards were filled with a collection of jelly jars, peanut butter containers, plastic cottage cheese cups, and the assorted eating effluvia of the period. Her prized possession, which she brought out only for State occasions, was a matched Shirley Temple sugar and creamer of dark blue glass. Our silverware consisted of Tom Mix spoons, Clara Bow pickle forks, and a Betty Crocker bread knife with rubber handle and cardboard blade.

Dish Borrowing and Dish Bringing were major social customs in the neighborhood. It was well known that my Aunt Clara had a set of six matched Mexican-motif coffee cups which she carried with her for any full-scale family ceremonial dinner. My mother, on the other hand, was the owner of a magnificent white meat platter with tiny violets spilling over the edges that had provided the underpinning for every turkey dinner in the family for years.

The effect of the Orpheum's incredible offer, hence, was galvanic. The word spread like the bubonic plague, and by the end of the week of waiting the air had become tense and fretful. It was as though the whole town was waiting for Christmas morning, which, like all great days, approached slowly and creakily.

It was announced in the local paper that, along with the first Free Dish offering, *Tarzan and the Pygmies* would be shown, along with Selected Short Subjects. Doppler was going all out!

Friday morning dawned crisp and clear. By 7 P.M. a nervous serpentine line wound its way halfway around the block, past the poolroom, the Bluebird Tavern, Nick's Hardware Store, and almost to the Willys-Overland showroom, a full football field length away from the Orpheum. Our family, about halfway back in the mob which had begun to gather early in the afternoon, was surrounded by a great waiting mass of suspicious skeptics. It was hard to believe that it would really happen, that a real *dish* would be given out free just to watch Tarzan and Lady Jane swing from the vines, and another paralyzing fear gripped the waiters—would the dishes run out before we got inside?!

Rumors spread. The Pearleen DeLuxe display was a phony, just a come-on, and the dishes we'd get would be cheap, hollow reproductions of the truly beautiful original.

Finally the doors opened and the mob surged forward. The Box Office roared with activity as we pushed and stumbled toward the marquee. Just inside the door Mr. Doppler and two ushers stood, packing cases stacked behind them, handing out to each lady a beautiful, gleaming butter dish.

What a start! Doppler, the master showman, realized that a smash opening was imperative for the success of any Big Time act. He could have opened with a prosaic cup or saucer, but his selection of a butter dish as an opener was little short of total inspiration. Handing a butter dish to housewives who came, almost to a woman, from Oleomargarine families was masterful. In fact, few people in the crowd had ever even *seen* a butter dish before and some had to be told how to use it. My mother, a reader of *Good Housekeeping*, recognized the rare object for what it was, a symbol of Gentility, Good Taste, and the Expansive Life. She was delighted. And my kid brother had to be forcibly restrained in his desire to look at it and feel it.

We were Oleo people, and my mother would mix the white,

lard-like butter substitute in a glass mixing bowl, adding color-
ing from the gelatin capsules which accompanied the package.
We always referred to this as "butter," and it was invariably
served on a cracked white saucer used only for that purpose. Our
new butter dish was a step into the affluent world of the
twentieth century.

Mr. Doppler beamed, his black suit crinkling as he clanked
out butter dish after butter dish, distributing largess to the
multitude.

"Next week there'll be a different piece, lady," he said over
and over.

"Maybe a bun warmer, who knows?"

Thus he insidiously planted the seed in the mind of each
butter-dish clutcher that next week could be even more Exotic.
The hackles of desire rose even higher as they filed into the
darkened auditorium.

"What is a bun warmer?"

"You warm buns in it, you idiot!"

Snatches of complex Table Etiquette debates drifted back
and forth as the mob went up the aisle, butter dishes clanking.

The Tarzan movie began. The popcorn bags ripped open, and
the evening was complete.

As soon as the kitchen light went on, even before my mother
had taken off her coat after the movie, she feverishly slammed
open the refrigerator door and the butter dish was put into
action. Loaded with Oleo, its Pearleen finish lighting up the
linoleum for yards around, it rested in the center of the white
enamel kitchen table. Dish Night had come to Hohman,
Indiana.

The incredible news of Mr. Doppler's largess spread through
the neighborhood almost instantly. Over back fences, through
tangled jungles of clotheslines, up alleys, into basements, up
front porches, into candy stores and meat markets, the winged
word spread. Red, chapped, water-wrinkled hands paused on
clothes wringers and washboards; bathrobe-clad figures hunched
over sinks nodded in amazement. Neighbors trooped into kitch-

ens all over town to observe firsthand the beautiful works of art that somehow had come into our lives.

The following Friday the Orpheum drew crowds from a three-county area, a jostling throng that stood in long expectant lines to see *Blondie Takes a Trip* starring Penny Singleton and Arthur Lake and to receive as compensation for that trial by fire a Pearleen-finish Bun Warmer. Mr. Doppler did not fail his public. Bun Warmers flooded Lake County in a massive deluxe Hollywood Finish tide. There were few buns to warm, but the Calumet region was ready.

The movies, and the Orpheum in particular, had never known such total and complete popularity. It was more than popularity; it was verging on True Love. The other movie in town, the Paramount, desperately tried to stem the rising tide of Mr. Doppler's popularity. A huge, glowing sign appeared on their marquee announcing that they were prepared to offer free a 187-piece set of Movieland Mexican Plasto-Ware, designed personally by Gilbert Roland and including his permanent, indelibly embossed, raised signature on each and every piece. It was too late. The incandescent Pearleen beauty of Mr. Doppler's dinnerware had a grip on the aesthetic fancy of the population that was unbreakable. A whole new dimension had been added to Art Appreciation in Northern Indiana, and even Gilbert Roland was swept under.

The first evening we actually used our bun warmer was a red-letter day in the family annals. Mr. Doppler was in the saddle and his power grew from week to week as each succeeding piece was added to the growing collection that began to gleam from practically every kitchen cupboard in town, crowding jelly glasses and peanut butter jars further and further and further to the rear.

The third week saw the first cup and saucer combination, a two-piece bonus. The fourth week a petite, delicately modeled egg cup, the first ever seen in the Midwestern states. Week by week the crowds grew larger. The tension mounted as piece after piece was added to family collections.

Speculation was rife as to what the next week would bring.

Doppler usually just hinted as he and his aides passed out celery dishes and consommé bowls.

"Maybe next week an Olive Urn, with pick."

He never exactly said it *would* be an Olive Urn, with pick, just hinted. A sort of question. Well, the audience would squirm in their seats as the sound track engulfed them, speculating, already anticipating next Friday.

The weeks flew by. The town was hooked. They had the Free Dinnerware monkey, a 112-piece specimen clamped on their backs and growing heavier every week. Ladies in the last stages of childbirth were wheeled into the Orpheum, gasping in pain, to keep the skein going. Creaking grandmothers, halt and blind, were led to the Box Office by grandchildren. Ladies who had not seen the light of day since the Crimean War were pressed into service. They sat numbly, deafly in the Orpheum seats, their watery eyes barely able to perceive the shifting, incomprehensible images on the screen, their gnarled talons clasping a sugar bowl for dear life.

I remember particularly the night we got The Big Platter, as it became known in our family over the years. The Big Platter— a proper name, like The House On The Hill, The Basement, The Garage. The Big Platter was important. There was only one Big Platter in every complete set of dinnerware, the crowning jewel in Doppler's diadem. For weeks we had filed past the magnificent display in the lobby and there in the exact center, catching the amber spots, glowing like the sun, was The Big Platter. And tonight it was ours!

One of the saddest sounds I have ever heard was the crash in the darkness as some numb-fingered housewife, carried away by a brilliantly executed scene by Joe E. Brown loosened her grip in laughter. A sudden panic and her platter was no more, scattered in a million Pearlescent slivers among the peanut shells and Tootsie Roll butt ends that formed a thick compost heap underfoot. Recriminations, suppressed sobs, and the entire family rose and filed out, their only reason for being there gone in a single split second. My mother held ours with both hands clamped over her chest in a death grip.

Few of us at the time realized in the exultation of the moment that the end of the party was already in sight. Without warning one night the patrons were handed a finely sculptured grape-encrusted Gravy Boat. This windfall was greeted with hosannas in our innocence.

The following week a strangely furtive Doppler dealt out to each female patron *another* Gravy Boat, all the while mumbling something over and over about:

"The shipment was wrong this week. You can exchange this Gravy Boat for a dinner plate next week."

Vaguely uneasy at this unexpected break in the rhythm of dish collecting, the women filed into the theater, bearing redundant Gravy Boats.

The third Friday was significantly marked by a sudden avenging rainstorm that grew in intensity until, as the Orpheum hour approached, it became a genuine cloudburst. Women scuttled through the dark, howling rain, carrying paper-wrapped Gravy Boats, to be met at the turnstile by Mr. Doppler and a shamefaced crew surrounded by cases of more dry, shining Gravy Boats.

"Bring *all* your Gravy Boats in next week. We will *positively* exchange them next week. The shipment. . . ."

The tide had turned. What had been, weeks before, a gay rabble of happy ticket buyers had become a menacing, pushing, dispirited mob.

All through that fourth week a strange quiet hung over Lake County. Even the weather seemed to reflect a sinister mood of watchful waiting. Fitful dry winds blew across the rooftops; screen doors creaked in the night, dogs bayed at the sullen moon, and children cried out in their sleep.

That fourth Friday turned unexpectedly cold, a chill, clammy cold somehow suggestive of the Crypt; mysterious tombs, deserted caves. Solitary dark-clad women bearing shopping bags full of Gravy Boats converged on the Arena.

By 7 P.M. a murky clot of humanity milled under the marquee and spilled out raggedly along the gloomy, shuttered street. The doors remained shut. Seven-five. Seven-ten. A few in the

forefront of the rabble tapped demandingly on the wrought
brass gateway. Seven-fifteen. It was obvious that something was
up. Seven-twenty, the doors finally, reluctantly, swung open.

As the vanguard approached the turnstile, they knew the
worst had come to pass. For the first time in many weeks Mr.
Doppler was absent from his post of honor. Two weedy substitute ushers, unknown strangers, eyes downcast, handed to
each ticket holder *another* Gravy Boat, the fourth in as many
weeks. Each Gravy Boat was received in stony silence, quietly
stuffed into shopping bag or hatbox, completing a set of four
carried hopelessly for exchange.

The feature that night was *The Bride of Frankenstein*, the
story of a man-made monster that returned to pursue and crush
his creator. For long moments the house lay in darkness and
almost complete silence, waiting for Mr. Doppler's next move.
On this night no gay music played through the theater loudspeakers. No Coming Attractions. The candy counter was dark
and untended, as though Mr. Doppler himself felt the impending end near.

The mothers waited. A sudden blinding spotlight made a big
circle on the maroon curtain next to the cold, silent screen
and then, out of the wings stepped Mr. Doppler to face his
Moment of Truth.

He cleared his throat before speaking into the ringing silence.
No microphone tonight. He seemed to have shrunken somehow, his eyes erased by black shadows in that blue light. His tie
was a little crooked and for the first time scuff marks and dust
marred the gleaming toes of his black pumps. His coal black
suit was vaguely rumpled.

"Ladies." He began plaintively, "I have to apologize for
tonight's Gravy Boat."

A lone feminine laugh, mirthless and arid, mocking, punctu-
ated his pause. He went on as though unhearing.

"I give you my personal *guarantee* that next week. . . ."

At this point a low, subdued hissing arose spontaneously.
The sound of cold venom landing on boiling lava began to rise

from the depths of the void. Doppler, his voice bravely raised, continued:

"Next week I *personally guarantee* we will exchange *all* Gravy Boats for. . . ."

Then it happened. A dark shadow sliced through the hot beam of the spotlight, turning over and over and casting upon the screen an enormous magnified outline of a great Gravy Boat. Spinning over and over, it crashed with a startling suddenness on the stage at Doppler's feet. Instantly a blizzard of Gravy Boats filled the air. Doppler's voice rose to a wail.

"LADIES! PLEASE! WE WILL EXCHANGE. . . . !!"

A great crash of Gravy Boats like the breaking of surf on an alien shore drowned out his words. And then, spreading to all corners of the house, shopping bags were emptied as the arms rose and fell in the darkness, maniacal female cackles and obscenities driving Doppler from the stage.

High overhead someone switched off the spotlights and Frankenstein flickered across the screen. But it was too late. More Gravy Boats, and even more. It seemed to be an almost inexhaustible supply, as though some great Mother Lode of Gravy Boats had been struck. The eerie sound track of *The Bride of Frankenstein* mingled with the rising and falling cadence of wave upon wave of hurled Gravy Boats. Outside the distant sound of approaching Riot Cars. The house lights went on. The Orpheum was suddenly filled with a phalanx of blue-jowled policemen.

The audience sat amid the ruin, taciturn, satisfied. Under the guidance of pointed nightsticks they filed into the grim darkness of the outside world. The Dish Night Fever was over, once and for all. The great days of the Orpheum and Leopold Doppler had passed forever.

Somewhere a million miles away a short man with a funny mustache, in a trench coat, was starting the cameras a-rolling for the next great feature, which was to star all the Male kids in the world.

The doors of the Orpheum never opened again. Mr. Doppler disappeared from our lives forever, leaving behind countless sets of uncompleted Hollywood Star Time Dinnerware, memories of Errol Flynn, stripped to the waist, climbing the rigging of a Pirate barkentine; George Raft, smooth and oily under a white, snap-brim fedora surrounded by camel's-hair-coated henchmen, Bobby Breen and Deanna Durbin on a rose-covered swing, with Nelson Eddy and Jeanette MacDonald waltzing endlessly under Japanese lanterns; José Iturbi at a piano made of ivory and mirrors playing great rhapsodies before thousand-piece orchestras in a perpetual MGM Grand Finale. Doppler had done his work well.

"Do you want me to warm up your cup?"

The counterman snapped me back from Screenland abruptly. Before I could answer he moved away. I knew what I had to do. Stealthily, moving like a cat, in one quick motion I swept the damp green bowl into my zippered briefcase. In my booming John Wayne voice, to keep him off my trail, I barked:

"Well, gotta push off."

I slapped a buck on the counter and quickly scuttled out with my priceless *objet d'art* concealed under my arm. For a brief instant I almost panicked as I thought I heard the sound of the high, tinny voices of the Andrew Sisters singing "Roll Out the Barrel" from my attaché case, but it was just the buzzing of a leaky neon-sign transformer.

An instant later I was out on the Turnpike, jaw set in my widely applauded Claude Rains smile, the hard-earned result of hundreds of hours logged in secret practice before the bathroom mirrors of my Adolescence, carrying with me safely a relic that would confound and bemuse as yet unborn future generations of anthropologists, a mute, lumpy Rosetta Stone of our time.

XXXI ॐ THE DAY SHIFT DROPS BY FOR A BELT

"You ain't seen nothin' yet."

With this, Flick hunched down under the bar and began rummaging around on the shelves next to the beer tap. He straightened with an air of transcendent triumph, concealing in each hand an object. Placing his fists carefully on the bar, he slowly opened them to reveal two dull, gleaming objects.

"What are these?" I asked.

"Take a look at 'em. Just take a look at 'em."

I bent over in the darkening light of Flick's Tavern. Full winter twilight had now settled down over the grim landscape. Outside, the wind rose, and I could hear the tinfoil streamers snapping and cracking viciously over at Friendly Fred's Used-Car lot. I bent closer to see what Flick had placed on the bar. Maybe it was the beer, or it might have been the light, but at first I didn't know what he was driving at. I picked one of them up, holding it so that the glow of the neon sign picked out its details in a dull, red-orange. I looked at it closely. There was something vaguely, naggingly familiar about that metal face that stared up at me. I couldn't quite put my finger on it.

"Okay, Flick, I'll bite. You've got me. What is it?"

"Pick up the other one," he said.

Again a peculiarly haunting, familiar face, this time feminine. Again I could not identify it.

"Okay, you win."

"That," said Flick, "is a genuine Fibber McGee and Molly salt-and-pepper shaker set. You see, the pepper comes out of the top of Fibber's head and the salt comes out of Molly's hair. My Old Lady bought 'em at the World's Fair in Chicago."

He tenderly replaced them on the shelf.

"Seventy-nine Wistful Vista. . . ." I said.

"You remember that closet?" Flick asked. "Old Fibber would swing open the door and down it would come, all that stuff. Digger O'Dell, the only gravedigger I ever heard on the radio. . . ."

The jukebox was now in high gear.

"I'll have to turn the heat up," Flick said, "temperature musta dropped outside."

He fiddled with a thermostat on the wall back of the bar. I swung around on my stool to look out at what little remained of the day. It was now almost dark. Darkness comes early in Midwinter in Northern Indiana. Kids shouted and shoved their way by the tavern front, going to the store, coming home from school, God knows what. Traffic had quickened outside on the street as the two lines of cars, one going to the mill, the other returning, crossed and converged.

I turned back to Flick, who was checking the cash register.

"Too bad Schwartz couldn't have been here," I said.

Flick grunted, busy with his change counting. We both knew that Schwartz had been shot down over Italy. They never found him.

A great crowd of Shift workers burst in. The day shift was home, and it was thirsty. They were going to hoist a few before heading home to the hamburger and the TV. Flick had galvanized into action, drawing beers and pouring shots like a man possessed. I called out:

"I hope they win tonight."

"Hell, it's a breather. They'll murder 'em."

I stood up stiffly, brushing a few crumbs of pretzel off my

coat and slacks. Turning, I pulled my light New York topcoat off the hook. As I buttoned it, I called out again:

"Hey Flick, I'll try to get back to have another drink with you before I gotta go back to New York."

He was at the far end of the tavern now, carrying a tray of steins. Faintly, I could hear his reply:

"Okay, I'll be seein' you, Ralph."

I glanced back over the mob of lumberjacketed, safety-shoed beer drinkers. Above the bar, under a Christmas wreath I noticed for the first time, a sign:

IN GOD WE TRUST

ALL OTHERS PAY CASH

How true. I swung the door open and stepped out into the bitter cold air. The refinery fumes, the aroma of a thousand acrid chemicals bit deep into my lungs. It was Home air.

I turned and walked against the wind that cut through my worsted topcoat as if it were cheesecloth. My stomach rumbled as the strong taste of beer welled up into my mouth. I fought it down. My conscience flared up. I had wasted a whole day. Well, what the hell. The company'd never find out. But I don't like to waste time when I'm working. Far off in the sky I could see the faint glow of the steel mills. I peered into the gloom at the grimy Mill traffic.

Dammit, it's gonna be hell getting a cab around here. Oh well. . . .

I waited briefly at the light and then turned left, toward the bus stop.